RAVES FOR
WHEN FIRST WE DECEIVE
AND CHARLES WILSON!

"Wilson may flat out be the best plotter of my generation."
—Ed Gorman, *Mystery Scene*

"A tightly plotted suspenser."
—*Chicago Tribune*

"An assault on the reader's nervous system. There is not a moment in this book when one is given the opportunity to catch a breath. My impulse at finishing this first-rate thriller is to press it into the hands of everybody I meet. But it won't be necessary; a book this good will find its audience."
—*The Clarion-Ledger*

"A page-turner thriller."
—*The Mobile Register*

Charles Wilson is a "wizard plotter."
—*Los Angeles Times*

"Non-stop thrills from start to finish. Be prepared for some sleepless nights."
—*Hattiesburg American*

THE FIRST BODY

Green stepped into the hall and crossed to the right. Pressing his back up against the wall, he pointed his revolver toward the first doorway on the left.

Brett crossed to the left wall. They both inched slowly down the corridor. Nearly to the two doorways across from each other, Green shined his light in front of Brett and said, "A bathroom on your side. I can see the commode."

Brett didn't say anything. He was shining the light back across the hall through the other doorway. His stare was locked on the slim body dressed in a short miniskirt and a pullover and lying sprawled on the blood-soaked carpet between the end of the bed and the wall. On a pale, outstretched arm and glittering in his flashlight's beam was the wide silver bracelet Trinity had worn since high school—the bracelet he had given her. He felt sick. Then he noticed the awkward angle of her head and realized it was nearly severed from her body, and his stomach turned.

Other *Leisure* books by Charles Wilson:
NIGHTWATCHER

WHEN FIRST WE DECEIVE

CHARLES WILSON

LEISURE BOOKS   NEW YORK CITY

A LEISURE BOOK®

June 1998

Published by

Dorchester Publishing Co., Inc.
276 Fifth Avenue
New York, NY 10001

ISBN 0-8439-4401-3

The name "Leisure Books" and the stylized "L" with design are
trademarks of Dorchester Publishing Co., Inc.

Printed in the United States of America.

To Pappy and Mom; Garfield and Annie; Dad and Mother; Lee Ann and Lila Jo; Linda along with Faye and Jewell; Charles, Cassie and Cas, and Destin; down to Ryder; from as far back as I can remember until now, how could anyone have been lucky enough to be blessed with such family.

Also, with special thanks to Police Chief George Payne of the Gulfport, Mississippi, Police Department, to Assistant Chief Tom Ruspoli of the Pass Christian, Mississippi, Police Department, and to Lieutenant Danile S. Gregov of the Long Beach, Mississippi, Police Department for the help they gave me on this book; to Kat Bergeron of *The Sun Herald* for her suggestions and insight into the Coast area; to Paul Stout of Senath, Missouri, for his careful scrutiny; and Tommy Furby, always too demanding critic.

CHAPTER 1

Trinity went out of her way to look her best that night, accentuating her high cheekbones and full lips with just the right amount of makeup, slipping on the pullover blouse that emphasized her small breasts and tiny waist, finally selecting the leather miniskirt that dropped barely to the top of her thighs. Her bare legs were eye-catching in the highest heels she owned.

And what had it gained her? she thought. She touched her fingers gingerly to her swollen lip; her eyes moistened and she shook her head. For the twentieth time her gaze moved to the telephone on the table next to her chair. But this time she didn't quickly look away.

Continuing to stare, she drew her mouth into a firm line, suddenly reached for the telephone directory lying next to the telephone, lifted it into her lap and opened it. In a moment she found the name she was looking for—Brett Dunnigan.

She reached for the receiver, but hesitated. There was a pencil on the table and she picked it up, rolled it in her fingers for a moment, turned the directory back to its front, printed the number at the top of the inside page and stared at it.

Then she shook her head. She was acting foolishly. She would have her revenge, but she needed to be careful she gained it in such a manner that she wasn't destroyed in the process. She needed to plan first—she had always been good at planning.

She moved the directory back to the table, sat a moment longer in thought, then raised her face toward the hallway at the back of the living room. "James!" she called.

After a moment with no answer she called his name again. Frowning, she came up out of the chair and walked toward the hallway.

Entering her bedroom, she saw the bathroom door to her right was closed. She could hear the sound of running water. She walked to the door and opened it.

"James?" she said, peering inside.

He wasn't there. The tub was nearly overflowing. She walked to it and turned off the water. Looking back toward the door, her brow wrinkled at her thought:

He couldn't have left the house without her knowing. He would've had to come up the hall and through the living room to go out either the front or back door.

The other bedroom, maybe he was in there; or maybe the bathroom across the hall. She hadn't noticed if its door was closed.

She looked back at the water lapping at the top of the tub and shook her head in exasperation. She couldn't take much more, not very much more at all.

She leaned to open the drain—and the lights went out.

Stopping her hand in its movement toward the tub, she straightened and looked back toward the bedroom, waiting for the power to come back on.

But after several seconds there was still only the dark.

Damn, she thought. She only hoped the lights were out on the whole street and not something wrong with the house's wiring. But if there *was* something wrong, that wouldn't be any surprise; not any surprise at all. The air conditioner had gone out only two days after they moved in. A couple of days after that, only the week before, the roof had leaked during a rain shower that swept down the edge of the coast. Lucky it had only been a shower, but even that caused enough leakage to ruin the ceiling in the kitchen. The old house was all they could afford, he had said. Yeah, with his habit it was.

But who else did she have to blame but herself? She had known from the very beginning how he was, and had still married him. What a fool.

Shaking her head in irritation, she reached back to the tub, felt in the darkness for the drain-control lever, opened it, then turned and moved carefully across the tile floor into the bedroom, dimly lit by the moonlight coming in through the curtained windows.

There was a flashlight in the nightstand on the far side of the room and she walked toward it, circling the end of the bed—

—and a flashlight suddenly came on behind her, startling her.

She frowned and turned into the bright light. "James, where have you ..." She saw from the position of the light that he hadn't walked into the room from the hallway to the left, but had stepped out of the walk-in closet a few feet in front of her. "James, what are you doing?"

She felt a gentle draft against her right side and something brush against her arm. The curtain billowing out toward her. The window was raised.

The light came quickly toward her.

"James?"

"Uh!" She grunted at the hard force that slammed into her forehead, jolting her head backward.

Uncomprehending, she raised her hand to her head. She felt the sticky warmth. Her eyes widened.

The dark shape stepped closer.

"Noooo!" she screamed in horror and raised her arms in front of her face. A second heavy blow came down through her hands, smashing into her head—and she grunted again and crumpled backward to the floor.

The flashlight was laid on the bed. A short section of lead pipe thudded to the carpet. A steel blade glinted the flashlight's beam. The figure stepped forward.

His feet straddling Trinity's limp form, he slowly lowered himself down to her body, his hard knees pinning her outstretched arms to the floor.

Down the street, a tiny, gray-haired woman stood at her open dining-room window. She narrowed her eyes quizzically behind a large pair of black binoculars as she swung the glasses quickly through the tree-lined yards.

A dog's yelp? she wondered. It almost sounded like the start of a woman's scream, abruptly cut off.

After a minute, still unable to locate an injured animal—or anyone being raped in plain view—she gave up her search and lowered the binoculars to let them hang against the front of her white terry-cloth robe.

Raped in plain view, she thought again, and herself running to the rescue. That would be a gasser, wouldn't it? All her life she had wanted to do something like that, or maybe break up a drug-smuggling ring. She smiled and raised the binoculars back to her eyes. Something like that.

The full moon brightly illuminated Brett Dunnigan's unmarked patrol car as he drove slowly along U.S. 90, the coastal highway running alongside the dark waters of the Mississippi Sound and comprising the southern limits of the small town of Pass Christian. Back to his right, away from the white sand beach on his left and at the top of a bluff gently sloping up away from the pavement, a continuous line of large houses, most of them wood-frame and some of them over a hundred years old, faced out over the top of his car toward the Sound, and the Gulf of Mexico beyond it. He looked at the houses. Though he had passed by them a million times, he always looked. How could someone *not* stare up at them? he wondered. Mostly built by wealthy New Orleanians when the Mississippi Coast was considered their playground, the houses' hand-carved woodwork, tall columns, and prominent roof lines represented a lifestyle that lasted for better than a hundred years, a way of life that thrived on luxury, peacefulness, and graciousness; a calm, slow way of life, and a closeness of family, a lifestyle that wouldn't be seen again. The equally as big, and some even bigger, modern mansions of brick and stone built later, farther east along the highway toward Long Beach and Gulfport just weren't the same.

He glanced back across the median and the two lanes to his left at the choppy waves building in the Sound, their tops fluorescing into foam before the strengthening wind. He reached forward to the dash, switched off the air conditioner and lowered his window.

Unbuttoning the collar of his uniform and loosening his tie, he let the fresh breeze blow across his lean face and taut neck and took a deep breath. With several hours passing since the sun had set, there was now some relief from the unusually warm spring temperatures the area had been experiencing. It would be mid-morning before the air conditioning in the small town would again go into full gear.

He glanced at his watch, his new watch with its heavy, solid gold band. He looked at the little box wrapped in bright red wrapping paper lying on the seat next to him, then reached to the two-way radio mounted underneath the dash and lifted its mike to his lips, calling in to the station.

In a moment the radio crackled at the voice of the old woman who served as the force's night radio dispatcher. "Yeah, unit two," she said.

"Martha, you mind telephoning Paige for me? Tell her my brakes are vibrating and I'm going to leave the car down at the garage. Ask her to meet me there and bring a pair of jeans and a shirt and I'll dress on the way to Biloxi."

"What's that?"

He smiled and shook his head in amusement. Martha had to know everything. "I'm taking Paige over to Biloxi to eat, Martha. If that's all right with you?"

The woman didn't reply, but he knew she was satisfied now. She knew what was going on. He smiled again, replaced the mike, glanced at the shrimp boats moored in their berths in the Pass Christian Harbor off to his left, then slowed for the turn leading off the highway. He steered up the gentle rise into the center of the old town, comprised of narrow streets and buildings that for the most part would not have been out of place in a movie filmed before the turn of the century.

In a minute, he had wound back along a road at the edge of the bluff, and turned away from the beach onto a narrow, alleylike street leading between a pair of massive, two-story antebellum homes. In another couple of minutes he was on a main street, driving toward the garage where he would leave the car for the night. He was almost there when his radio crackled again.

"Unit two."

"Yeah, Martha."

"I'd be ashamed, Brett."

"What?"

"I thought you young ones would be a little different. You sound just like my husband. That's what I've just been telling

Paige. That's what he would do on my anniversary—if he took me out to eat in the first place. You ever thought about waiting until tomorrow, when it's early enough to go to a really nice place? I mean, it's almost eleven, Brett."

A telephone sounded in the background, and he heard the woman snort her irritation. "Hold on, Brett. This phone's been ringing tonight like I'm *Larry King Live* or something."

She didn't come back on the radio, and in a minute he guided his car up to the front of the garage. Seconds later, Paige drove her Maxima in behind him and stopped. He didn't move to open his door, but instead lifted the little box from the seat and held it up in the glare of her headlights where she could see it through his rear windshield.

Her door opened and in a moment she stood at his window and looked down at him. "Brett, you're not fair." He had given her a thin gold bracelet studded with tiny diamonds when he had wished her Happy Anniversary that morning, had a dozen roses in his hand when he met her for lunch, and now this.

She still stared down at him, trying to look serious. But a smile played at the corner of her lips. "Brett, we're supposed to be saving money, remember—for when we're at the academy."

"You bought me a watch."

"One watch."

"Worth more than all my presents together." The watch *was* a beauty, especially with the heavy gold band her grandfather willed to his "favorite tomboy" at his death, a gift that meant the world to Paige. He raised his wrist up to the window and showed the watch to her, as if to remind her she had given it to him.

Her smile broke through. "Let me have it," she said, and reached for the little gift-wrapped box.

The radio crackled. "Unit two."

He reached for his mike. "This is unit two."

"Brett, I just got a signal 56. It's close to you and you still have ten minutes on duty. Sorry."

Brett closed his eyes. A signal 56, a damn prowler who would already be gone by the time he got there. He looked at his watch. He was scheduled to switch to the morning shift the next day. It would be two hours at least, eating in Biloxi and getting back to the house before he could get into bed. He wasn't going to get much sleep. He lifted his mike, but before he spoke the radio crackled again, this time with the heavy voice of a large male— Sergeant Armont Green.

"Brett, you take Paige on to the big eat-out. Arnie's already on duty. I saw him drive by a minute ago. He can back me up."

"Thanks, Armont."

The dispatcher spoke again. "Same address as before, Armont."

"What before?" Brett asked.

"I tried you, Brett," the old woman said. "You didn't answer. Radio's working now. Bet it was then."

The call had to have come when he was out of his car checking an open window at the back of a restaurant on the east edge of town.

"Brett," Sergeant Green said.

"Yeah."

"There was nobody around when I went by the first time, or they were keeping out of sight if they were still there. I'll go up on foot this time. Martha . . ."

"Uh-huh, Armont."

"You holler back at whoever called in the report. Get the name of the people at the house where the prowler was seen. Give them a call and tell them I'll be walking around in their backyard. I don't need to be getting shot. Tell them not to do anything other than what they're doing now—just stay inside. Arnie, you on the line?"

There was no response to the call.

A waft of Oscar de la Renta drifted inside the window, replacing the smell of salt air. "It's my favorite," Paige said as she slipped the spray bottle back into its box. She glanced past him at the radio. "If the prowler's been back twice—could be the burglar."

He raised the mike back to his mouth. "Armont, you saw that the occupants were home?"

"Lights were all on, and that old red MG I been seeing all over town is there. Guess that's where that woman lives who drives it."

Trinity.

Paige looked at him.

He felt awkward.

"Arnie," Sergeant Green called.

There was still no response.

"For God's sake," the old woman exclaimed in an exasperated voice. "Am I the only one working full-time tonight? Arnie, you out there?"

Brett depressed his mike button. "Forget him, Martha. Armont, I'm on my way to the location."

"Copy that," the sergeant came back, "but it'll take me a couple of minutes to get there. I'm down near the yacht club."

"Let me get my purse," Paige said, and hurried toward her car.

In a few seconds she was back and slipped inside the car onto the passenger seat. Brett drove back out onto the street.

After a minute, still staring straight ahead through the windshield, she casually asked, "Have you run into her since she moved back into town?"

"I saw her at the grocery store a few days ago."

She looked at him. "Talk to her?"

He had for just a moment. "No."

As she faced forward again, he glanced at her clothes. It had been her day off duty and she was still dressed in the white blouse and dark slacks she wore when she met him for lunch. The slacks were okay, but the blouse would stand out noticeably in the bright moonlight.

He nodded over his shoulder into the rear seat. "I have an old sweatshirt back there on the floor. Put it on."

"What?"

"Your blouse is too bright."

She leaned over the seat and looked down at the floor. "Brett— that old nasty thing."

"Put it on—Officer Dunnigan."

She frowned but reached for the garment. Turning back around, she quickly slipped it down over her head, fluffed her hair out from under the collar, rolled the sleeves up to her elbows, and leaned forward to peer through the windshield.

With her brown eyes open wide and her slim body lost in the folds of the sweatshirt, she now looked more like a college student than a cop. But he wouldn't dare mention that. She hated that she looked so young, always saying it hurt her authority as a policewoman. That was almost all she cared about—police work. With her gung-ho attitude it wouldn't surprise him if she ended up being the first woman director of the FBI—if, after they entered the academy, she didn't get kicked out for telling off one of the instructors. She was quick to voice her opinion when she didn't think she was being treated right. He smiled at the thought, turned off the headlights, and guided the car to the right, onto the street where Trinity lived.

The street was a blacktop shaded by the kind of oak trees common to the Mississippi Gulf Coast, many of them hundreds of years old with massive, short trunks and long, heavy limbs hanging out over the streets, some draping so low that a pickup truck could barely drive under them. The old houses were mostly of a moderate size and a mixture of wood-siding structures and those finished in brick. The occupants ranged widely in age, from gray-haired couples who had lived there most of their lives to young marrieds who mainly worked in Gulfport and Biloxi but who had been attracted down the coast by the relatively cheap prices of the lots and homes, and the almost nonexistent crime rate—prior to the burglar.

CHAPTER 2

In a few seconds, Brett stopped his car just before a curving turn on the narrow residential street. Trinity's small, one-story brick house was around the curve and two or three hundred feet ahead of them on the right, past several of the old homes and large oaks draped with clumps of Spanish moss. He pulled the flashlight from its bracket on the dash, and stepped outside.

Paige joined him as he went around the curve. "Somebody on the right," she said in a low voice.

A hundred or so feet down the street, a figure stood at the front of a salt-silvered, wooden, one-story house which was separated from Trinity's house by a vacant lot.

Brett unhooked the safety strap of his holster. Paige unsnapped her purse. As they neared the house, he saw that the figure was that of a short, frail-looking, gray-haired man dressed in a bathrobe and wearing glasses.

When they were almost to the lawn in front of the house, the man leaned slightly forward from the waist, peered toward them, then nodded his head and walked to meet them.

"Wanted to make sure you were a police officer first," he said in a soft voice as he stopped before them. "Weren't sure about your uniform until I saw that badge glint. Can't never be too careful, you know—not nowadays."

He looked back across the vacant lot toward Trinity's, which was completely dark. Sergeant Green had said lights had been on when he first went by. "It's that house there," the man said.

Brett nodded. "Yes, sir. You're the one who called in the report?"

"Sorta. Me and Mildred both did. I'm Henry Winford."

Brett smiled politely. "I'm Lieutenant Dunnigan and this is Officer Dunnigan. Where was he when you saw him?"

"Mildred or me?"

"The last time he was seen."

"That was Mildred. Maybe you'd like to hear it from the first?"

Paige had closed her purse. "Yes, sir," she answered. "We would."

"Well, I caught sight of him when I was out in the back goin' through the trash, tryin' to find where Mildred threw my paper. She's always doin' that before I can finish with it. I looked up and there he was, near the back corner of the house. I thought it was Mr. Anderson at first. Then it came to me it was Wednesday night and I told myself, uh-oh, that's not Mr. Anderson, he don't never get in off the road until Friday nights. That's when I up and called you all. Mildred's the one laid eyes on him the second time. He was up on the back step then." He dropped his eyes for a moment before looking back up at them and speaking even softer. "I suppose I owe you a little apology here, Lieutenant. Mildred was a little upset at that first officer who went by and didn't get out of his car to check around the house. So when she saw the prowler back over there again, she didn't call you all right off. Said it wouldn't do no good, hadn't done no good when I called—I mean, that's what Mildred said. I finally talked her into it. Was maybe twenty or thirty minutes ago when she laid eyes on him, though, so he could be long gone by now." He shrugged his narrow shoulders. "Sorry about that."

Paige nodded. "We'll see if he's still around."

The door to the man's house opened and an old woman came out and walked toward them.

Her gray hair in curlers, a thin robe pulled tightly around her angular frame, she stopped beside the man, wrapped her long arms around her chest, and stared down at him from a height a good six inches above his.

"Well, Henry," she said in a sharp voice, "they gonna do anythin' this time or did we just waste another call?"

"Yes, ma'am," Paige said, "we're going to check on it. Your husband said you saw the prowler on the back step."

"If you're askin' if he went inside or not, I don't know. Sounds like he might've least been tryin', don't it?"

She looked down at her husband. "Henry, did you tell them there's one other possibility for what we seen?"

He shook his head. "That wouldn't have anythin' to do with this, honey."

"Maybe and maybe not. Lord knows it wouldn't be the first time a man slipped out of there at night. When Mr. Anderson's not at home, that is."

Brett noticed Paige's eyes revolve around to his. Her stare said, Look what your old girlfriend is, Brett. As if he didn't already know! He ignored the look.

At the woman's remark, the old man had briefly closed his eyes. "Now, Mildred," he said, "that's really none of our concern."

She glared down at him. "Speak for yourself, Henry. I got a right to say what I seen."

"Now, Mildred, we don't even know she's there. We was only a minute ago wonderin' about that." He looked back at Brett. "Mrs. Anderson sells hosiery to stores. Most nights she's home by dark, but occasionally she stays out on the road at night."

"If she's not home," the woman said, "then what's her MG doin' there, and who shut off the lights 'while ago?"

"I don't know, Mildred. Maybe she had friends come by, left with them. There was a spell there we wasn't lookin'."

The woman sneered. "Going out? After ten o'clock?"

"She's still a young woman, Mildred."

"No, Henry, she's a married woman is what she is."

She looked across her shoulder at Trinity's house. "But then again, wouldn't surprise me none if she was out. Wouldn't surprise me none what she might be up to. I've been tellin' you ever since she moved in here and started paradin' around in them strings that she was trouble."

The woman looked back at Brett. "And Mr. Anderson is such a nice man," she said, her voice suddenly soft. "Of course it always happens to that type of man, though, don't it? They give their wife the upper hand, then she don't never turn loose of it. Make life hell for their husbands."

The old man glanced up at her. Paige smiled. Out of the corner of his eye, Brett caught the glow of a car's lights approaching the curve down the street behind them. Then the lights went off. A few seconds later, Sergeant Green, a tall, heavily built middle-aged black man with flecks of gray in his closely cropped hair, walked around the curve and came down the street.

When he stopped before them, he nodded his greeting to the older couple, then looked toward Trinity's house. "See anybody?" he asked.

"They said somebody was on the back step. The lights just went off."

"Not just," the woman said. "It was a while ago, good fifteen minutes now."

Brett smiled politely at her and looked back at the sergeant. "Paige can watch the back while we go around to the front."

"I'd rather go to the front with you," Paige said.

"No, you take the back."

She frowned but started toward the vacant lot next to Trinity's house. He stared after her as she left the street and angled across the tree-covered lot toward the back of the house. He felt guilty at where he was sending her. If the burglar was inside and ran when they appeared he could go out the back way. But, then again, if the prowler was fleeing, he wouldn't be that dangerous, and it would be Paige who surprised him, not the other way around. Besides, Brett thought as he continued to watch her now halfway across the lot, what else could he have done but send her around to the back? He certainly couldn't have her walking up to the front door with him and Trinity blurting out that she hadn't seen him since they talked in the grocery store. Why had he not said yes when Paige asked him if he had talked to Trinity? The answer to that was simple enough. It would have just led to more questions. And there hadn't been anything to the conversation—not really.

CHAPTER 3

Brett gave Paige another minute to get safely into position behind Trinity's house, then he and the sergeant started down the street. In a minute they had stepped up to the front door. He pushed the doorbell.

After several seconds without any response, he knocked twice on the door and jabbed the button again. After another minute had passed, still without any lights coming on or any other indication anyone was home, he tried the doorknob and it turned.

Gesturing with his head for the sergeant to step to one side of the doorway, he did the same, then turned the knob the rest of the way and pushed against the door. It swung open.

They shined their flashlights inside, playing the beams into a small living room, sparsely furnished with a couch nearest them and a couple of easy chairs. A lamp and telephone stood on a table next to one of the chairs. Halfway down the wall on the right there was a wide doorway leading to another room. A second opening was on the left near the rear of the room. The entry into a hallway divided the far back wall.

He knocked hard on the door facing. "This is the police—anybody home?"

Still no response.

"Mrs. Anderson!"

Only the continued deep silence.

He felt around the wall, fumbled until he found a light switch, and flicked it on.

The living room remained dark.

The sergeant's brow wrinkled. "I'd say that makes it pretty plain our man's been here," he said. "The only question remaining, is he still here or has he left?"

And was Trinity here when he came in? Brett wondered. He pulled his automatic from his holster. "You ready?"

"This is why I went to work over here instead of in Biloxi or Gulfport," Green said, shaking his head in disgust as he reached for his revolver. "So I could escort school children across the street, occasionally investigate a shoplifting—not have to be worrying about getting shot by some doped-up damn burglar. Yeah, I'm ready, I guess—ready as I'm gonna get, anyhow." He leveled his revolver over the top of his flashlight into the house.

Brett stepped inside and angled toward the wall to his right. He moved down it to stop just before reaching the wide doorway on that side. He dropped into a crouch and, moving his automatic in sync with his flashlight, swept the beam back and forth across the rear of the living room as the sergeant hurried to the left wall.

His big body pressed back against the wall's paneling, Green shined his light through the door in front of Brett.

"Looks like it's a family room, Lieutenant."

It was, a small one with a hardwood floor, the only furniture a couch, a throw-rug, a couple of chairs, and what appeared to be a small wet bar in a far corner. Brett shifted his gaze back into the living room and pointed his light toward the opening at the room's left rear.

The sergeant moved in that direction. Hesitating at the opening, he leaned forward and shined his light around the corner, then disappeared around it.

In a few seconds he stepped back into view and spoke in a low voice. "It's a dining room, leading to the kitchen and the back door. Lights don't work in there, either."

They moved toward the entrance of the short hallway at the back of the living room. Green stepped to the left of the entrance and he went to its right.

There were three doorways. One of them went off to the left near the rear of the hall. The other two were directly across from each other and not more than ten feet down the corridor, not far unless you were walking exposed down the hall and somebody with a gun in his hand suddenly stepped from one of the rooms.

"Trinity! This is Brett!" he called down the hallway.

The sergeant looked at him, stared for a moment, then peered back toward the doorways.

Brett realized he had begun to perspire. Trinity's car was in the carport. Had she left with friends? Or was she still there? She could have walked in on the burglar. He didn't like that thought.

He glanced toward the front of the living room and the bright, moonlit yard in front of the house. It would be nice if she suddenly drove up with friends, if they had been to buy some new fuses after the fuse box in the house had blown while they were talking in the living room. Then he heard a barely perceptible sound back to their left. Something had bumped.

Brett turned off his flashlight. "Someone's in the kitchen."

The sergeant switched off his flashlight, turned, and knelt on one knee. His wide shoulders hunched forward, he pointed his revolver toward the opening.

"Brett," came the whisper.

Christ, doesn't she ever do what she's told? "We're in here, Paige."

In a few seconds, gun in one hand and her purse in the other, she walked from the kitchen. Ignoring his frown by refusing to look at him, she moved to Green's side. The top of her head didn't come to much more than the level of the big man's shoulder. She leaned around him to peer down the dark hall.

Brett frowned again when he caught her glance in the glow of the flashlights.

"I saw somebody with a light moving around in the kitchen," she explained. "I didn't know who it was. Was afraid maybe somebody was in there you didn't know about. What was I supposed to do—wait until I heard a shot?"

He stared at her for a moment longer before looking back at the sergeant. "We'll go down each side. You watch the doorway on my side and I'll watch the one across from it. Don't forget the one at the end of the hall."

Angry at being ignored, Paige laid her purse on the floor, stepped out from behind the sergeant, and, clasping the butt of her revolver in both hands, leveled the weapon at the far doorway.

Green stepped into the hall and crossed to the right. Pressing his back up against the wall, he pointed his revolver toward the first doorway on the left.

Brett crossed to the left wall. They both inched slowly down the corridor. Nearly to the two doorways across from each other, Green shined his light in front of Brett and said, "A bathroom on your side. I can see the commode."

Brett didn't say anything. He was shining his light back across the hall through the other doorway. His stare was locked on the slim body dressed in a short miniskirt and a pullover and lying sprawled on the blood-soaked carpet between the end of the bed and the wall. On a pale, outstretched arm and glittering in his flashlight's beam was the wide silver bracelet Trinity had worn since high school—the bracelet he had given her. He felt sick. Then he noticed the awkward angle of her head and realized it was nearly severed from her body, and his stomach turned.

"My God!" Green exclaimed.

"What?" Paige said as she started down the hallway.

"You don't want to come down here," Green said.

Brett shut his eyes and leaned back against the wall.

Paige looked into the room. She stiffened and drew her hand to her mouth.

Brett pushed off the wall and took a deep breath. "Call the chief," he said. He handed her his flashlight. "There's a phone on the table in the living room. Probably need to call the sheriff, too."

As he looked back into the bedroom, Paige moved up the hall, stopping to pick up her purse lying at the living-room entrance. At the table with the telephone, she covered her hand with a handkerchief she took out of her purse, sat in the easy chair next to the table, and lifted the receiver to her ear. She punched in Information.

When she was answered, she asked for Eddie Seales's residence in the town, then told the operator she would also be needing Sheriff Hasting's home number. Balancing Brett's flashlight on her knees, she reached for the pencil next to the telephone directory.

When the recording began to give the number, she flipped open the directory and, barely able to see what she was doing with the beam of the flashlight pointing under the table, she wrote the digits at the bottom of the inside page.

*   *   *

Back inside the bedroom, Brett knelt besides Trinity's body. He stared at the gaping wound that had nearly decapitated her.

"I'm sorry, Trinity," he said. "I'm so sorry." He felt sick. He couldn't think of anything else to say. *I'm sorry, Trinity*. He touched her arm gently.

"Brett," Green called in a low voice from the doorway. "Maybe you shouldn't be touching her anymore until the lab boys get here."

Her arm was not just warm, it was almost hot. Brett looked at the wide circle of blood only partially soaked into the carpet. His eyes narrowed and he reached out his finger tips and touched the sticky substance. Coagulating, but not anywhere close to drying.

He came suddenly to his feet, looked at the curtains rustling gently from a passing breeze then faced back to Sergeant Green.

"This just happened, Armont," he said, and hurried across the room into the hall.

Outside, he walked toward the vacant lot and looked back at the wooden fence behind the house. The sergeant joined him.

"Armont, I want you to look around back there. Then stay here until some other officers arrive. Be careful." He hurried on across the yard toward his car parked down the street.

Paige caught up with him. "What are you doing?" she asked.

"She hasn't been dead but a few minutes at most."

She had to hurry her steps to keep up with him. "Chief wasn't in," she said. "But his wife thinks she can find him. I told Martha, too. The sheriff's on his way."

Brett nodded. His lip trembled, and he broke into a trot toward his car.

CHAPTER 4

Paige barely made it inside the car before Brett drove away. As they passed Trinity's house he reached for his radio and contacted the police station.

"Martha, get the rest of the shift out here. Then get on the line to every off-duty officer. Tell them the killer might not be back to his car yet. And tell them not to use their sirens. If he is still on his way back we want him to keep taking it easy."

He replaced the mike and turned off his headlights as he turned left onto a narrow street a half block over from Trinity's house. Paige watched out the passenger window, carefully running her eyes over each yard they passed.

In a few minutes, they had circled the block and then stretched the circle wider to the next succeeding blocks. As they passed through a street crossing, they saw down to their right a marked patrol car with its floodlight playing out to its side as it drove through the next intersection.

"We might as well go back," Paige said. "He would've had his car parked closer by than this. He's gone."

Brett nodded, but didn't make any attempt to turn back toward the area in which Trinity had lived. He tightened his hands on the steering wheel in frustration. In a moment they drove over the hump of a railroad crossing and down into a lesser populated section of town. Now there were more, vacant tree-studded lots interspersed with smaller homes. He tried to see into each yard as he passed them. A few more minutes and several turns later, and Paige glanced at him again.

"Okay," he said, and nodded. "Okay."

"Look!" Paige said suddenly.

A few hundred feet ahead of them, a dark figure walked along the left side of the pavement. Brett pressed down hard on the accelerator and flicked on the headlights.

At the sudden bright lights and sharp screech of the rear wheels, the figure whirled and stared at them. Suddenly, he dashed off the pavement and into the thick trees at the side of the street.

"He's running!" Paige shouted.

Brett drove off onto the shoulder and jammed on the brakes, grabbing his flashlight and throwing open his door as the car slid to a stop.

Paige, her revolver in her hand, leapt from the other side.

Pulling his automatic from his holster, Brett dashed into the trees at the same spot the figure had disappeared.

Paige hesitated a moment at the front of the car. The patch of woods wasn't very deep. There were lines of small houses on its far side. The man running would have the best chance to escape them if he went parallel with the road.

She dashed up the pavement, running until she was sure she had gone far enough to cut him off, then ran into the trees.

The moonlight was suddenly dimmed by the thick foliage above her, and she had to slow her pace. A thin branch slapped her a stinging blow in the face and she slowed even more, at the same time holding her hand up in front of her, protecting her eyes. And it grew dimmer—she felt a nervousness beginning to settle over her like a blanket.

She wasn't scared of things women were said to fear. Crawly bugs were nothing, rats and mice were only rodents, snakes were only to be taken seriously if poisonous. But the dark—it bothered her. Nothing had ever happened to her to cause the fear, she had no background of a scary brush with darkness, it just bothered her, always had, ever since she was old enough to remember. She stopped walking.

As she did, she felt moisture seeping into her shoes. Ahead of her the undergrowth thickened as the soil got richer and damper. The trees were bigger. There was still a trail of dim moonlight ahead of her, illuminating draping limbs festooned with ghostly gray wisps of Spanish moss hanging limp and still in the humid, thick air. But deep black voids, too, where the moonlight was completely cut off by the heavy canopy of leaves at the tops of the trees.

Then off to her left she heard a faint sound—the noise of branches gently rustling against each other as a person moved through the undergrowth. Her throat tightened. Brett or the one they were chasing?

She faced in the direction of the movement and raised her revolver in both hands.

Then behind her she heard another sound of branches moving, and she whirled in the direction of that sound—and stared into more darkness. She heard it again.

"Over here, Brett!" she shouted across her shoulder. The noise out in front of her suddenly increased. The man running again. "Over this way!" she repeated loudly, and hurried forward as fast as she could.

Fifty feet farther and she stopped to see if the man still ran in the same direction—and heard nothing.

Her brow wrinkled. He had stopped. When? If it had been right after she started after him, he couldn't be very far away. She realized she couldn't hear Brett's movements, either. He would have come running at her shout. Maybe he was circling ahead of her. Her eyes darted back and forth, trying to pierce the dark voids. But it didn't help; there were so many places she couldn't see. She caught her lip in her teeth and gripped her pistol tighter.

Where had he stopped? she wondered again. Behind a trunk of one of the trees? She looked at the dim shape of the thick oak a few feet to her left.

Or maybe he was behind the one a few feet to her right. She moved back a step. She glanced over her shoulder to see another thick, dim trunk.

Jesus! She turned partially sidewise and tried to look at both trunks at the same time. And there were those that she couldn't see in the dark voids.

Then she couldn't stand it any longer. "Breh-ttt!" she screamed, the sound almost seeming to jump out of her on its own. But he didn't reply. *Damn you, Brett, answer me.*

A twig snapped off to her right and she whirled toward the sound and pointed her revolver at it. She licked her dry lips and swallowed, tried to keep her voice from breaking as she spoke.

"All right, I see you now," she said into the wide, black area a few feet in front of her. "Put your hands up and come out of there. You're under arrest."

No sound. No movement. She couldn't have seen it if there was. So dark. *Always dominate the situation when making an arrest,* they preached in training; take charge, be in control at all times. How could you be in control of somebody you couldn't damn see?

Then another thought as her revolver began to waver—the killer smiling at her bluff as he edged silently through the dark toward her. She imagined the bloody knife blade.

"Dammit, I mean it. You put your hands up or I'm going to shoot." And those words caused an even scarier thought—what if he had a gun? *Jesus!* At that second, back at the very far edge of another dark patch to her left, she thought she glimpsed a slight movement—and she yelled at the same time as she jabbed her revolver toward it.

"I'm going to shoot! Right now!"

"Paige!" Brett shouted from close behind her.

"Here!" she squealed in a strange voice. "Hurry!"

The sound of branches slapping hard against one another came from behind her, and Brett emerged not ten feet away. He switched on his flashlight and swung it in the direction she pointed her revolver.

The figure was gone—if she had ever really seen it in the first place.

Then there was the low, barely perceptible voice.

"Mr. Brett?"

She jerked her revolver toward the right of the earlier movement. Brett swung his light in the same direction. But there was nothing but the stark tree trunks.

"Mr. Brett?" the voice repeated, an unmistakable nasal tone to it now. "Is that some of you?"

Brett lowered his arm to his side, no longer pointing his automatic. "J. B.?" he asked. "Is that you?"

"Yeah, this is me, Brett."

"Dammit, J. B., what are you doing? Come on out here where I can see you."

"I'd feel a sight better about doin' that if that woman would quit swinging that pistol around."

"Come on, J. B."

A slim figure slowly stepped out from behind a trunk twenty feet in front of them. He was an older, gray-haired black man in coveralls, his bare skin taut under the garment's faded blue straps. Paige realized she had seen him in town before.

Brett shone his light toward the ground and stepped forward to meet him. "What are you doing running from us, J. B.?"

"Maybe I'm the one oughta be askin' what you all chasing after me for?" the man replied.

Paige realized she was still pointing her revolver at the man and lowered it.

He looked at her and smiled. "I never met the wife, Brett," he said, "but that's her, ain't it?"

"Yeah. J. B., this is Paige. Paige, this is J. B. Browning. He was the janitor at the high school when I was there. His son's the one I told you about signing off our football team."

Browning smiled proudly. "Older boy signed, too. That un's with the Saints now. I haven't had to hit a lick since."

Brett slipped his automatic into his holster. "Why did you run, J. B.?" he asked again.

"I's mindin' my own business walking over to my sister's and you slip up on me with your lights shed, then come at me like you've a mind to flat run me down—what'd you expect me to do?"

Brett nodded. "Yeah, I guess so. We thought you might be somebody we're looking for."

"You're workin' mighty hard at it, too. Not that burglar again, is it?"

"No, a woman was murdered."

The man's narrow face twisted in shock. "Lord, have mercy! Who?"

"A woman named Trinity Anderson. She had only been in town for a little while."

"Red MG?"

"Yeah, how do you know?"

"I know'd her, all right. Seen her 'round town, anyhow . . . Kilt, huh?" He shook his head. "Lord," he said again. "I don't guess with your chasin' after me that you have any ideas who done it yet?"

"Not yet."

When they reached the road, J. B. stopped at the side of the car as Brett slipped inside and shut his door. Then the old man looked down through the window.

"Mr. Brett, you ever hear of an old boy they call Blue Tick?"

Brett shook his head.

"Well, Sergeant Armont knows him, you ask him. When I's first laid eyes on that woman in her MG, Blue Tick's the one what pointed her out to me. Said he'd mowed her yard last week. Said there was somethin' 'bout her made him think she might not half mind if he'd done more than mow her yard. I didn't put no stock in that, not knowing Blue Tick like I does. But I figured you oughta know what he'd said—considerin'."

CHAPTER 5

"He goes by the name of Blue Tick," Brett said, and glanced across his shoulder at Trinity's house, brightly illuminated with the flashing lights of half a dozen police cars parked in the street.

Sergeant Green nodded. "Yeah, I know him. Last I heard, he lived over close to Gulfport. I'll get somebody to check him out." He walked to his car and leaned inside the window for his radio mike.

Brett looked back at the house again. Several officers shining flashlights before them searched the side yards for anything the killer might have dropped in his hurry to get away. An ambulance backed slowly toward the open front door. When a car drove up to the edge of the street behind him, he turned toward it.

A stocky man dressed in a brown suit stepped from the car. He appeared to be in his middle to late fifties, with his closely trimmed brown hair showing flecks of gray. He looked familiar. The slimmer, younger man who had been driving the car came around its hood and the two walked toward the house.

Brett moved to cut him off. "Excuse me," he said.

The stocky one ignored him, striding on toward the house without slowing his pace. His companion stopped and pulled a small I.D. case from an inside coat pocket.

"F.B.I.," he said, holding up the case.

Brett nodded, and the agent hurried to catch up with the other one.

25

Brett stared after them. F.B.I.? he thought. Then another car stopping behind him caught his attention. The driver's door opened and a well-built dark-haired man in blue sports jacket and gray slacks stepped outside—Vic McIntyre. In a moment he came around the car and toward the lawn.

"Hey, Brett," he said as he reached to shake hands. "I've been thinking about you ever since I heard the victim's name. That had to be rough on you, finding her like you did. I heard talk over my radio about a print. Are we going to be lucky?"

Brett shook his head. "He had on gloves." He glanced back at the house and the two F.B.I. agents now talking to Dr. Felter, the county coroner. "Vic, the F.B.I.'s here, and now you. You all thinking—"

"F.B.I.'s thinking you could have surprised him before he finished is the word I got over the radio. We'll know for sure in a minute with Applewhite here. He has something they can verify it with—something they've held back."

Applewhite. Brett knew why the stocky agent had looked familiar. He had been on television before—the man sent to the area to head up the search for the psycho. He had opened a headquarters in Gulfport, a location roughly equidistant between the murders that had taken place in New Orleans and Mobile, and due south of Memphis up I-55, where the psycho had also struck.

"Was there any other sign?" Vic asked. "Other than the near decapitation."

Brett shook his head. "I didn't even take it as a sign. I just assumed it was the viciousness of the attack. He's never struck outside the cities."

"We'll know pretty soon," Vic answered, and glanced back across his shoulder as another pair of vehicles stopped at the edge of the street.

The first was a TV van. A long-haired young man hopped from the driver's side and hurried around to the rear door. An attractive brunette in a light-colored skirt and matching blouse stepped from the passenger seat. She leaned to look at her reflection in the sideview mirror, fluffed her hair, ran her thumb around the corners of her mouth, and then strode toward the house.

The other car double-parked in the street next to one of the cars belonging to the sheriff's deputies. Police Chief Eddie Seales, dressed in khaki slacks and a camouflage shirt, moved his blocky body outside and shut the door. Brett walked to meet him.

"Chief."

Seales nodded his greeting and looked toward the house. "I was out fishing. First night I've taken off in a damn month—and this." He pulled a folded handkerchief from a rear pocket, mopping his brow before he spoke again. "He came in through a bedroom window?"

"It's open and the screen's off."

"What about this Blue Tick I been hearing about over the radio?"

"He worked for her before. Armont's having him checked out."

Seales looked at the F.B.I. agents, still talking to the county coroner. "I heard they were on the way over here. They seen the body yet?"

"No, sir, they just got here."

Seales nodded and started toward the house. The brunette from the TV van noticed him and cut him off. The long-haired young man, balancing a camera on his shoulder, hurried after her. The camera's lights came on as she lifted a mike toward Seales and said something to him. He ignored her and continued around her on toward the house. The camera lights went out, leaving the brunette, her hands on her hips, staring after him.

Brett stared at the house for a moment and thought about the psycho, then glanced across the narrow street at the assembled onlookers. As he did, the gray-haired woman in the white terrycloth bathrobe stepped from the group and walked to Sergeant Green in the middle of the pavement. With her hair in a bun atop her head barely level with the big man's chin, she talked to Green a moment, then the two came on across the street.

"Lieutenant," Green said. "Lady's got something you need to hear."

She smiled pleasantly.

Brett nodded his greeting. "Yes, ma'am."

"I'm Mrs. Wylie," the woman said. "Virginia Wylie. I think her husband did it."

Brett narrowed his eyes at her statement. "Excuse me?"

"Her husband," the woman repeated. She drew a pair of spectacles from her robe pocket, slipped them over her short, pointed nose, and smiled up at them.

"Her husband, James," she said. "He came in with her tonight. They were arguing something terrible. And now he's gone. Isn't that right?"

"Ma'am, let me get this straight. You *saw* him come in with her?"

"You heard that right. I was looking out my window when they drove up. They were in her sports car, there."

Brett turned toward Green. "Get the chief."

As the sergeant hurried toward the house Brett turned back to the woman. "If you don't mind, I'd like for the chief to hear this."

"Don't mind at all. I want to help all I can." She smiled pleasant again, her eyes big behind the thick lenses of her glasses.

Vic stepped up beside him. "What is it?" he asked.

"She said Trinity's husband was here."

"Was," the woman said softly.

In a moment, Applewhite, the other agent, and Seales, strode toward them. When the chief stopped, he nodded at Vic and looked at the woman.

"This is Mrs. Wylie," Brett said.

Seales nodded. "Mrs. Wylie, I'm Chief of Police Eddie Seales. This is Special Agent Jerry Applewhite of the F.B.I."

The little woman's eyes brightened as she looked at Applewhite. "I never met me an F.B.I. agent before," she said. "That's what I always wanted to be. Or a C.I.A. agent, maybe. 'Course, back when I was coming up, women didn't do things such as that." She held out her hand to him. "So glad to meet you, sir."

As Applewhite awkwardly returned the woman's handshake, Seales got back to business. "You told Lieutenant Dunnigan you thought you saw Mr. Anderson tonight."

"Just a minute, Chief," Applewhite said, and looked at Vic.

"This is Vic McIntyre," Seales explained, "a private investigator working on the Lloyd murder—the man killed along with the maid last month."

"I know who he is," the agent retorted gruffly. "I didn't know if you wanted to be asking questions in front of him."

Vic smiled, glanced at Brett, and turned away, walking toward the rear of the house.

Seales looked at the F.B.I. agent for a moment and faced back to the woman. "You said that you thought you saw Mr. Anderson tonight?" he repeated.

"No, sir, Mr. Seales," the woman said softly. "I didn't say I thought. I did see him—both of them. They drove up in her MG and walked to the door together. I saw them as plain as day."

"His boss said he's supposed to be out on the road. Somewhere around New Orleans."

"Yes, sir, Mr. Seales, I'm sure that's right—supposed to be."

"Where were you at the time?"

"At my house. It's that one down past the curve on the far side."

The house she pointed to was almost a hundred yards away and hard to see due to the large oaks lining each side of the street.

Seales looked back at her eyes, at how widely magnified they were through the lenses of her glasses.

"Would you mind showing us exactly where you were when you saw him?" he asked.

"Of course not. It was from my dining-room window. Come on and I'll show you—had a clear view of their front door. That's where they were when they were arguing."

Mrs. Wylie's house was a small one-story. As she neared the front door, she said, "You're just gonna have to put up with the mess inside. It's Roger's doing. He never picks up after himself. I think it goes back to his mother babying him."

She held the door open and they filed inside. There wasn't any mess, unless she was referring to the newspaper draped over the arm of an easy chair in one corner of the room, or the two copies of *Original Spy* magazine on the coffee table. Otherwise, the room appeared freshly cleaned. Roger must be the one whose snoring could be heard coming from down a hall leading toward the rear of the house.

After leading them through an opening off the right side of the room into a small dining area, the woman pointed past a mahogany table and four ornate wood chairs to a window.

Seales stepped to it.

"I was standing right there the whole time they was carrying on. You can plainly see there's a clear view of their front door."

There was. More important were the binoculars to a side of the window sill and partially concealed behind a drape. Brett looked at the chief and saw he had noted them, too. When they turned back toward the woman, she showed an embarrassed smile.

"I sorta forgot I left them there," she said. "But I guess you believe me, now, don't you? They came with my *Original Spy Kit.*"

"A damn wife killer," Applewhite grunted in a low voice and shook his head. "I hear about her nearly being decapitated and rush over here, and it's nothing but a wife killer. A damn plain-run-of-the-mill-son-of-a-bitching wife killer." He shook his head again. "Arguing when they came in, were they?"

Even though he was musing aloud rather than asking a question, Mrs. Wylie nodded. "Yes, sir, sure was."

"Probably been arguing since the day she met him," Applewhite added. "You're going to find out he'd been slapping her around for a long time. Things like this don't happen all at once. It was coming and she didn't have the sense to leave him. Dumb broads."

Brett caught his lip in his teeth and stared.

"Well," Applewhite said to the other agent, "let's give the body a look anyway."

Brett would just as soon the agent went on back to Gulfport. If the bastard handled Trinity's body roughly . . .

CHAPTER 6

Paige, her purse strap slung across her shoulder and Brett's flashlight shining before her, walked slowly toward the graying wood fence surrounding Trinity's backyard. A pair of deputies worked with gloved hands at a dark smudge near the top of the bannister. Sheriff Richard Hastings, a rangy man in his late forties, monitored their work while absentmindedly cleaning his finger-nails with a small pocket knife. With no tie on under his coat, and his hair mussed, it was obvious that he had been asleep when he received the call about the attack.

He looked up as Paige stopped before him.

"Where he came over?" she asked

"Uh-huh. We're taking a blood sample. But I doubt she had a chance to hurt him—it's going to be hers."

"They found more blood down the street?"

Hastings nodded back across his shoulder toward the spot where she and Brett had first parked at the curve. "He went over a fence behind one of the houses facing the beach; guess his car was parked over there somewhere."

One of the deputies said something and Hastings turned back toward the fence. Paige looked down the street. Seeing a flashlight cast its beam behind a house past the curve, she walked in that direction.

Brett stood near the edge of the street in front of Trinity's house and stared at the front door. Inside, FBI agent Jerry Applewhite knelt before Trinity's body, which was partially covered by a sheet. He held her wrist in his hand and slowly lowered it back to the carpet. He looked up at the other agent. Neither of them spoke.

Paige climbed over the short cyclone-wire fence into the rear yard of a massive, two-story antebellum house facing across a frontage road and U.S. 90 toward the beach. Only one dim light shone through a second-floor rear window; the occupants were obviously asleep.

Traffic whizzed by along the beach and past the house, many of the vehicles undoubtedly loaded with those coming and going from the large casinos lining the coast. Beyond the beach a brightly lit large motor yacht cruised slowly west along the Mississippi Sound toward New Orleans. Everybody having a good time, she thought, with no one other than a few of Trinity's immediate neighbors aware of the horror that had taken place. Well, they would know by morning, and then the small towns along the coast would be full of anxious people. For though New Orleans was only a little over fifty miles away, and a vicious killing there not big news, it would be earth-shattering here.

She looked to the left of the home in front of her, at the huge stucco contemporary next to it, also darkened and with no sign of life.

Facing back to her right, she looked at one big house after another rising in a long line of expensive dwellings, some of them the old wooden structures restored to the grandeur of the last century, some of them new, constructed of brick and stone and replacing the houses that had formerly sat there and had either burned or been blown away by Hurricane Camille. They reminded her of those houses dotting the sprawling luxury area where her father lived in Biloxi. According to him, the kind of future lifestyle she was throwing away when she made up her mind to make a career out of law enforcement. She didn't even listen anymore. A light played across her and cut off.

She saw a pair of officers coming toward her from the rear of the house off to the right of the antebellum home. She walked toward them, her hair whipping about her face from a particularly strong gust from the Gulf.

"Paige."

It was Arnie Hatcher, the officer who had failed to answer the dispatcher's call. Knowing Arnie, there was no telling what he had been doing. A short, slightly built man, he was at twenty-two both the youngest and newest officer on the force, having only been hired the past spring.

The man with him was a little older and dressed in the uniform of the sheriff's department. She thought she knew almost all of the deputies but didn't recognize him.

"Find anything?" she asked.

"You heard about that spot of blood on the fence there?" He nodded toward the next yard.

"Yeah."

"It looks like he fell when he went over it," Arnie said. "Squashed down a bunch of big flower bushes on this side of it." He raised his hand and brushed his thin, brown hair back away from his forehead. He was constantly doing that, a nervous habit she had noticed the first time she met him.

He glanced across his shoulder down the line of houses. "Deputy down that way found a little piece of material in a hedge. Might be torn from a shirt. He's waiting for one of the lab boys to come and see if it looks like it got there recently, but it looked old to me."

He glanced at his watch. "I guess we'll be going on, make another sweep through the yards. Want to walk with us?"

"I might catch up to you. I'm going to go look at where he came over the fence."

"Okay. We'll be down in this direction." He and the deputy started across the grass in the direction of the line of houses. Then he stopped and looked back at her.

"Oh, yeah, Paige. If you happen to run up on a big black dog out here—I mean a *real big* black dog, don't let him throw you for a scare. He comes on looking bad but he's a regular pu— a wimp when you call him down."

"Thanks."

As the two men walked off, she smiled. If Arnie called the dog down, then the animal had to be a wimp. In the short few weeks he had been on the force, Arnie had already twice threatened to quit because of being forced into situations he considered unduly threatening—once when he had to transport a straitjacketed patient up toward Jackson to the state mental hospital, and the second time when he had been asked late one night to check on shots being fired out toward the swamps north of town.

Well, it took all kinds. She glanced at the full moon hanging out over the water and, clutching Brett's flashlight comfortingly in her hand, walked toward the place where the killer had left the second spot of blood.

"Her husband planned it a little too hard," Sergeant Green said, looking back at Trinity's house. "His taking the screen off and raising the window made it look like a break-in, all right. But how would anyone not familiar with the place have any idea the fuse box was in the closet?"

Brett nodded.

"Oh, yeah," Green added. "For what it's worth now, Blue Tick was playing cards with half a dozen others. Gulfport P.D. said the game started before dark."

Brett looked toward Trinity's house as the front door opened and the two F.B.I. agents stepped out into the bright light of the TV camera. They strode across the lawn toward Sheriff Hastings and Seales, and Brett moved toward them to see what they had to say.

"We need to get more men out here," Applewhite said in a sharp voice as he stopped in front of the sheriff. "Nobody but the psycho knows what that man did to her—nobody."

Brett was sure what he had heard, but he didn't believe it. Hastings's forehead wrinkled questioningly. "What?"

"Nobody but the psycho," Applewhite repeated. He looked down the street toward Mrs. Wylie's house. "If that old woman's not totally blind—if it really was the husband who drove in with the victim—then we don't only have ourselves a wife killer. And he was surprised in the act; that's obvious because he didn't finish what he started."

Brett stared back at the house. He still couldn't believe it. And *surprised in the act*—Trinity's body still warm and the blood not dried into the carpet. He looked down the street past the curve, beyond Mrs. Wylie's house toward the fence where the spot of blood had been found. Officers' lights swept the yards behind the big houses facing toward the beach.

CHAPTER 7

The big flower bushes that Arnie had told Paige were squashed when the killer came over the fence were azaleas; there were millions of them in bloom all up and down the coast. Her father had them planted along the boundary fence that circled his estate. The depression in the soft ground next to the fence was deep; the killer had fallen hard. Too bad he hadn't broken his damn neck.

She looked at the darkened stucco contemporary at the head of the deep yard—and noticed movement. She narrowed her eyes. The huge German shepherd Arnie had spoken of came slowly toward her.

As he neared, he grew in size to the biggest shepherd she had ever seen. She smiled faintly. "You're a wimp," she said softly. "Don't forget. Okay?"

The animal stopped directly in front of her—and held up his paw.

She smiled and leaned to squeeze his foot. "And glad to meet you, too, fellow. I'm Paige." She glanced back in the direction she had come. "Want to go find Arnie with me?"

The dog's tail wagged. He fell in beside her as she started back toward the yard where she had entered the subdivision.

After crossing that yard and two more closely mowed lawns, she came to a tall, matted hedge. It had to be the place where the piece of material had been found, and the lab technicians must have already been there; the deputy was gone.

She walked along the hedge, saw a place where the limbs weren't as thick, and, holding her forearms in front of her face, pushed her way through the branches to emerge onto the property of a large two-story brick house. An oversize, rectangular-shaped swimming pool was set directly behind it. The dog came through the hedge at another spot and hurried to her side.

She walked to the pool. The water was dirty, almost black, leaves, bits of trash, and dead bugs floating on the surface. Back to her right a few feet from that end of the pool, a large pool house built out of the same brick as the house showed bare windows.

She switched on her flashlight and shined it toward the main house, saw its windows were without curtains.

Looking down at the German shepherd staring into the dark water, she leaned and patted its head. "Which one of these houses do you live in, fellow? Hope it's not this one. If it is, I hate to be the one to break the news to you, but you're an orphan."

She saw a patrol car pass by the house. The vehicle's spotlight shone back and forth into the lawns along the pavement.

Looking farther down the yards, she saw another beam of light flash between two houses.

A half mile away, a highway patrol helicopter hovered a few hundred feet above the ground, the craft's brilliant spotlight sweeping the yards below it.

Arnie and the deputy were nowhere to be seen. They must have moved to the lawns in front of the houses—that probably was the beam of their flashlights she had seen from a front yard. She glanced at her watch. Brett and the others would soon be finished back at the Andersons', if they hadn't already. He would be wondering where she was. She decided to go back.

Feeling uncomfortably warm, she slipped off Brett's dark sweatshirt and folded it across her arm. Turning in the direction she had entered the line of houses, she noticed the door to the pool house was cracked open. A little slit showed dark behind it.

A nervous sensation played over her. She smiled at her anxiety and again started to head back—but her eyes went to the door once again.

No, she thought, the killer would be trying to get as far away from here as possible. Besides, one of the deputies or officers would have already looked; there had to be several of them already by here. Still, her gaze went back to the door.

Damn, she thought. *What are you out here for—to take a stroll?* She walked toward the pool house—like a cop would be expected to do.

At the door, she hesitated a second, then reached for the door-knob. As she clasped it, she felt the warm stickiness on the back of the metal and jerked her hand back.

She dropped the sweatshirt, threw her body against the wall next to the door, and fumbled in her purse for her revolver. Grasping the butt, she yanked the weapon out and held it toward the door.

Her heart beating rapidly, she glanced down the row of houses toward the antebellum home where she had entered the yards. And then for the second time that night her shout almost seemed to jump out of her by itself. "BREH-TTTT!"

The silence was the deepest one she'd ever heard. Except for her breathing—it was too loud; she couldn't hear above it. She tried to muffle the sound. Then she visualized the slight movement she had seen in the dark woods earlier. She had come out okay on that. Now, here she was again. Why in the hell hadn't she just stayed with Brett? And then her next thought:

What if the stickiness wasn't blood?

Her brow wrinkled. Though the big house at the far end of the pool was deserted, someone was taking care of the lawn. The mower would be stored somewhere. She had yelled out like a banshee. Brett and the others would come running in a minute and she would have oil on her hand where a yardman had worked on a lawn mower and then passed through the pool-house door, leaving the smear.

She raised the revolver and lifted her fingers from the butt, shining the flashlight on them.

Her heart skipped another beat at the bright red. Her lips were so dry, they felt like they were cracking. Her surging adrenaline made her head swirl. She glanced back toward the Anderson house again and then back to her other side and up the row of houses.

Where were Arnie and the damn deputy? Where was *somebody?* Then she thought, *Pull yourself together.*

She looked back at the door. If the killer had entered the place,

he would only have darted inside to hide a moment when an
officer passed. He wouldn't have continued to stay there. He
couldn't be *that* crazy.

She took a deep breath, slipped her hand around the facing, and
felt for a light switch. She found it and flicked it on.

Nothing happened.

The dirty pool, the pump not running— *No electricity.*

Dark.

But not like in the woods. She had a flashlight with her this
time. She took another deep breath, waited a moment longer, then
reached out with the light and used it to push the door open the
rest of the way, making sure it went far enough back so that no
one could be hiding behind it. Slowly, shining the light around
the corner ahead of her, she leaned forward and peered around
the door.

There was no furniture, only the empty space with high walls
rising to a vaulted ceiling and a bare tile floor. She felt her muscles
relax—and then noticed in a back corner of the room a single
closet with double doors.

She stared at the closet.

He wouldn't be.

She smiled wryly. No, not that, not in the closet. He might have
looked inside the pool house. He *did* look inside, the blood proved
that. But then he would have left. He wouldn't have let himself
be trapped like that, not just standing in there, just waiting to be
caught, just— No, of course not. She could go on back to the
Anderson house and tell the sheriff or the chief about the blood.

But she couldn't. What if he *was* hiding in there? If she left,
then he could, too. They would never know whether he had been
there or not. What if she left and they came back and there was
a pool of blood in the closet, where he had been standing, waiting,
dripping? She closed her eyes at that thought, then glanced again
back in the direction of the Anderson house.

She was too far away for her voice to have carried above the
brisk breeze blowing in from the Gulf and the sound of the traffic
on Highway 90. No one there could have heard her shout. She
looked back at the closet again. Even as nervous as she was, an
amusing thought occurred to her:

She could fire her gun in the air.

That would certainly stand out above the other sounds, certainly bring somebody running—a bunch of somebodies.

She stayed amused only a moment, then looked back at the closet once again. What was she going to do, she wondered, keep peeking in and out of the place, stand there until Brett finally came looking for her? Stand there until dawn maybe? For the first time she noticed the German shepherd had left. Wimp.

She looked back at the opening into the pool house. She closed her eyes in exasperation, trying to summon the courage by telling herself all her advantages. She had a gun. She could blind whoever was there with her light—hold the light out to her side just in case. And why not her? If Brett and a half dozen other officers were here with her, one of them would still have to be the one to open the door and look inside. She had once overheard an officer make a remark about a woman cop, a typically male remark. Why *should* she wait for a man to get there—to prove the officer was correct in what he had said about women cops? That did it. And, besides, not even a nut would hide in such a place, she told herself once more. Right?

She kept repeating this to herself again and again as she took a deep breath, clasped her hand tighter around the butt of her revolver, and suddenly stepped away from the wall and into the doorway, crouching, her light and revolver directed rigidly toward the closet.

Though the room was empty, she kept her eyes on all four sides at the same time. She couldn't help it. Her revolver trembled noticeably. She steadied the gun by bringing it against the flashlight.

She took a step forward, and another, and another, doing as she had been taught, legs wide, a slow shuffle—stay in control.

The closer she got to the closet, the harder it was to see both sides of the room at once, and she didn't want to quit seeing them. She felt her throat tighten.

Tighten up, Paige, you're in control. You've got the gun. It's only a closet. Even in the tight grip of both her hands, the revolver began to shake again.

Suddenly, she was there. The worst was over, she didn't have to take another step. Now she had only to move to the side and open the damn doors. Simple. The only problem was, she now visualized his smiling face as he lurked just behind the doors, waiting, the knife raised in his bloody hand. *Dripping.* She shuddered at the thought.

Damn it, go on, she told herself, ashamed of her thoughts and scared by them, too. She forced her flashlight away from holding her revolver steady, stepped to the side, and reached for the door.

She stopped her hand.

She decided to get on her knees and open it by reaching up. He wouldn't expect that. She'd hold the light up high where he would think she was, blinding him, and shoot up at him.

She knelt and reached for the doorknob, almost dropping her flashlight as she moved her fingers to clasp the knob—then hesitated. She held her breath again, once more shut her eyes briefly, then squinted in fear and jerked on the knob.

Her heart stopped—dead still. But all she looked at was empty space. Blessed empty space. Her revolver slowly quit shaking. Still holding onto the doorknob, she slumped in relief.

After a few moments, she raised her head, struggled to her feet, glanced again for a moment into the closet, and closed the door. She turned toward the doorway—and saw the wide, cavernous shadow near the top of the wall to her left.

A cold chill ran up her back as she jerked her pistol and flashlight up toward the loft. She had walked to the closet without ever noticing it. Another chill swept over her, this time causing her to shake noticeably.

Then out of the corner of her eyes she caught the ladder bolted to the side of the way—*the way up into the loft.*

She continued to stare at the ladder with one eye and the black void of the loft with the other. She began to shake her head back and forth.

No. No. No. Not this time. There wasn't any way. The woods— the blackness there and the man staring at her out of the darkness, then standing in fear outside the entrance to the bathhouse, shaking inside as she came across the tile floor toward the closet—that was enough, that was too much.

She continued to stare at the ladder. She couldn't do it. Her legs wouldn't let her. She didn't want them to let her. The hell with him; she didn't care if he was up there.

"Come on down!" she suddenly shouted, slapping the flashlight

back to the side of her revolver and pointing them both at the dark space. *"Now!"* She couldn't believe she was doing this for the second time tonight.

Then she heard the barely perceptible sound come from the loft—or thought she did. The revolver trembled, the light's round beam vibrated against the edge of the loft.

She heard it again—a scratching sound.

"Oh!" she moaned, and cocked her revolver.

A large rat jumped from the loft to an exposed rafter and dashed up it toward the top of the vaulted ceiling.

Jesus!

"Paige!"

She whirled toward the door.

Brett stared at her. She jerked her revolver toward the floor. He was lucky she hadn't shot him.

"What in hell are you doing in here?" he asked, his tone both sharp and nervous. He stepped inside the room. Green appeared behind him.

She looked back at the loft. "Up there," she said.

Brett, his eyes toward the loft, walked up beside her. *"What* up there?"

"I don't know if there's anything, but there's blood on the door."

Green knelt and pointed his light and revolver toward the loft.

Brett saw the ladder and moved toward it. He had someone else's flashlight.

Hesitating a moment at the ladder he glanced back at the sergeant and Paige, both of whom were pointing their weapons toward the top of the ladder.

Using the hand in which he held his flashlight and the elbow of the arm that held his automatic, he started climbing awkwardly up the rungs.

One rung from the top, he hesitated, raised his automatic beside his head and jerked himself up to shine the light into the space.

His body slumped visibly. He hung there for a moment, and then he looked back down at her.

"I can't believe you came in here by yourself," he said in an exasperated voice. "You had to have been out of your damn mind.

You're going to get your butt killed one of these days. If you haven't got any more sense than to—''

She walked toward the door, silencing him. She wasn't angry at his remarks; she knew he said what he did out of his fear for her. But she was in no mood to listen. She noticed her pulse had slowed—too slow. She felt dizzy. Now was she going to faint? What a hell of a time. It would ruin everything.

But she didn't, and her legs became stronger as she walked on to the door. She stopped there and looked at the dark stain on the knob. She shined her light on it. The blood went on around the knob, under it.

She saw the edge of an imprint, and her brow wrinkled. She knelt, shined the light up under the knob, and looked closer.

"What?" Brett said.

"Somebody stepped in here to look around before I did. There's a partial impression here, in the blood. It's not from my fingers, either. I caught the knob from the top."

The sergeant knelt beside her and looked where the beam of light fell.

He smiled when he came back to his feet. "I'd give a month's pay if it was Arnie, and I'd been here to see his expression when he felt it on his hand." He chuckled and shook his head in amusement. "Two months' pay."

CHAPTER 8

Leaving Sergeant Green at the door of the pool house to wait until someone could come back and check on the smear of blood, Brett walked to Paige, who was standing out in the fresh air.

"Her husband killed her," he said.

Her brow wrinkled. "Her husband?"

"Yeah, the window open and all that—he tried to make it look like a break-in. But there was a woman down the street who saw him come in with Trinity in the MG. And the F.B.I. says he's the psycho."

At his last words, Paige's brow wrinkled. "What?"

He nodded and started back toward the fence and the place where he had entered the yards. "No doubt about it."

Paige hurried to keep up with him. "You said no doubt about it?"

"Vic says there's some way they know for sure when it's the psycho—something they've held back that he does to his victims. It was her husband and he's the psycho—they're one and the same. Hastings has everyone he can think of on his way over here. There's the possibility he might be trapped somewhere around here."

When they stopped at the short cyclone fence to climb into the yards of the houses closest to Trinity's, Paige looked back in the direction of the pool house, and her brow wrinkled. Brett hoped that the thought scared her as badly as it had him when he couldn't find her earlier.

But Paige had something else on her mind. "I didn't like you talking to me like that in front of Armont," she said.

He didn't answer, and she spoke again. "You made me sound stupid. What would *you* have done if you'd been there? In fact, what did you do when you got there? You climbed up to the loft and looked."

"I had a backup."

"What difference would that have made if he had jammed a knife in your neck? You'd be just as dead. I was a lot safer only opening a door and having a light to blind him with. And if I'd left there, we would never know whether he was there or not, would we? What was I supposed to do?"

What about nothing? he thought, what about just waiting—somebody would have eventually been by there.

As they left the fence behind them, Paige looked over at him again. Her tone was softer now. "Brett, it doesn't make sense that he would have driven up in her car with her, taken a chance on somebody seeing he was back in town, then killed her—not if that was his plan all along."

"You're probably right. The old woman said they were arguing when she saw them at the front door. Maybe he just lost his temper—lost it, period. Then he could have tried to cover up what he did—blame it on the psycho and hope no one saw him come in with her. Or maybe he lost it so bad that he did whatever the F.B.I. knows about before he got his control back. *If* he got it back."

Her face wrinkled again. "But if he didn't plan it, where's his car? That sounds more like he planned it, had her come after him so his car wouldn't be seen. But then he would have left it far enough from the house to warrant her coming after him—more than a block or two. Maybe he hasn't gotten back there yet."

"Seales has officers looking everywhere for it. He's hoping we find it parked somewhere, that he didn't get away."

Two Gulfport police cars drove down the street and parked in front of Trinity's house. Behind them came another two cars loaded with men in civilian clothes—F.B.I. agents. In a minute they all clustered in a small group and quickly started up the pavement. They nodded as they passed Brett and Paige. Brett saw Chief Seales and Vic standing in front of the house, and he and Paige angled across the lawn to them.

"Anderson's boss says he's scheduled to be at a sales meeting in New Orleans in the morning, Brett," Seales said as they stopped before him. "If he did get away and is on his way back there, the highway patrol will probably get him. If they don't, then New Orleans P.D. will have officers waiting for him when he shows up at the sales meeting."

Vic wasn't so sure. *"If* he shows up there, is more like it," he said. "And the only way that's going to happen is if he planned this from the very beginning, was out to kill his wife and make it look like the psycho did it, and I don't think that's the case."

"What do you mean?" Paige asked.

"I think their argument continued when they got inside the house and she said something to set him off and he just went bananas—something shook him up so bad he lost control. If it wasn't that way, if he had it planned, then why did he just drive up to the front door with her for everybody to see he was back in town?"

Paige nodded. "That's just what I was saying to Brett."

Vic continued. "The psycho has never been careless before. I don't believe he had it planned at all. He lost control over something, went all the way through his act, at least got as far as whatever it is the F.B.I. knows, and then you two surprised him before he decapitated her. And he's running like hell now. He'd have to be after he came down and realized what he had done— that he might've been seen with her."

"Maybe and maybe not," Seales countered. "Where is his car? He damn sure had her come somewhere and pick him up. Besides, how do you figure how a maniac thinks? Maybe he thinks no one knew he was in town. No one would have except for the old woman, and that was just an accident."

"Chief," Brett said. "Paige found another blood smear. It's at a pool house behind one of the homes on the beach."

Seales's brow wrinkled. "Which house?"

"Cross over into the yards directly past the curve. Turn back to your right. The bathhouse is to the far side of the first hedge you come to. It's on the doorknob. I thought you might have already heard. Somebody touched it before Paige did. You can see his print.''

Seales looked at Paige. "What does he mean, you touched it?"

"I didn't know the blood was there before I looked inside. But I didn't touch it on the bottom."

"You've lost me."

"The print that was there is on the bottom of the knob. I touched it at the top."

Seales's tongue washed his top lip as he thought. "Okay, I'll go take a look at it." He looked at the house next to Trinity's as a car turned into the drive. It parked under a carport at the far side of the house and they couldn't see who got out and went inside the house.

"Wonder where it's been?" Seales asked. "Did you notice if that car was here when you first came up?"

Brett hadn't, and he shook his head.

"Go ask them. Then I guess you need to start checking houses all along the street. Somebody might have seen something, heard something."

Brett looked at Hastings, who was talking to one of his deputies in the street. "You want me to ask the sheriff if someone reported the blood to him?"

"No. You get on to the houses and I'll check with him when I get back from seeing it."

As Seales walked away, they crossed the lawn to the small, one-story redbrick house next door to Trinity's.

The couple who had just arrived there appeared to be in their midtwenties. The husband, Edward Gregory, had a strong face accentuated by a square jaw. He wore his sandy-colored hair mounded high above his forehead and was maybe an inch taller than Brett's height of slightly over six feet, as well as more heavily built.

His wife, Paula, was a statuesque blonde, with her long hair done up in a French roll. They were both well dressed, him in a suit and her in a beige cotton skirt and a white cotton blouse with a stand-up collar. They had spent the evening in Vancleave eating dinner at his parents' home, but had heard about the murder on their car radio.

Brett nodded as the husband finished explaining. "Mr. Gregory, how close were you with the Andersons?"

The wife answered. "We weren't."

Her tone was sharp, and he looked at her. "Was there a problem between you?"

She shook her head. "No, not a problem. It was just that Mrs. Anderson was a, uh—" She shook her head again. "With her dead now, I don't want to be talking about her."

"Was what?"

"Officer, I, uh—I don't even know if this is the right word for it, but I think she was some kind of exhibitionist."

"Paula," her husband started, but she cut him off with a quick look.

"She was, Edward. I mean, always coming out in her backyard in that tiny bikinilike thing. You know she was."

She faced forward again. "There almost wasn't anything to the suit, Officer—you know what I mean. When Edward was outside, she especially showed off then."

Brett went on to the main subject. "What about Mr. Anderson?"

"He seemed nice enough; always waved when he happened to see us. You know, just normal."

"Did you ever notice them arguing, having a fight?"

"No."

As Brett stepped from the Gregorys' house outside into the muggy night air, he saw that Chief Seales had returned from the pool house and stood by his car at the edge of the street.

"How did it go?" Seales asked, tucking his camouflage shirt tighter around his thick waist.

"They didn't see anything. They were in Vancleave having dinner until after Trinity's body was discovered—that's where they were coming back from. They did touch on Trinity's character—the wife's opinion of it, anyway."

"Like the Winford woman did?"

"No, not men coming out of the house. It was more the wife thought Trinity was making a play for her husband. She didn't actually come out and say it, but that's the impression I got."

Paige nodded. "Yeah," she said.

Seales glanced toward the couple's house. "So, the Winford woman talked about men," he said, "and now the woman here—what's her name?"

"Paula Gregory."

"Gregory—she didn't like how Trinity was acting, huh? Evidently Anderson didn't like it, either. Maybe that's what he got fed up with." He looked at Paige. "I thought you said there was a partial print at the pool house—one you could see."

She nodded. "Yes, sir, I did."

"The way you talked—the way I understood you, anyway, I thought the print would be able to be lifted. All I saw was a smudge where it looked like somebody might have handled the knob."

"The smudge was where I handled it at the top. The print was under the knob, behind it."

Seales shook his head. "There's no way it's liftable."

Paige brought a confused look to her face. "But, sir, Sergeant Green and Brett saw it, too. It was there, clear, almost like a print on tape, but in blood instead of made with ink."

When the chief's eyes moved to his, Brett shook his head. "No, sir, I didn't see it. I never looked. But Sergeant Green did, and I heard him say it was there."

"Well, it's damn sure not now. As far as the print goes, I could care less, since we know Anderson wore gloves. But somebody, in fact a couple of somebodies—the one who first grabbed the knob and whoever messed the print up later—neither one of them said anything at all to me or the sheriff about the blood being there. *That* I really don't like. Didn't it occur to you to leave someone there to watch it until the lab boys could get to it?"

Brett glanced at Green standing beside the Anderson house as he talked to Arnie.

Seales looked toward the sergeant. "Him? You told Green to stay there?"

Brett nodded.

Seales shook his head. "He was coming back from up near the street when I got to the pool house. He walked on back with me." He looked toward the house and called for the sergeant.

In a few seconds, the big man walked up to them. "Sir?"

"Sergeant," Seales said. "Officer Dunnigan said you saw the print at the pool house."

"Yes, sir."

"Could it be lifted?"

"I don't know, sir, with it being in that blood. You saw it. If nothing else, though, I believe forensics could take a picture of it with a camera."

"You can't even tell for sure there was a print there, Sergeant. It's smeared all to hell."

Green's brow wrinkled. "Sir, did you see any officer near the head of the pool, near the main house, before I saw you at the pool house?"

"No."

"When I first came back out of the main house, I saw one. I couldn't tell if he was a deputy or one of our men, maybe even highway patrol, but it was someone in a uniform. I guess he stepped in there to look around and smeared it when he opened the door."

"What were you doing at the main house, Sergeant?"

"Right after Brett started back I thought I saw somebody up there next to the bushes around the house. I thought it was an officer, maybe trying to see inside—it was deserted. But then I didn't see any more movement and I got to wondering and went up there. It was only a big dog; he had laid down in the bushes. Then I started thinking that if the killer stepped into the pool house looking for a place to hide, then he might have also thought about the main house being deserted, ended up going in there. A highway patrol cruiser and a deputy's car stopped out on the street and I got them to go inside the house with me. When we came out is when I noticed the man down by the pool house. I talked a minute to the patrolman and then came on back to the pool. I thought you'd already taken a blood sample when you didn't say anything about me continuing to stay there."

"Sergeant, the house isn't more than thirty or forty feet from the pool, and you couldn't tell who he was?"

"From the rear of the house, it is about that distance, that's right. But I came out the front and was walking to the patrol car with the officers when I glanced back and saw him. I was probably a hundred and twenty or thirty, maybe as much as a hundred and forty feet from him. And when I noticed him he had his back to me.''

Seales looked up at the bright moon and back to Green. ''Even at a hundred and forty feet, Sergeant, that's still less than fifty yards. The moon's bright. You said he was in uniform. We wear navy blue. Sheriff's department wears dark-blue shirts and French-blue pants. Highway patrol uses gray. You couldn't even make out which force he belonged to?''

''No, sir. I'm color blind, sir.''

CHAPTER 9

The morning sun was beginning to cast a faint glow in the east when Brett stepped out onto the porch of one of the small brick houses across the street from Trinity's. Paige said something to the family they had interviewed and joined him. The elderly husband, wearing a flowered robe and sitting in a wheelchair, rolled to the open door and watched them as they stepped off the porch and walked across the lawn to the street.

There was only one police car left in front of Trinity's house and another parked down by the curve. It was obvious that Anderson had gotten to his car and left despite all of those looking for him. And there had been no word from the highway patrol.

"Would you admit to it if you had smeared the print?" Paige asked.

"Not now, I wouldn't. If whoever stepped inside the pool house had reported finding it, there wouldn't be any problem. The pool house was a long way from Trinity's. No one could have been expected to be careful about handling the doorknob. You weren't. What Seales and Hastings are upset about is not that the print was smeared but that whoever did it didn't report finding the blood. Nobody's going to come forward now. Be hell to pay if they did." He cupped his hand to his mouth and yawned. "What a hell of a time to be scheduled for a make-up on the day shift."

"I nearly forgot. You want to go home and get a nap before you go on? And I have to take a shower and put on my uniform."

He glanced at his watch. "Two hours? I'd feel worse if I lay down and then had to get back up." He looked down the street toward Trinity's house. "A few hours more and we'll know if Anderson showed up for his sales meeting. I'm beginning to feel more like Vic about that."

"And me," she said. "Don't forget that's what I said, too. I don't think he'll show up, either."

At nine-thirty the radio in Brett's unmarked car crackled. He reached for the mike.

"This is unit two."

"Brett, Anderson didn't show for his sales meeting in New Orleans." Brett's eyes narrowed as he slowed his car for a red light ahead. The brakes were still vibrating.

Paige heard the report, too. She nodded to herself, then played her fingers against the top of the steering wheel of her patrol car as she wondered where he might be. Certainly not still in the area. If he hadn't made it to his car then it would have already been found. Or was it that he hadn't come in his car? That might make even more sense with the highway patrol in a two-state area watching for the car and not yet seeing it. But if that was the case, if Trinity had picked him up in some other town, then how did he get away?

At ten A.M. the radio again crackled in Brett's car, and shortly after that in law-enforcement vehicles up and down the coast. Anderson had left his car at a service station in town the night before—to have the oil changed and the tires rotated.

"Then he damn sure wasn't planning to attack Trinity when he came into town," Brett said across the table in the small beachfront restaurant where they took their lunch break. "He just lost it. For some reason he just lost it."

Paige nodded, then leaned back for the waiter to fill her iced tea glass. The man stared at her nametag and shook his head. "Lady," he said, "you're one up on me with those kind of guts."

"Excuse me?"

"I was looking at your nametag there. You're the one who went in that pool house last night, aren't you?"

She smiled a little and nodded.

"Not none of me," the man said. "I'd still be running." Shaking his head, he moved on to the next table.

Brett smiled. "He thinks you're as crazy as I do."

The familiar strain of the tune leading into the news came over the small TV set on a table in the far corner of the restaurant and they looked that way.

The murder and the uncovering of the serial killer's identity was the lead story. The anchorwoman, the same willowy brunette they had seen at the house the night before, gave a brief introductory statement. Scenes of the Anderson home flashed on the screen as she continued with the story.

Several minutes later, she ended the piece with a jab at Chief of Police Eddie Seales because of his initial refusal to release the identity of the killer to the media. Then she reminded the audience that Seales was the same man who, a few years before, had been forced to resign from his job on the New Orleans police force "—after a television commentary had put pressure on the New Orleans chief and the mayor's office in regard to the beating then Homicide Detective Seales had administered to a prisoner in his custody."

The implication was clear—at least part of the reason for Seales's initial refusal to talk to the media had been due to his resentment of their past treatment of him.

"That's not fair," Paige said. "For all Seales knew at the time the reporter questioned him, Anderson was under the impression he had gotten away with the murder and was on his way to New Orleans. Nobody knew any better until he didn't show up there this morning. What did they want Seales to do last night, warn Anderson we were looking for him by naming him for every radio and TV station in a thousand miles of here to broadcast?"

She looked back at the TV set. "I've been thinking about him leaving his car at the service station. He knew the attendant at the station saw Trinity pick him up, knew that everybody was going to know he was in town, even if he didn't know he had been seen entering the house with her. Then to top that off, he did whatever it is that the F.B.I. knows about. As hard as everybody would be looking for a man who killed his wife, it wouldn't be anything compared to how hard they'd work to catch the serial killer. He'd know that. Why did he make it obvious that he was the psycho, which guaranteed there was going to be a massive hunt for him?" Then she shrugged. "But then again, like Seales said last night, how do you figure a maniac? Who knows what he was thinking, if he was thinking at all?"

Brett leaned back in his chair. "The attendant said that as soon as Trinity pulled up to the station she laid down on her horn, kept honking it until Anderson was nearly to her car. And not much more than an hour and a half after that, I'm finding her body. Whatever caused him to lose it happened quick."

"What was she like, Brett? I mean really."

"Just a person."

"I won't get jealous—not now."

"You've heard it before. She lived the way she wanted to. She did what she felt like doing and didn't care what others thought about it. To her, sex wasn't any different than any other way of having fun. But she didn't come across cheap, not in the way she presented herself, and she wasn't a hard person. I think, at least as a person, you would've liked her."

"Yeah, maybe, but I sure didn't since I met you. When I heard how you two were always saying in high school that you were going to get married, I was jealous of her without ever meeting her. Now I'm feeling guilty about that."

He didn't say anything. He thought about the silver bracelet he had given Trinity when they were seniors—their sign they were going to get engaged.

"Brett, I wonder if it's heredity or environment? Or is it a mixture of the two?"

"What do you mean?"

"Her husband—how he became a maniac."

He shrugged.

A reflective look crossed her face and she smiled.

"What?" he asked.

"Maybe we'd be better off if it is environment rather than heredity. I had a great-granddaddy who was a horse thief, stole horses down here and sold them to army posts in Arkansas, was hanged over near Little Rock."

He smiled. "I think it's safe for us to go ahead and have kids—not a lot of army posts buying horses anymore."

She smiled again and took a drink of water.

"Brett, you were a sophomore in college when your father went broke, right?"

He was taken aback. "What brought that on?"

"I was still thinking about environment and heredity. And I started thinking about the pressures everybody seems to experience. How some people are able to handle them and others can't. I thought about you and how, especially at your age then, you had to have been under a tremendous strain when it happened, especially with your mother having just passed away. Damn, that must have been terrible."

He shrugged rather than replied. There had been some bitterness, wondering why so much bad was happening to him; his faith had even been affected at the time. But, mainly, after a while, after he had learned to accept all that had happened so close together, his worry had been for his father, a man who had deeply loved only one woman and was without her forever—then financially broken at the very time he was getting too old to start over again. But there were good memories, too, mainly the compassionate reactions of the people in the town, something he would forever be grateful for and never forget.

"You decided on law enforcement then?" Paige asked.

"Had to decide on something. I needed a job."

"Why didn't you stay in school? I saw your transcript from your freshman year. You could've applied for some kind of scholarship."

"It wasn't just tuition and books—you have to eat. And my dad—I didn't want him to worry about having to keep supporting me on top of everything else he was facing. Going to night school and making a living at the same time looked like the thing to do, and being a cop seemed exciting at the time. Turned out it was a good choice. I enjoy what I do."

"Yeah, I know. I do, too. But I wonder if I would've ever had the nerve to try it if it hadn't been for knowing I always had my trust fund to fall back on if I ever changed my mind. I probably wouldn't have, would probably be sitting in an office in some kind of nine-to-five job, hating every minute of it." She smiled at her next thought. "I'm going to love it even more when we're working for the bureau."

He nodded. Things in his life—their life—would soon change drastically. He was finished with night school and had his degree. The F.B.I. training academy was next. Then starting a family right after that—they had planned it down to the very last detail. And only a little over a year ago he didn't have any aim in life except to enjoy it from day to day. Then he had seen her one night. It hadn't been love at first sight, more like *lust*. Before he knew it, though, his first feeling was replaced with one he never had before. He just plain liked her, enjoyed being with her, saw in her someone he would like to be around the rest of his life. She felt the same. After they married, she transferred to be on the same force with him, but told him her goal all along was to be an F.B.I. agent—and that he needed to finish getting his degree if he wanted the same. And he had.

"You know, Brett, I thought Daddy would act a little bit better after he saw I really was going on to the F.B.I."

"I think it's the other way around. As long as you were in Gulfport, and then over here, just testing the waters, he still thought there was a chance you'd change your mind. Now, with you going on, he knows you're going to stay with it. I can understand his point—a daughter he had his mind set on following in his footsteps in the medical field, and with enough brains to do it, ending up as a cop. However we feel about it, it's still a disappointment to him."

"Daddy chose his way of helping people and I chose mine. And I did as he asked. I tried this for a couple of years. Now, it doesn't make any difference whether he understands it or not, he's just going to have to learn to accept it."

R. C. Dillon geared his riding lawn mower into neutral and raised the back of his bony, dark hand to remove the sweat from his brow, then wiped it on his coveralls. He didn't like being so close to a house where a dead woman had been found, especially one with her head nearly off. He wouldn't be there, except for the fifty dollars he earned every time he mowed the big yard.

He looked at the pool house. There had been blood found on the doorknob, he had heard. The crazy bastard must have peeked inside after running from murdering his wife. What was he looking for, a float? The nut.

R. C. raised the back of his hand to his forehead again and glanced at the sun, sending its merciless rays of heat despite starting to sink toward the west. There wasn't much breeze from the Gulf, a few hundred yards in front of the house. He glanced over at the strip of uneven grass next to the thick hedge the killer came through. He had started mowing there first, but felt uneasy at riding along with his shoulder so close to the thick, tangled branches and had pulled a few feet out into the yard. He would have to go back and get that before he left. Needed to get to it next, before the sun got too low. He wouldn't be getting to it at all if on top of everything the hedge became thick with dark shadows.

He looked at the pool, then switched off the ignition, stepped down from the tractor, and walked to the water.

For several seconds he stared at its brown surface. He decided it wasn't any worse than some of the bayous he played in as a kid. He slipped off his shoes and socks, glanced toward the pool house, the hedge, and the main house, then sat down on the pool ledge, rolled the legs of his overalls up above his knees and moved his feet over the side.

The water was warm, unusually so, but still refreshing. He wiggled his long toes as he watched them disappear from sight. Leaning back on his hands, he glanced about him a last time, then began to relax.

He felt the gentle touch on the bottom of his soles. His eyes widened and he jerked his legs back out of the water and scrambled to his feet.

The body, its back surfacing first, gently broke the surface.

CHAPTER 10

James Anderson's bloated corpse, clad in slacks and a slime-streaked white dress shirt, the material straining to contain his swollen stomach, lay on its back on the end of the pool nearest the pool house. Dr. Martin Felter, his shoulder-length brown hair giving him more the appearance of one of the coast's narcotic unit undercover agents than a county coroner, knelt on one knee beside the body. Sheriff Hastings, Chief Seales, Paige, and Brett stood in a cluster off to one side of the pool.

Seales glanced toward Felter. "It's a damn shame that he's not going to be around after this fall. He's the best I've seen in my thirty years in law enforcement."

Brett had heard others go even further in their praise of the doctor, saying Felter was the best coroner who had *ever* worked for the county—an M.D. no less. But he was also the most controversial.

First there was his long hair hanging down his back, at the moment swept back into a ponytail, but sometimes hanging loose and covered with a wide-brimmed, drooping old hat—giving him the appearance of a pale-faced Geronimo.

Then there was also the fact that, still a bachelor at forty-eight and independently wealthy from a fortune his family had left him, he attracted hopeful women everywhere he went, including the one who had been the final straw as far as his job was concerned—the wife of one of the coast's most prominent men, a man who also happened to be the brother of the owner of an independent paper in the area.

After the divorce proceedings had begun, Dr. Felter had been mercilessly crucified in column after column. Then one of the New Orleans TV stations became fascinated with the story. Though a round man of five feet ten burdened with a noticeably soft two hundred pounds could scarcely be labeled a Casanova, that was exactly what the station had dubbed him: Dr. Casanova. It wasn't long until a group of concerned citizens in the county began circulating petitions asking for his immediate removal. Mississippi was, after all, still the center of the Bible Belt.

Felter had already announced he wouldn't be running for the office again. The only good news as far as Brett was concerned, since he liked the doctor, was that the man's career wasn't going to suffer. His professional reputation was such he had already received a half dozen other job offers—all of them paying much more than he currently earned.

Felter rose to his feet and walked in their direction. The sheriff and Seales walked to meet him, stopped, shook hands with him, and asked several questions. When he answered all that they asked, they shook hands again, and Hastings and Seales walked toward the body.

Felter proceeded to where Brett and Paige stood, extended his arm, and shook hands with them.

"Doctor," Brett said. "Why in hell did the killer go to the trouble to bring the body down here and dump it in the pool? Wasting the time he took to do it, taking such a chance? He had to be out in the open when he crossed the street on his way over to these yards—it just doesn't make sense."

"I realize you're only asking rhetorically, Brett. But I've been thinking along the very same line. How about this. Perhaps he wasn't planning on leaving him. Think about what it might portend if our maniac was only thinking along the lines of temporary storage, planning on coming back and retrieving the body later."

Felter looked at the water as he paused. "He certainly picked a good place to conceal the corpse if that is what he had in mind. If the last few days hadn't been so blessed unusually hot, warmed the water to such a degree, I imagine the body would have stayed submerged for at least another day, possibly two."

As if his talk about the heat reminded him that his forehead was beaded with sweat, he reached to his rear pocket and pulled out a grayed handkerchief, mopping his face before continuing.

"Of course, I want you to understand I'm only thinking aloud. No, actually I'm playing a type of game I'm always into. Speculating about crime and mystery and all their various nuances is my favorite pastime. When I saw the dark water and realized what a superb job it had done concealing the body not only from sight but from any scent that might be given off if police dogs had been used, I immediately thought of Jack the Ripper. Though I subscribe to the idea he died a patient in a mental institution, there are some mystery buffs who contend that he retired. They, of course, base that on the fact he was never apprehended and yet ceased killing." He glanced toward Anderson's body as he paused.

"So, with that as a foundation for my thoughts, my mind started jumping from possibility to possibility. I came up with two theories. That is, I came up with two if he indeed contemplated coming back to retrieve the body and dispose of it where it would never be found.

"First, as I said some believe Jack the Ripper did, he could be planning to retire. If that is indeed the case, then he could spend his golden days in a great deal more comfort if the police were directing their main effort toward trying to find Anderson—the purported serial killer. You and the chief and I were only last night discussing how sure we were of the fact that he *was* the serial killer.

"The second possibility is that instead of thinking along the lines of retirement, he was floating a decoy—pun unintended. If that was the case, then every time the killer attacked a victim, law enforcement would be using a great deal of their available manpower in an effort to locate Mr. Anderson, again relieving the pressure on the real killer."

He smiled again. "Don't wager your inheritance on the likelihood of either of the possibilities being what he really had in mind. But isn't it fun to try and think like a murderer?"

Paige didn't roll her eyes until Dr. Felter turned and was walking away. Brett smiled at her gesture.

Another car stopped on the road in front of the house. It was the two F.B.I. agents who had been at Trinity's house, the younger agent and Applewhite. As they came across the lawn toward the pool, another car stopped on the frontage road and Vic climbed out and slipped on a bright red sports jacket, then started in their direction.

Behind his car, a TV van stopped and a long-haired young man and an attractive brunette hurried toward the pool.

"I didn't think about this," Vic said as he paused in front of them and glanced toward Anderson's body. "I knew something wasn't right. I couldn't see her husband being so stupid if he was the psycho—not to the extent of leaving his signature. But this never occurred to me. He's been playing games all along, the bastard leaving his signs, telephoning the cops, taunting them. He was taking Anderson with him—for God only knows what. That's what he was planning. Then you two arrived at the house quicker than he expected. He knew he had to run. He killed Anderson right here, I'll bet you, then took off."

Anderson had been strangled. Right here, Paige thought. She pictured him on his knees, his eyes bulging as his life was taken from him by some hulking psycho. Or maybe the killer looked just like everybody else, a nondescript person to whom you wouldn't give a second glance. She wondered what he *did* look like.

Bobby was rather average in appearance, if a little on the heavy side and with wide shoulders. The most noticeable thing about him was his wide face and how his hairline had receded halfway back up his head and hung long in back.

He came down the long, ramplike walkway leading from the front of the Harrison County Detention Facility into the parking lot which was bathed in the hot sun, but didn't walk to a car. He didn't own one—and wouldn't know how to drive it if he did.

Turning right at the bottom of the ramp, he walked past the tall, razor-wire fence surrounding the sprawling gray-and-maroon contemporary buildings where the prisoners were housed. In a few minutes, his broad shoulders slumped and his thick thighs straining at the material of his faded work pants, he had walked the quarter mile or so to the main gate leading from the widely spread complex. There, he let his eyes slide sidewise, looking at the sign near the gate that read, "Harrison County Correctional Facility," different from the "Harrison County Detention Center" sign on the main building—and that confused him. Correctional Facility or Detention Center, which was it? They were always doing something like that to him—everybody did. But he smiled. Always better to smile no matter how you feel, the nurse had told him—and hadn't it always worked?

The smile frozen across his face, his neck muscles bulging, droplets of sweat starting to form on his head where his hairline receded, he continued on his way out to the main road and then turned right toward 49 leading into Gulfport.

CHAPTER 11

By eight that night, Brett, still in his uniform and feeling like he hadn't taken it off for a week, was worn out as he sat in a window booth at the Hook Line & Sinker. Even the fried scallops and oyster combination he always liked so well only tasted normal. He had to get sleep, a lot of it, and soon. He felt so bad he almost wondered if he was coming down with something.

But Paige, she was a different matter. Bright-eyed, looking as fresh as her crisp uniform, she seemed to be running on jet fuel, one question after another coming from her mouth.

"Brett, the screen being off makes sense now—especially with the dust on the window sill smeared. He came in that way. But how did he know the fuse box was in the closet?"

Brett shook his head. "I don't know. Had to stumble up on it. Maybe after he knocked the husband out, he hid him in the closet—saw the box then."

Paige nodded. "Yeah, I guess. It would have to either be that or that he already knew where it was—been in the house before."

Brett looked up from his plate but didn't say anything.

Paige took a sip from her tea and looked across the table at him. "Brett, what do you think Gregory thought when he saw Trinity in her backyard in the kind of bikini his wife spoke about?"

"I assume we're changing the subject again? Or is this just a different verse? Wish you'd just finish eating so we can go. I've got to get home and get some sleep or I'm going to end up in intensive care.''

"He'd be interested, wouldn't he, Brett?"

"Yeah, I guess."

Paige took a quick bite of the crabmeat filling in her stuffed flounder, swallowed it, and narrowed her eyes as she looked back across the table at him. "Guess, my foot—of *course* he would be interested. Now the question is, is he the type that plays around?"

"What are you getting at, Paige—specifically?"

"The killer's first three victims were prostitutes."

"Uh-huh."

"Then he suddenly killed the maid."

"Go on."

"Well, when that happened, the victim profile was blown all to pieces. The police psychologists started pulling their hair out. Just like Vic was wondering—why did he suddenly change his type of victim, three prostitutes and then a non pro? Now, with Trinity, two non pros in a row."

"I assume you've come up with an idea."

"What if he hasn't changed his type of victims?"

"You lost me there." He yawned and glanced at his watch, then looked out the window west up the beach toward the bright lights of the Broadwater yacht marina and the President Casino.

She frowned. "Brett, will you please pay attention to me for a minute?"

He looked back across the table at her. "I am, Paige."

"Well, you can at least look at me while I'm talking."

"I'm looking."

"Good," she said. "Thank you. Now what I was trying to say is—you've seen the files on all the killings, what was unusual about the maid? I just thought about that a minute ago."

He shrugged and shook his head.

"Brett, the car she drove. The one you saw in the paper—that old antique Thunderbird. And she supposedly had a diamond on that cost a couple of thousand. She had too much money, Brett, too much for a woman who worked only a half a day five days a week—as a maid. And that was the only job she had. Where did she come up with what it took for the car and the ring—some of the clothes she had?"

He nodded. "So you're suggesting she might have been a pro on the side."

"It's possible, and Trinity might have been, too. Maybe the killer *is* still selecting the same type of victims."

She took another bite of her flounder as she waited for him to comment. Somehow she had already managed to eat most of the huge serving despite her almost continuous questions. "Well?" she asked.

"I really don't think something like that was Trinity's cup of tea."

She laid her fork in her plate and stared at him for a moment. "Brett, until she moved back here you hadn't been around her in six or seven years. How do you know *what* her cup of tea had grown to be over time? With the way she was, you don't think she was capable of becoming a pro?"

No, he didn't. But then he had never met a woman who understood Trinity—*could* understand someone like her.

The waitress leaned to fill their tea glasses. "Did they really find the husband's body in a swimming pool?" she asked.

Brett nodded. "Yes."

"He was strangled?"

Brett didn't know if the cause of death had been officially released, or was going to be. "I don't have any idea," he said.

The woman nodded a couple times. "Well, that's what I been hearing," she said. She moved on to the next booth.

Brett shook his head in amusement. "Talk about living in a small town."

"What about what I was asking, Brett?"

"Okay, Paige, assume she and the maid were both selling it. What difference does it make?"

"God, Brett, it makes an enormous difference. After the first three attacks, the teams working the case were concentrating their efforts in known areas of prostitution. With him suddenly changing victims they're now spread out all over the place. If in fact he hasn't changed the way he selects his victims, it would allow them to go back to concentrating their efforts. And if Trinity was into something like that, then that could also explain why he attacked over here. He could have met her at some kind of . . . of party in New Orleans or Mobile and ended up following her over here."

He stared at her for a moment, then nodded. "Okay, it won't hurt anything to ask around about her. Maybe somebody she worked with will know something about her, another saleswoman, *somebody* anyway. She'll have a good friend somewhere. I'll mention it to Seales. He can have the F.B.I. check on the maid, too. They can call up to Jackson where Trinity lived the last couple of years, have the cops there check on what she was doing then. Applewhite's the type to go hard on it. He should be able to come up with a pretty good idea in a few days."

"No, I don't want to wait a few days. It's on my mind and I want to find out one way or the other—now. That's why I want to go speak with Edward Gregory again. He was her nearest neighbor, and about her age. Add to that the fact it's obvious his wife thought Trinity was making a play for him—that makes me wonder how maybe he responded in a way she doesn't know about."

He finished his tea and set the glass back on the table. "Okay, so what if he was involved with her? You think he's just going to up and tell us about it?"

"Yeah, I do, maybe—if we approach it just right."

"What?"

"We can ask him in a way that sounds like we already know he is. Do it away from his wife, but leave the impression with him that we're going to tell her what we know if he doesn't come clean with us."

He smiled. "He's going to tell us we've gone crazy, we can go to hell."

"In that case it'll mean he wasn't involved, doesn't know anything special about her. But if he does, then I believe he'll say so to keep us from going to his wife. I can tell you right now that from what I observed when we talked to them, she not only couldn't stand Trinity, but she also expected him to feel the same way. I'm a woman; I know. He wouldn't want us going to her insinuating anything whether he's innocent or not; it could be the end of their marriage."

The end of their marriage, Brett thought. That was how Paige looked at a wife catching her husband stepping out on her. What else could a wife do? she had once asked him; there would be no way to ever trust the man again, she had said. It'd be all over. The thought made him uncomfortable.

"Brett, if he has something to hide, I'm betting he'll fall to pieces. Okay?"

When he didn't answer right away and remained with his thought, she said, *"Brett."*

"Hell, Paige, I don't know. What are you asking?"

"If you don't think we should confront him—that it's a good idea."

"You're half crazy, Paige. Accuse a man of infidelity, of having a relationship with his next-door neighbor— Sure, why not, that'll be as good a way as any to start tomorrow. Maybe he'll fall to pieces so badly he'll end up suing us, give us something to do between now and when we go to the F.B.I. academy—spend our time in a courthouse defending against a slander lawsuit. But your dad's put plenty of money in your trust—what's a lawsuit or two?"

"Come on, Brett, I'm serious."

He looked at her for a moment. "Paige, I just got off of back-to-back shifts. I was going to sleep late in the morning."

She stared at him.

He shook his head. "Okay, it's a crazy idea, Paige, but okay."

Excited, she quickly ate the rest of her meal, ordered bread pudding and a cup of coffee for dessert, then drove her Maxima back toward their house while he dozed in the passenger seat.

He was jolted awake when the car suddenly swerved hard into a tight right turn. Paige floored the accelerator.

"What in the hell are you doing, Paige?"

"A car just flew across the railroad tracks with its lights off," she answered. They were nearing the tracks.

He grabbed the dash to brace himself. "Slow down!"

They went up the hump over the tracks and flew through the air for several feet before the car crashed back hard to the pavement. "Paige, dammit!"

He looked ahead of them and saw the shape of the darkened car in the distance. He glanced back behind them and saw blue lights. The police car wasn't gaining on them a bit. He wished they were in his patrol car where they had a radio and he could find out what was going on.

An S-shaped turn was ahead of them. *"Paige!"*

She ignored him, taking the turn at full speed. When they didn't flip, he took a deep breath and shook his head.

A mile ahead and the car they were chasing suddenly hit its brake lights and skidded off the road onto the shoulder. Paige kept her accelerator depressed until she was nearly on the stopped car, then hit the brakes, and again he had to jam his hand against the dash to brace himself.

Their headlights bracketed an old brown Chevy fifty feet in front of them.

"Be careful," he said, and opened his door. Paige, pulling her revolver from her holster, stepped out the other side of the car.

A lanky, stooped figure in bib overalls over a short-sleeved T-shirt came around the front of the Chevy.

It was old man Pennebaker.

Brett reholstered his automatic. "What are you doing, Jerome?"

The man lifted his hand in front of his face as he tried to see into the glow of their headlights. "Who's askin'?"

"Brett Dunnigan."

"Oh, hi, Brett. Just relieving myself."

Brett smiled a little. "You must have had to go awful bad."

"You got that right. I was startin' to hurt some kind of bad."

The old man raised his hand again to shield his eyes as he looked toward Paige. "That you, Miss Paige?"

"Yeah, Jerome."

He showed a toothless smile. "Don't mind tellin' you it worried me some little bit when y'all stopped. Thought maybe you might be hooligans out lookin' for trouble." He came on toward them. The police car that had followed them, the vehicle's blue lights still flashing, braked to a stop behind them. Sergeant Green turned off the lights and stepped outside. He had his revolver in his hand, but holstered it when he saw whom they were talking to.

"Jerome," he said, "what in the hell you mean running from me?"

The old man's eyes widened in astonishment. "I did no such thing, Armont."

"Yeah, you did. Ran a stop sign and then tried to lose me. Don't guess you have your license with you?"

"As a matter of fact, I do," the old man said, and began searching through his overall pockets. "Got it back just today."

"Well, I hope you didn't get attached to it."

"What do you mean, Armont?" the man asked, stopping his search and staring at the sergeant.

"Attached, Jerome, like you're going to get it back again as easily this time. Now find it."

"Aw, come on, Armont."

Green held out his hand, waiting for the license. "Find it, Jerome."

The man dropped his eyes and started searching again.

Brett smiled and walked on past the old man to the bank of the swampy lowlands beyond them.

Paige stepped up beside him, stared for a moment at acre upon acre of swamp grass stretching out before them, and shook her head.

"It's pretty, all right," she said. "But there's no way you would ever get me back out there at night again." She shook her head. "What a girl will do to marry somebody; I can't believe I went with you."

He smiled. Though hesitant, she had gone frogging in the swamps with him twice during the time they were dating. She had told him after they had gotten married that those two cloudy nights were the most nervous she could ever remember experiencing. City girl and country boy, her rich and him poor, her with a master's degree and him in night school when they met—and they had married? It was a wonder they had even met. He had to be the luckiest man who ever lived, he thought, and yet had risked it all a month after they became engaged, the night when he had met up with Trinity in a casino in Biloxi and drove to Back Bay with her.

Nothing had happened. They had only left the casino and driven over there after laughing about one of their youthful antics in the bay, in particular when he lost his bathing trunks after hitting the water hard when skiing there. The boat's motor had died and wouldn't start again. An old couple had finally come to their aid.

But then something nearly happened. During a lull in their conversation after they parked above the bay, Trinity suddenly said, "I love you." He had stared back across the seat at her and felt a strange mixture of sexual desire and guilt. What was he doing out there in the first place? He had quickly driven her back to her

car, then wondered for a week if anyone might have seen him
with her. Who would have believed he had done nothing—especially Paige. Then, after swearing he would never be tempted
again, he found that resolve evaporating when Trinity moved back
into town the week before. He had run into her in the grocery
store and stopped to speak with her for a moment. And she laid
her hand on his arm and looked in his eyes the way she could.
He had to be a fool even to think about it; he would've had to
have been crazy had he done any more than just thought.

CHAPTER 12

Paige was up by dawn the next day and excited as she hurriedly fixed them scrambled eggs and toast. Brett sat at the kitchen table watching her. Despite her trying to get him out of bed soon after she had arisen, his eyes hadn't really opened until she had slipped her nightgown off just before she disappeared into the bathroom. When, ten minutes later she had stepped back into the room, she was pulling her bathrobe around her and he had gotten a glimpse of a tanned, bare leg. He had followed her into the kitchen.

Now he moved his gaze from the soft movements under her robe and stared at her face. Even without the first bit of makeup, and with her long brown hair wet from her shower and slicked toward the back of her head, she was beautiful, stunning—perfect. He could think of a much better way to spend the morning than going to talk to Edward Gregory. But he knew better than to waste his time trying to interest her in anything else. Maybe afterward, he thought. And he decided to get it straight right then.

"Paige, I'm going with you to talk with Gregory, then we're going to have to get something else on our mind. You're going to have to do that in particular."

"What do you mean?" She scraped the eggs onto the paper plate in front of him and then onto hers.

"I mean, we find out what we can from Gregory, and then if there's anything to it, we tell Seales and let him get it to the F.B.I. They can take it from there."

Her brow wrinkled in confusion. "What do you think I want to do other than that?" she asked as she took a seat across the corner of the table from him.

"I know you—it'll be something."

"No. I just want to see if he knows anything about her, that's all."

"Yeah, and I've thought about that, too. Just to know he might have made a pass at her, scored, who cares? What would that tell us about the possibility of her being a pro? Whether he did or didn't have a relationship with her, there's no reason she would have told him that."

"There would be if she charged him," she said, and stuck her fork into her eggs.

"Charged him?" He shook his head in amusement.

"Yeah, charged him. Isn't that what pros usually do?"

An hour later they waited in his unmarked car off the beach side of 90 leading from the east end of town toward Gulfport and Biloxi. "This is the limit," he reminded her again. "This one thing, that's it."

She didn't answer, only kept staring out her window toward the bright, cloudless sky hanging over the water.

"Brett," she finally said, her voice with a wistful tone to it. "Maybe Daddy's right; maybe I am in the wrong business."

"What brought that on?"

"It's only that I was looking at the sky, thinking what a nice day it was, and Trinity popped into my mind. She'll never see it again, the blue sky, the water—anything."

He nodded but didn't say anything, then tried to get his mind off the thought by looking out across the white sand at the children playing near the edge of the water. On out in the far distance he could see the faint shapes of the trees rising from a barrier island—and he pictured Trinity's body again.

"Here he comes," Paige said.

The blue Toyota came in a break in the traffic, only one other car close to it. When the two passed, he pulled out behind them. Waiting until the other car had gone around the Toyota, he pulled up alongside it and honked his horn.

Gregory glanced toward them, and Paige signaled for him to

pull over. He stared a moment. A smile crossed his face and he slowed the Toyota and drove it off onto the side of the pavement into a parking area along the beach.

As Brett and Paige parked behind him, she said, "Be sure and ask him in the way I told you."

He nodded. "But I'm only going so far."

"Make sure you act like you *know*," she added. "And don't shake hands. We want him to think this is official."

He smiled. "With us out of uniform?" They didn't go on duty until three o'clock that day and were both wearing blue jeans and pullovers.

"Come on, Brett," Paige said. "I was out of uniform when we first met him—what difference does it make?"

Gregory, in a light-blue suit, his thick, sandy-colored hair moussed high above his forehead, was already walking back toward them. He had a polite smile on his face but also a quizzical expression.

They met him between the cars. Brett smiled politely and nodded. "Mr. Gregory."

"Yes " He extended his arm and Brett couldn't help but shake hands. Paige frowned.

"I'm Lieutenant Dunnigan and—"

"Oh, I recognized you. You all have any leads on the killer yet? It blew my mind when it turned out it wasn't James. Glad, though, that it wasn't."

"We have a couple of questions we'd like to ask you."

Paige spoke then. "But we didn't want to in front of your wife."

Brett looked at her. Gregory's forehead wrinkled in puzzlement. "I'm sorry," he said. "What did you say?"

"We didn't want to ask you in front of your wife," Paige repeated.

"I don't understand."

"We were hoping maybe you would tell us a little bit more about Mrs. Anderson," she said.

"I don't . . . Like what?"

"There were times when your wife wasn't home and you were—and Mrs. Anderson was."

Gregory was silent a moment, glanced at a car whose driver

honked a greeting when he drove by. When he turned back and did speak, his tone was noticeably colder.

"I'm probably taking what you said the wrong way, miss, but it sounds like ... like you're maybe suggesting I had some kind of relationship with her."

"That's what we're asking you to talk to us about."

"That's crazy!" he exclaimed. His cheeks flushed. "I'm going to be late for work. I have to go."

He turned and moved toward his car. But Paige wasn't through. "Mr. Gregory," she called after him. "Mrs. Anderson had mentioned you and her to one of her friends. Would you mind taking a lie detector test to prove we have been misled?"

Brett frowned and spoke in a low voice. "Come on, dammit, Paige. That's enough." She was going too far on her own. If Gregory became upset to the point of causing trouble, there could be hell to pay without their having received permission from Seales to question him. A trailer truck whizzing by blasted them with wind, whipping their hair, filling the warm air with the stench of a load of oyster shells on their way to a crushing plant somewhere toward Bay St. Louis and New Orleans.

Gregory had stopped at Paige's words. Now he slowly turned to face them. "Y'all really are crazy."

"A polygraph might not be necessary," Paige continued, then twisted the knife. "We might not feel one is called for *after* we discuss it with your wife."

Brett clasped her forearm and squeezed it purposely hard. "Go back to the car, dammit." He looked at Gregory to see him now walking toward them. When he reached them he looked directly into Paige's face. But rather than the angry words Brett had expected, the man's voice was suddenly low, his tone almost pleading.

"Please," he said. "My wife is suspicious like you wouldn't believe. If you started her to thinking something might have gone on between me and Trinity ..." He shook his head. "I don't know what it'd lead to. Please."

"We understand that," Paige said. "That's why we went to the trouble to stop you and speak with you when your wife wasn't present. In fact, if this wasn't concerning a murder investigation, we wouldn't go to her even if your answers didn't satisfy us. But this *is* a murder investigation."

"Who said Trinity mentioned my name?"

"I'm sorry, Mr. Gregory, but we would no more divulge that information to you than tell anyone what you say to us. It's all strictly confidential. Strictly. You can rely on that."

The man shifted his eyes from hers to Brett's and back again. He spoke slowly. "If I had a relationship with her and told you, that'd only lead to more questions, wouldn't it?"

Christ, Brett thought. She's getting him to admit it. This time Gregory didn't even look over as a driver in an old pickup honked a greeting.

"You're not any kind of suspect, Mr. Gregory," Paige said in a soft voice. "We're not the least bit interested in you except for what you can help us understand about her. So if we're satisfied with what you say, we won't be back—to question you or your wife. I promise you that. The thought of our having to go to her was really bothering me in the first place."

What a con artist, Brett thought. Keep speaking in a low voice but keep mentioning the wife—the threat.

"And if you're not satisfied with what I tell you?" Gregory asked.

"I think we're going to be," Paige said. "In fact, I'm pretty certain of that."

The man was silent for a while, ran his hand around the back of his neck, and glanced out over the water. Finally, he looked directly into Paige's eyes.

"Okay, I went to bed with her," he blurted out. "Once, only one time. There, are you satisfied?"

"Why only one time?" Paige asked.

"What?"

"Why only one time?"

"I just never did again."

"Why not?"

He looked exasperated. "Her kind of sex didn't do anything for me—okay?"

Paige's eyes brightened. "She was a prostitute. You had to pay her."

Gregory stared for a moment, then shook his head. "No, nothing like that. She was, uh . . . just flaky after we got started. I've been around flaky ones before. I mean, before I got married. But she takes the cake—you know.''

"No, I don't know."

Gregory's eyes narrowed in thought. His mouth partially opened, then closed as if he had started to say something but wasn't sure how to put it in words. Finally, he shrugged and just told her.

"I mean she started saying how she shouldn't be doing it as soon as we started taking our clothes off. I laughed at first, thought she was only making a teasing remark. You know, to break the ice, relax us a little. But the entire time we were making love she kept throwing in remarks like that, even talked about needing to be punished. There I was bustling at the seams and she was acting as if she was some kind of embarrassed kid, not really knowing what she had gotten herself into. Even began to look a little bit like a kid—the expressions she made. Hell, I was there because I'm a man and she was a damn good-looking woman—know what I mean—not for games.''

Finished, he took a deep breath. "There. Now, I have to go. Okay? I told you all there is to tell.''

Paige smiled politely and nodded.

As he walked off, she stared after him. *"Games,"* she mused aloud, then turned to Brett. "That hadn't occurred to me. All I was thinking about was the possibility she was selling herself. It does sound like she was playing games, doesn't it? Maybe that was something she had gotten into since you knew her, maybe really into it. He said she was even talking about needing to be punished.''

"Paige, she was just kidding around. She—''

"Maybe, and maybe not. Submissive acting, wanting to be punished—games. We studied about people into things like that in some of my psychology courses." She dropped her eyes in thought for a moment before looking up at him again. "It doesn't have to be just pros. Group sex, parties, games—prostitutes could be brought in to spice up something like that. There could be pros and non pros at something like that. If she was into that, then that could be the common thread that might link all of them together, why the killer went after them. I mean Trinity and the maid and the pros, too. Maybe he wasn't going after prostitutes at first and changed to a different kind of victim, but is still going after the same type of woman he has been after from the very beginning, those into some sort of games, maybe even dominant and submissive games—rough sex. Something like that could attract a nut; he could have met them all through that. But how would we find out?"

He didn't know whether to take her seriously or laugh at her. Despite what Gregory said about Trinity, there was no way she would be into anything rough; he knew that. Still, group sex—there *was* a possibility she'd do something like that. Finally, he said, "We can check the victim case files, see if any of the pros had arrest records and for what, look through whatever else the investigators might have cataloged about them. If any of them were into those activities, maybe there'll be something in the files that will catch our eye." He smiled and shook his head in amusement.

"What?" she asked.

"Jesus, Paige, I told myself that after we talked to Gregory, it would be the end of it for us. If we came up with anything, we'd give it to Seales to hand over to the F.B.I. and we'd get back to our normal routine. But I'm damn sure not going to say anything to Seales about this idea. Not yet I'm not, not with as little as we've got—really just a wild guess. Yet I can't just ignore it, either." He stared at her for a moment. "You can come up with the damnedest ideas. Let's go look at the case files, Sherlock."

Paige smiled. She could feel it. They were going to end up with something—she just knew it. But she tried to play down her feelings. She didn't want to get her hopes too high and then be disappointed. And for them to find something that easily that would give them the hint at how the killer was selecting his victims would be almost too simple, especially considering the trouble the task force had gone to and not come up with anything. But she could feel it, sense it; she knew something was going to come of it. She just knew it.

CHAPTER 13

After they arrived at the sheriff's office, a stocky deputy with a burr haircut informed them that a complete set of copies of the victim case files were on hand, but that the cabinet they were in was kept locked. They had to go to Hastings's office and explain to him why they needed access to the files.

To Brett's surprise, the sheriff showed immediate interest in Paige's idea and then personally led them to a small storage room where he opened a file cabinet.

He stood off to the side, absentmindedly working with a pocket knife at his fingernails as Paige opened the labeled drawer and pulled out a folder containing a mixture of local and F.B.I. computer-supplied information about the serial killer's first victim.

Lying the folder on the table across from the cabinet she opened it and began to scan the pages.

"Angela Cummings," she mumbled, "a.k.a. Polly. She was the one found in New Orleans. Man named Abe McLaurin I.D.'d her four days after her body was found. Said she was a pro."

Brett remembered the cringe he suffered when he heard about Cummings's body being found. He had been at his desk working on an arrest report. Sergeant Green had come in shaking his head. "Got a dope head gone crazy in New Orleans," he had said. "Sheriff's department there just reported a hunter finding a body in a swampy area northwest of the city—her head's missing."

There had also been an X cut on her torso. Since she hadn't

been raped or further mutilated, Brett remembered thinking at the time that her murder must have been a hate crime rather than a sex crime. He had wondered if the X was almost like crossing her off—finished with her.

Although the decapitation had garnered national attention, the murder had been judged an isolated event, the F.B.I. computer listing no other such unexplained decapitation and murder occurring anywhere else in the nation for several years. (The small piece of cardboard with the number 4 on it that the police found in her bedroom remained a mystery; maybe even something she had fashioned.) Nor did the calls to the police station that came in three days in a row prior to her body being found cause any particular notice. The caller had simply said "three" the first time he telephoned. The next day he called to say "two," and the next day, the day prior to her body being found, he had said "one." The victim's rotted head was discovered a month later in a garbage can in the south part of the city.

Paige turned to a second page in the folder and, her forefinger leading her eyes, hurried down the eight-by-ten sheet, occasionally voicing aloud what she was reading.

"Five feet five . . . Apparent saw blade used in the . . ." After a few seconds more, she shook her head. "Nothing here."

She removed another folder from the filing cabinet and laid it on the table. "Ellen Fulton. Killed over in Mobile. Anonymous caller said she worked as a pro under the name Bunny. Residence was a cheap apartment complex. Nobody there had any idea what she did for a living—I'll bet."

Fulton had been the second victim. Her death had come eight months after the first. She had first been reported as missing after she didn't make it to a hotel where she was to entertain at a bachelor party. The next day someone had called the police headquarters and said, "six." The calls kept coming, every time a husky male voice voicing a number smaller than the one he had said the day before. The day after the last call, the woman's headless body had been found shortly before dawn in a drainage ditch on the south side of the city. The medical examiner said that she had been dead for less than six hours, meaning she had been held alive for several days. A search of her apartment turned up a piece of cardboard, the number 6 on it and the word "surprise" written at its top. The psychopath was into games, taunting the police with his countdown, exulting in his power to make something happen the day he indicated it would. The woman's head had shown up a month later, impaled on a cypress knee in a swampy area east of the city.

Paige moved a third folder on top of the others. "This one was found in her home in Memphis. Paula Evans a.k.a. Honey ... Woman living next door I.D.'d her but didn't know she was a prostitute."

This third victim, killed four months after the second one, was found in her home. The main differences noted in this attack and the previous one in Mobile was that the victim had been immediately decapitated and left lying in her bedroom alongside her strangled common-law husband—the killer obviously didn't kidnap all his victims, nor was he above killing any companion who might be with the victim when he struck. A section of cardboard with the letter O on it and the words "getting bored with playing" written at its top was lying under the woman's bed. Her disintegrating head turned up a month later on the east bank of the Mississippi River under the old Interstate 55 bridge.

Paige stopped her forefinger at the middle of the page she was reading. "Brett, the same woman who didn't know the Memphis victim was a prostitute said, however, she did know the woman dated frequently, had an obvious arrangement with her husband. Now, listen to this. The woman said that the victim, in addition to having a worthless husband, didn't do much better with some of the men she dated—that the victim had exhibited bruises more than once on days following a date." She raised her eyes from the folder.

"Bruises, Brett."

The sheriff closed his pocket knife, replaced it in his hip pocket, and leaned forward to look. She lifted the page to scan a sheet stapled to its back.

"Two counts of soliciting under the name of Honey. Pulled in on a drug charge but never prosecuted ... Here, listen to this. A man charged her with theft of his wallet but then dropped the charge when she countercharged him with assault. After that she withdrew her charge even though she had the marks on her body to back it up."

Brett nodded. "So you're saying he hired her for the pleasure of working her over, but didn't pay up. At least didn't pay her what she thought she had earned. So she copped his wallet. Maybe and maybe not. It's possible. But also remember that she wasn't any big-time call girl but rather a cheap streetwalker. All three of the first ones were. They took on any John who came along. Those kinds of hookers occasionally get slapped around. Just that she had bruises on her doesn't mean she was into any kind of rough sex. That's not enough to confirm anything, not even to make it likely."

Certainly not enough to make him believe it. He hadn't known what Trinity had been up to in the last few years. But knowing her like he had—at least once had—it just didn't seem possible that she would have gravitated into that kind of life. Sex, yes, almost any kind of sex—but in a gentle, loving sort of way. That's what she had always really been into—love—even if she didn't know how to express the emotion in any way but through sex. But love—not pain.

Paige pulled the fourth folder from the filing cabinet as a deputy called from the doorway. "District attorney's here to see you, Sheriff."

Hastings looked back at them. "Be sure and lock the cabinet up. If you need me, I'll be in my office."

Paige opened the folder as Hastings walked from the room. The victim was Melissa Vilander of New Orleans, the second woman killed in that city and the first non-prostitute the killer had sought out. Like the Memphis victim, she had been immediately decapitated and left in her bedroom and, also the same as in Memphis, a man had been killed during the attack, her longtime employer, Mr. Robert Lloyd, who had gone to pick her up after her car wouldn't start.

That attack had occurred only two months ago and was the case Lloyd's widow had hired Vic to work on. There had been another piece of hidden cardboard with another O on it, and the words "still bored" at its top. The maid's head had been found in a roadside ditch off Interstate 10 the month before.

Paige was still looking through the folder. Finally, she shut it. "Nothing. Nothing at all except the bruises on the one in Memphis, and even I'll admit that's nothing."

She was silent for a long moment and then raised her face to his. "The two in New Orleans, Brett. You know we could check—" She shook her head. "No, my idea's so far out."

He'd rather end it there, not say anything, leave with Paige and try to get his mind back on something else. But for him to ignore the obvious, stop short of what could be checked, no matter how far out it might seem, wasn't right. He looked at her staring at him and he smiled to himself. She wasn't about to let him stop short, anyway. Her mind was already on what they should do next; she had started to suggest it. She just wanted him to be the one to say it. And he did.

"Let's call Vic and see if he knows anything about the maid that's not in the files," he said. "Then we could call the man who identified the first victim, see if he knows anything."

"Yeah, that's a good idea," she said quickly.

He nearly smiled. "What was his name?"

"McLaurin. Neither one of the victims over there had any next of kin around the area, but they would have had friends. We could talk to them, too. A good friend might know what they were into."

They walked to the telephone on a nearby desk, Brett making the call.

"No," Vic said after he had been told what they were trying to find out and why. "No, I hadn't even thought about her being involved in something like that, and I don't know any of her friends' names; didn't talk to any of them. Knowing who her killer was, there wasn't any need to be questioning them . . . Hang on for just a minute."

After a few seconds, Brett heard the sound of a drawer opening and shutting, and then he could hear the sound of paper rustling.

"Just a minute," Vic repeated. A few seconds later the pages stopped turning.

"The case report shows the cops didn't talk to any of her friends, either," Vic finally said, his voice low, a musing tone to it. "Didn't talk to any people who knew her, except for her employer and immediate neighbors. Tell you what, I'm going to see if I can get Mrs. Lloyd on the line. Hang on for a second more."

A good two minutes passed. Vic's voice came back. "Brett."

"Yeah."

"I have Mrs. Lloyd hooked in on a conference call. Mrs. Lloyd, this is Lieutenant Dunnigan."

"Hello, Lieutenant." Her voice was soft and cultured.

"Hello, Mrs. Lloyd. Did Mr. McIntyre explain to you what we're interested in?"

"Yes, and I told him I'd do anything I could to help you. Anything. I don't know any of Melissa' friends' names, but I do know where one of them lives. I think I do, anyway. Melissa was always having difficulty with her car. One day when she had a problem with it, I delivered her to this friend's house. I think I can get back there again. I'll try. If I'm able to, then I'll get the woman's number so you can telephone her."

"Thank you very much, Mrs. Lloyd."

"Lieutenant Dunnigan, even though I'm going to do that, I want you to understand it's only because you have asked and because I will do anything that could conceivably help find my husband's killer. But I don't believe there's even the remotest possibility of Melissa being involved in some kind of kinky sex. She had worked for us for years, ever since she was eighteen, and I knew her quite well. I'm not a prude and, in fact, discussed some of her men friends with her in quite personal detail. But *normal* relationships. I can assure you of that, Lieutenant."

Paige wasn't disappointed that Mrs. Lloyd was putting a damper on one of her ideas. There was still McLaurin. "Tell Vic, Brett. See what he thinks about our going to talk to him."

Vic didn't think much of the idea—but there *was* always the possibility.

When Brett replaced the receiver, he looked back at her. "Paige, this has got to end."

"New Orleans is only an hour away."

"Better than an hour, Paige, and there's the drive back even if we find this character right off. We'll be on duty by then, if we can even make it back on time."

"Brett, please. I can feel it. I really can."

Vic stared down at the file on the serial killer. The psycho always used a heavy section of steel pipe to stun his victim, had a particular habit of removing much of the skin of the neck complete with the head. There were a half dozen things he always did—the exact same thing every time. Then suddenly, with no apparent reason, he had changed his victims from prostitutes to non pros. That wouldn't especially raise eyebrows if it weren't for the fact that he had also killed a man along with the victim in Memphis—something else different. The telephone rang and he reached for it.

"McIntyre Security."

"Vic."

He smiled and leaned back in his chair. "Hey, baby."

"You going to be able to get away from Peggy tonight?"

"What's this 'get away' stuff? If I want to come, I'll come."

"I know. I was just wondering."

"Yeah, I'll be there. Might be late, though. I've got to get through some bills here first."

"You want me to have something cooked?"

"I'll catch something before I come over."

"Don't make it too late."

When he replaced the receiver, he opened his checkbook and stared at its balance—eighteen hundred dollars. What a joke. He flipped the book closed. He had quit being a cop to make some *real money*. Hell, he had carried more than that in his account when he had been a rookie officer. He shook his head in disgust. He had known six months into opening the agency that it wasn't going to work out like he planned. But he'd starve before he'd go back to being a cop again, taking that bureaucratic shit from the top and dealing with slime each day. He'd rather be dead first.

He moved his eyes back to the psycho's file. Applewhite was an asshole, but a smart one, too. He didn't just sit and wait back for the obvious leads—he had a shotgun approach. At least that was how he was doing on this case, working both himself and his agents without rest, hitting everything at the same time, having everybody talked to. Before he was through, Applewhite would know more about Trinity than anybody ever had—and about everybody who had ever been around her, had anything to do with her. It might work. There might be some yokel who had seen something that he thought not very important at the time, but something that might ring a bell in Applewhite's mind.

Still thinking, he closed the file and leaned back in his chair. The hundred thousand dollars he had been offered if he found a lead to the killer was public information. It was a lot of money, especially to an FBI agent who probably didn't make any more than half that in a year. He wondered if maybe Applewhite had thought of that, maybe was pushing a little harder than usual, hoping that if he found the psycho there might be a way he could get his own little grubby hands on the money? But he couldn't, at least not in his official capacity he couldn't, and as much as it was, it still wasn't enough to shuck the years he had put in at the bureau. That probably pissed the little stocky bastard off, maybe so much it was part of the reason he worked so hard at solving the case—and being an asshole at the same time. Vic smiled. There was something Applewhite damn sure didn't like about him. That was obvious.

CHAPTER 14

The traffic was unusually light on I-10 toward New Orleans, and it didn't take Brett much over an hour to drive there. Abe McLaurin lived in a part of the city that had once teemed with blue-collar subdivisions but had since turned into a largely industrial and commercial area. After locating the street his house was on, they drove down it only to find the pavement dead-ended at the property line of a sprawling cement plant. They cut over a couple of blocks, circled past the plant complex, and came back where the street started once again but now showed nothing to each side but boarded-up and abandoned houses. A couple of blocks farther, the deserted houses gave way to trash-strewn, weed-infested fields on both sides of the street. Then, on the right, another line of houses started.

"This is the block," Paige said.

Brett slowed the car.

The houses were nearly identical—small two-story wooden structures jammed close together, with only a shallow patch of grass between their fronts and the rough potholed pavement. McLaurin's house turned out to be the eighth one down the row. His name was printed in block letters on the mailbox near the curb.

"Well," Paige said. "He might not have a telephone listed anymore, but he's still at the same address, unless somebody just never took his name off the mailbox."

As Brett parked his car and he and Paige stepped from it, Vic

and a New Orleans police department detective, a man who had
been one of Vic's closest friends when the two worked together
on the force, stopped behind them. Brett had asked for Vic to
come along and bring an officer with him so that they would have
somebody with them who had authority in the city. Not a lot of
people would admit into their home a man and woman dressed in
blue jeans and pullovers who said they were cops from a small
town in Mississippi.

Vic stepped outside his car, slipped his blue sports coat on over
a light-blue open-neck shirt, and walked toward them. The detective, red-haired, stocky, and about the same height as Vic's six
feet, was in a rumpled brown suit, his shirt collar unbuttoned and
his tie loosened.

Brett stared at the two-story house with its shallow, roofed
porch. Though the dwelling wasn't any newer than any of the
others in the line, it recently had been painted an off-white, and
its few feet of yard were mowed and clean.

They heard a laugh and looked to their right. An old, white-
haired black man continued to move his rocking chair back and
forth as he watched them from his porch a couple of houses down.
When he saw them looking his way, he flashed a big smile, waved,
and laughed loudly.

"I don't suppose he knows something we don't," Paige said,
and nodded up McLaurin's short gravel driveway to the rear of
the black BMW projecting slightly out of the one-car garage built
onto the side of the house.

Brett glanced back to the smiling old man and then to the windows of the house. "Shades are pulled, Vic. We walking up on
a crack house?"

"Not any reports of activity in this area," the stocky police
detective answered. "Never can tell, though. They set up fast."

"Maybe Paige should stay here while we go up to it," Vic said.

"Why me? One of you stay here."

Brett stared at her. "You stay here."

She frowned but nodded. "Be careful."

Vic started forward, and Brett and the detective followed. Somewhere in the distance there was the sound of a train whistle.

They paused for a moment at the steps leading up onto the
shallow porch. A gust of warm wind blew the odor of something

rotting down the line of houses to their left. A paper bag followed the gust, tumbling across the narrow strip of grass behind them.

The shades had not moved, neither the ones across the two front windows nor the one behind the glass panel in the upper half of the door. They moved up the steps and onto the porch.

After walking across the creaking boards to the door, they divided to each side of the entrance. Vic knocked.

A shade was edged aside and one half of a dark face peered outside. A moment later the door opened and a skinny, middle-aged black man with his hair in an old-fashioned wide Afro stood in the doorway. He was wearing white tapered slacks and a pink shirt, the sleeves turned up to his forearms and the front unbuttoned and spread open almost to his navel.

When he smiled at them, he displayed a gold tooth that was in vivid contrast to the thick silver chains he wore around his neck. His smile faded as he looked toward the street.

Brett glanced back over his shoulder to see Paige, her hand resting on her purse slung over her shoulder, on her way toward the porch.

The detective produced his identification. "Are you Abe McLaurin?"

The man looked at the I.D., raised his face to the detective, and stared for a moment.

"What am I doin' to cause you to be botherin' me?" he asked incredulously, and shook his head. "Yeah, man, I'm McLaurin." Without another word, he turned and went back inside the house, leaving the door standing open behind him.

Brett, the detective, and Vic all glanced at each other, then quickly followed McLaurin inside, passing a wooden staircase leading to the second floor before they emerged into a small living room.

It stank of strong, cheap perfume. Two brown-skinned women in their early twenties sat on a green couch against the far wall. They had long, braided hair and wore shorty nightgowns so thin that nothing was left to the imagination. They smiled as they rose and turned sideways to better display themselves.

Paige stepped into the room. The women glanced at each other. Brett relaxed at the realization of what kind of house they were in. Paige frowned.

McLaurin had stopped in front of an easy chair, the only furniture in the small room besides the couch, and a TV on a card table against the left wall. He gestured with his head toward the two women.

"Alicia and Mary," he said. The two women once more brought fixed smiles to their faces.

"These are cops," McLaurin said to the two. "And bein's the lady's with them, don't 'magine they're here for no freebies."

The smiles disappeared again. The women sank slowly back to the couch. Brett could hear the sound of rap music coming from a radio somewhere in the kitchen back to the right of the room.

"Alberta is upstairs," McLaurin said. "Man with her. That's it. Nary 'nuther soul in the place." He shook his head in exasperation. "Man, I'm not believin' this. Who am I hurtin'?"

Somebody was coming down from the second floor. The detective stepped back and looked up the staircase.

It was a short, red-haired man wearing sunglasses and dressed in a slick three-piece suit. His vest and coat were open, and he was working with his tie as he came down the stairs. Seeing the detective, he turned his face and continued toward the door.

The detective stepped up behind him and tapped him on the shoulder.

When the man turned around, his pale forehead wrinkled questioningly. He saw the badge the detective held in his hand, and the color drained from his face.

"If you'll step into the living room," the detective said.

The man remained where he was, his mouth open. He shook his head. "I can't—I mean I . . ." He glanced across his shoulder at the door. "Officer, could you step outside with me for a moment? Please."

"No, you just come on into the living room."

"I can't afford to get in trouble . . . It would . . . Please." He bit his lower lip, then spoke in a voice so low Brett could barely hear it. "It's financially important to me, Officer—You know what I mean. You know . . . if you'll step outside."

The stocky detective's wide, lined face hardened. His tone was sharp. "You better get on along into the living room, mister. Now!"

The man briefly closed his eyes, then stepped around the detective and moved toward the room. When he entered it, he looked at McLaurin and frowned angrily. The black man shrugged his narrow shoulders. Brett vaguely remembered having seen him before. Then he remembered—from a TV commercial beamed into Pass Christian. The owner of a car lot in the city. Brett thought about the BMW in the garage, and guessed how the monthly payments were being made.

"Mr. McLaurin," Vic said. "You're the one who I.D.'d Angela Cummings—Polly?"

The dark eyes narrowed. "What does— Yeah."

"She worked for you?"

"For a while. Put the whore back on the street."

"Why did you have her leave?"

"Drugs." He looked back toward the woman on the couch. "Not gonna have a lady here can't stay off drugs." One of the women dropped her eyes and the other one glanced at her.

"Why did you come down to I.D. her, Mr. McLaurin?"

McLaurin didn't answer for a moment. When he finally did, his voice was measurably softer than it had been before.

"When I heard tell 'bout the angel tattoo, I knew it was her right off. Thought she oughta be put in the ground with a name. She weren't all that bad afore she got strung out on coke."

"Who did she work for after she left here?"

"Worked the streets for a spell, then from her house after she came up with the idea of using ads."

"Ads?"

"Yeah, you know, man—dainty lady of color lookin' for free-spendin' gentleman who likes to party, *do anythin'* to have fun. That'll pull in some real nuts. Had it figured that's why she got knocked off. Some dude got goin' and couldn't stop. That's before I heard tell about there bein' a crazy out on the streets goin' after workin' ladies."

When McLauren had stressed, "do anything," Paige's eyes brightened. She looked directly at him and said, "You said you thought somebody got carried away. I think I know what you mean, but you tell me."

"Lady, most men coming to a place like this are looking for what they can't get from their wives. But there are some that can't get what they're looking for from nearly anybody. When they do find someone willing to go along with them, they pay big. I mean, real big. Polly learned that when she worked here—met a couple of those types. Wanted to accommodate them. But I wouldn't let her. I run a clean house—straight one, too. When she got away from here, there was no one to control her and she needed the big bucks for her habit.''

Paige was nodding. "You're talking about S and M, aren't you?"

The train they heard when they first arrived now began passing behind the house. McLaurin had to raise his voice in order to be understood.

"The greater the pain, the greater the gain. Big bucks. That's what she was doing, all right, lady."

CHAPTER 15

$\mathfrak{I}$n an office at the back of the Pass Christian police department, a wide, one-story metal structure, sitting near the middle of town and across from small St. Paul's Catholic elementary school, Brett sat in one of two straight-backed chairs facing the chief's desk. Paige sat in the other chair as she explained her theory to Seales. She had told Brett he should be the one to explain it, but he had told her no, she had come up with the idea in the first place; if there proved to be anything to it, she deserved the credit.

But now he wondered if he had done wrong in having her be the one to make the presentation. Seales, his broad body leaning back in his chair under a faded, framed photograph of J. Edgar Hoover, had slowly developed a frown as she had talked. Now he clasped his hands across his slightly protruding stomach and began to revolve one thumb around the other—(a well-known sign) that he was growing impatient.

Paige quickened the tempo of her words. "So you see, even in his first three attacks maybe it wasn't prostitutes he was attacking, per se. We know from what McLaurin said that the prostitute killed over in New Orleans was advertising she was into S and M. The neighbor who I.D.'d the prostitute killed at her home in Memphis said that the victim often had bruises after returning from dates.

"Now, if you do assume the killer is attacking victims involved in S and M, Chief, then the maid and Trinity might not involve a change on his part. Both of them *could* have been into S and M. Mrs. Lloyd doesn't believe the maid was capable of that. But how could she really know? From what Edward Gregory said, it's possible Trinity was what the psychiatrists call a submissive type, a type that has been known to gravitate toward a desire for punishment. I know I'm not giving you very much concrete information, but I'm sure you can see that there's at least a possibility of a common thread among the victims.''

Seales remained silent for several seconds. Finally, he sat upright in his chair and leaned his heavy forearm forward on his desk. The look on his wide face told Brett that whatever was coming wasn't going to be pleasant.

He looked at Paige and saw her glance at him out of the corner of her eyes. He wished again that he had been the one to make the presentation—or that it hadn't been made at all.

"When did you find the time to come up with all this information?" Seales asked.

"We did it earlier today," Paige said.

"Today, huh?"

"Yes, sir."

"Got a lot done, didn't you?" There was no escaping the sarcasm in his tone.

"Well—uh, yes, sir."

"Why didn't you say anything to me about it first? Maybe even ask me if I had any objection to you doing all this investigating on your own."

Brett had feared that was the problem. They had done the worst thing possible; they had stepped on Seales's ego by not first consulting him about what they were going to do. Brett knew he should've thought of that and told Seales what they had in mind before they went any further. But Paige had made her idea sound plausible, and one thing had led to another without him ever really stopping to think about how far they were going on their own. He had been a fool, and now both of them were going to pay for it—but it was his fault.

"Well," Seales said as he stared at Paige. "You can't talk now? You were going on quite steady just a second ago. I asked you why you didn't consult me first."

"I—uh—didn't think about it. It was on our free time and I didn't see how it—"

Brett shifted in his seat. "Chief," he said. "I was the one who made the decision to do what we did."

Seales moved his gaze to him for a moment and then looked back at Paige. "You think ads—that might be how the killer picked them out?"

She nodded. "It's possible, sir. McLaurin said the prostitute he identified used them. If somebody could get a judge to subpoena the magazine's records, maybe we'll find out that the other victims did, too."

"Which magazine?"

"Well, McLaurin told us which one the prostitute in New Orleans used. That's a start. Subpoena that one's records and see if any of the others used it. If they didn't, I'm—" She shook her head. "I don't know—there can't be that many magazines carrying ads like that."

When Seales briefly closed his eyes, she said, "Well, maybe there are a *lot* like that. But that's not the important thing, anyway. We know the one magazine for sure. The one the prostitute used. If my theory's right, then maybe, at least in her case, the killer did respond to an ad in it. We could use the same magazine."

Seales slowly nodded. "To run our own little ads."

"Yes, sir."

"So now you've decided that this department is going to take the lead in this investigation. Going to take it away from the F.B.I. and Memphis, New Orleans, Mobile—gonna tell them that little old Pass Christian is taking over."

"No, sir. Give what I've said to anybody you want to. Let them do it. The sheriff didn't think it was such a bad idea."

Seales's eyes narrowed. "Will you tell me, Officer Dunnigan," he said, "what you were doing going to him before me? Looking for a change in jobs, a little varied experience before you go off to the F.B.I.? That can damn sure be arranged. At least you're leaving this job."

"Chief," Brett said. "That's out of line."

Seales's eyes narrowed, but Brett continued. "We went over there to go through the case files. We had to get him to open the file cabinet. It was just a comment he made. Paige didn't ask him for his opinion.''

Seales's eyes continued to burn. "And you, Brett, it must be the lack of sleep going to your head. That's it, isn't it? You pulled the late shift, stayed up the rest of the night during the investigation, then pulled the early shift. That has to be it, because a cop with your experience would know better, wouldn't he?" Seales's mouth tightened.

But when he looked back at Paige, his face suddenly softened. "Okay," he said, in a much gentler tone. "Let's say you're right about your theory, Paige, and, furthermore, say the F.B.I. would agree to set up the kind of ad you're talking about. Even if the killer did respond, how would they know which one he was?"

"However many respond, that'll give them somebody to question. They don't have that now."

"So you're saying that everybody who has a different idea of sex than we do, they should be snared with an ad and pulled in to interrogate. What do you think the ACLU would say about that?"

Paige dropped her eyes without commenting.

"You didn't like my shooting your theory down?" Seales asked.

She raised her face to his and said, "It's not that I don't like it, sir. I thought I had a good idea, at least good enough for it to be checked out further. I'm sorry."

At her apology, Seales was silent for a few seconds. Finally, he said, "Well, it wasn't a particularly good idea the way you presented it, but maybe it's not altogether as bad as I'm making it sound. And though I don't like hearing about something my officers have done after the fact, maybe I've been a little bit rough on you—both of you. But then I've been rough on everybody today after finding out that we might have had the killer's print right in our hands and then some dumb ass blew it—it's got me uptight, I guess.''

"Print?" Paige said. "Are you speaking about—"

Seales nodded several times. "Yeah, yeah, the print. Arnie was out near that pool house today—looking around. You remember where the deputies saw that old piece of cloth hanging in the hedge? Well, a few feet on down the hedge he found a piece of a rubber glove with blood on it, a part that would've covered a finger and a small area of the palm. He must have torn it off going through the bushes. Then we up and just smeared the print all to hell—somebody did.''

He shook his head. "But I need to put that behind me. All I'm doing is causing my ulcer to act up.''

He shook his head again, stood, and walked around his desk past them to a water cooler sitting against the back wall. He spoke over his shoulder as he mixed a couple of Alka-Seltzers into a glass of water.

"Tell you what. Even though as far as I'm personally concerned, this idea of yours sounds more than anything like you two have got a hell of an imagination, what's there to lose by checking it out a little further? I want you to go back out to the Anderson house. Look around for telephone numbers, names. Meanwhile, I'll call the district attorney and ask him to have a judge draw up an order for their telephone records. After you've finished at the house, you can run over to the telephone company and go through the Andersons' long-distance calls, see if anything jumps out at you—a lot of calls to the same number, or maybe some to a place you're not sure what it is. If she was into the kind of activity you two are guessing at, then she had to have somebody to do it with.''

He came back to his chair and sat down, placing the glass of foaming water on his desk as he began speaking again.

"You find what I just told you, get me a list of all the names and numbers you can and then I'll call over to Gulfport and talk to Applewhite, explain your theory. He'll follow up on it, follow up on about anything at this point. But he'll need the names out of her house first, something concrete to go on so the civil liberties people don't say it's just a fishing expedition—need to be able to tie the names directly back to the Andersons. Then let's leave the people that are equipped to handle the psychopath to worry about him, and you two get your mind back on our business, in particular, that damn burglar that keeps hitting us. Rory Kellum and his wife got back in from vacation this morning and found their house had been ransacked. I'm sorry about Mrs. Anderson, but that was just a fluke as far as our business is concerned. The psychopath spotted her someplace and followed her over here. He won't be back. The burglar *will* be.''

Quitty Corning, the large, stockily built secretary who Seales had hired his first week on the job, stuck her wide, dark face around the doorway into the office.

"Chief Seales," she said, "that newspaper reporter is here to interview you."

He nodded and immediately stood, stuffed his shirt tighter into the broad waistband of his pants, and adjusted his tie. He started to run his hand across his short-cropped hair but stopped when he noticed their stares. "What are you waiting for?" he asked.

As they started toward the door, he added, "By the way, I had a call this morning that Trinity's husband was strung out on coke. Caller said bad strung out. The guy who called wouldn't leave his name, but he said he was telling us because he thought maybe it was a drug-related killing, said Anderson owed a lot of money to someone who had advanced him on an IOU. The gist of the conversation was that somebody made it look like the serial killer— a copy cat."

That didn't sound right to Brett. "I don't know of any dealer who advances on credit."

Seales agreed with a nod of his head. "Yeah, and unless there's an awful big mouth in the F.B.I., I don't know anybody who can imitate the psycho's attacks—what he does."

"Do you know, Chief?"

"No. But I wouldn't tell you if I did. You don't have any need to know."

When Brett and Paige walked into the outer office on their way to the front door of the station, they saw why Seales had primped. A squat, young blond with short hair and an enormous jutting bust stood waiting beside Quitty's desk. She smiled and ran her gaze up and down Brett as he walked across the floor toward the door of the station.

Paige didn't even notice, she was so occupied with her thoughts. "Brett, if somebody doesn't figure out something about this psycho, if somebody doesn't catch him. . . . The times he strikes are getting closer and closer together. There's got to be something that stands out, something that we would notice if we just knew what we were looking for. If somebody could just think of it."

After the reporter entered Seales office, he showed her to a chair across his desk and waited for her questions. He was prepared for her to dwell on the serial killer, but she didn't, most of her questions instead touching on his background and the memorable cases he had worked on. She had been impressed, too; that was evident in the wide-eyed looks she had given him from time to time.

She finished writing his last answer onto her notepad and looked back across the desk. "I know you can't give me anything confidential," she said, "but is there some way you can give me at least a general idea of what you're doing to find the killer? So much of the stories in all the big papers have been slanted toward the killer being at large. I would like to frame this story more along the line of what is being done—reassure the public some, show them how their interest is being served."

He liked that.

CHAPTER 16

Nearing Trinity's house, Paige said, "There's Dr. Felter's van."

It was parked at the side of the street in front of the house. There was another vehicle, too, an old wrecker backed down the gravel driveway to the rear of the red MG, and Brett felt suddenly angry. He parked behind Felter's van and strode across the lawn to the wrecker.

"What are you doing?" he asked of the tall, lanky man in grease-stained yellow coveralls standing between the two vehicles.

The man's thin eyebrows tightened at the top of his narrow face. "I'm takin' this in for lack of payments," he said.

"You have a judge's order?"

"Don't need none. This was on a chattel mortgage. Who are you to be askin', anyways?"

"How many payments are they behind?"

"Mister, I don't know what your problem is, but I got work to do."

"No, I don't think you do. Not here, anyway. I think you just need to get on out of here."

The man stared a moment, then stepped around the rear of the wrecker to an open tool box. He pulled out a wrench and patted it into his palm as he looked back across the truck.

Brett had his police I.D. and badge in the hip pocket of his jeans, but staring at the skinny vulture who hadn't even waited until Trinity had been buried to come after her car, he didn't feel like showing it.

"Brett," Paige said.

He didn't answer her.

She stepped up beside Brett, glanced at him, then produced her badge and showed it to the man.

"We're police officers," she said. "I think you need to go on now. You tell whoever sent you that this car belongs to an estate until a judge says otherwise."

The man looked at her, back at Brett, and again to the badge. His face flushed but he dropped his hand to his side and walked to the side of the wrecker.

Climbing inside the truck, he threw the wrench clanging to the floorboard and slammed the door. In a second, the loud motor roared and the truck jumped forward. The sling the man had worked with still down and swinging barely above the gravel driveway, he drove rapidly out of the yard and turned back left toward the curve at the end of the street.

Paige looked at Brett staring after the truck. "He was just doing what he was told," she said.

Brett stared a moment longer without answering her, then turned and walked past her toward the house.

She shook her head and followed him.

Bobby looked down at his bed, which was covered with his hunting equipment—the big shiny knife, its thick blade both razor sharp and strong enough to pry cervical vertebra apart without breaking; his hacksaw—in reserve—he preferred the knife; the nylon hood he had painstakingly fashioned and sewn himself; a set of master keys; a pair of surgical gloves; a narrow thin-bladed stiletto for slipping under window screens; and a snub-nosed .38 caliber Smith & Wesson revolver. He didn't like the gun; any no-talent nobody could use a gun. But he carried it just in case he should ever run into more than his knife could handle—highly doubtful.

And of course, the small piece of folded cardboard. Above an O written with a Magic Marker were the words, BACK AFTER MY REST AND NO LONGER BORED.

He worried sometimes about taunting the cops like that. Making the calls and the countdowns were bad enough. If he wasn't careful he was going to give away too much. But then that was what the devil had told him to do, what he had to do. His cheek twitched and he smiled broadly.

As the wrecker—the still-extended swing swaying behind it—disappeared around the curve down the street and Brett and Paige neared the front door, Dr. Felter stepped outside into the bright sunlight. He wore a thigh-length white lab coat unbuttoned over his white dress shirt and baggy dark slacks. His long brown hair was hanging loose down his back and his head was covered with a wide-brimmed felt hat pulled low down over his forehead—he *did* look a lot like a pale-faced Geronimo. He removed the hat as he nodded at Paige, then reached into a coat pocket and pulled out a round, striped piece of hard candy wrapped in cellophane. He held it out to them.

From somewhere a scent of honeysuckle reached Brett and, inexplicably, made him think of the smell always present in the morgue where Felter had his office. He looked at the candy and shook his head. Paige smiled, "No, thank you."

The doctor smiled. "Well, you've caught me in the act of examining the scene," he explained. "Not in my official capacity, mind you, but along the lines of my hobby, seeing if I might notice anything that would give me a hint what went on other than the obvious." He unwrapped the candy and popped it into his mouth.

"Attempting to quit smoking," he said. "So far I've been through two pounds of peppermints and three cartons of cigarettes." The candy cracked between his teeth.

He smiled sheepishly. "Can't suck it like I'm supposed to—keep biting down. Now that you two have discovered what I'm about, what are you back here for?"

Brett answered. "Looking for names."

"Names?"

"Yeah, names and phone numbers. By the way, did your autopsy show any drugs in James Anderson's body?"

"No. You were saying, names and numbers?"

"Paige has a theory that the victims might have been into a common activity. Just a wild guess. But we're going to send the names and numbers to the F.B.I so they can question them."

Felter looked puzzled. "I'm sorry. Obviously, there's some evidence I am unaware of."

"Sort of," Paige replied. "The autopsy report on the woman in Memphis mentioned that she had bruises on her body that were inflicted a few days prior to her death. Trinity was into acting out some kind of submissive behavior. At least that's what I think she was doing. It's not much to go on, almost nothing, but it made us wonder if maybe the victims might've been into some kind of rough sex—S and M. If they were, then maybe the killer's selecting his targets out of a group like that."

"I see. That's interesting." The candy cracked again. "But if that's all you have to go on, it sounds like you've made quite a leap to come up with your hypothesis."

"Yes, sir, you're right," Paige said, "but anything is worth trying to check on—however far out it might be. If it turns out there is something to it—if we're right—then the teams working on the case will be able to narrow down the type of victim he's drawn to, because everything else about them is still the same as it was when he first started. They've all been relatively young women. All of them had dark hair. All had comparatively slight frames."

A smile lifted the doctor's round cheeks.

"What?" she asked.

Felter chuckled under his breath, raised the back of his hand to wipe the beads of sweat from his forehead. "I guess I have to occasionally entertain a less than serious thought in order to maintain my sanity in the profession I'm in," he said. "I was wondering if it had occurred to you that you just described an individual remarkably similar to yourself—young, dark-haired, and small."

"Yeah, but I'm not into S and M. At least not yet, I'm not."

Felter chuckled again. "Well, must be on my way. Have a pile of things to work on."

Halfway across the lawn toward his van, he shook his head and chuckled again.

CHAPTER 17

As Dr. Felter left and Brett stepped inside Trinity's house, the first thing he noticed was how hot the interior was, and the strong odor coming from the bedroom where she had lain in her own blood.

He tried to ignore it at first, and not breathe deeply. Then he tried the opposite tack and took in as much air as he could through his nose—hoping to dull his sense of smell. Paige was already going through drawers in the living room as she looked for something with names and addresses or numbers.

As he forced his attention to his job, the first thing he noticed was the black fingerprint powder present on the telephone receiver and all the doorknobs in sight. Neither the lab technicians nor the deputies had lifted any prints from inside the house the night of the murder. There hadn't been any need to with Anderson as the prime suspect. There was nothing unusual about his prints being in his own house. Since his body had been found and the discovery made that he wasn't the murderer, somebody had been back to the house—the sheriff's deputies or the F.B.I.

He hesitated a moment at Trinity's bedroom door, then glanced inside the room.

A telephone directory sat on the table on the far side of the bed. He didn't want to lower his gaze to the carpet but did anyway, and looked at the wide round circle now crusted hard and black.

He raised his eyes and stepped into the bedroom, trying to keep the now-stronger odor from his nostrils by breathing through his mouth as he walked toward the left of the bed.

The directory didn't have anything written on the cover. He thumbed through it quickly and saw no underlined name.

Opening the drawer of the table, he looked at its contents—a flashlight, loose change, twine and a needle, a set of keys, several pencils, an ink pen, and several packs of grocery-store stamps.

He shut the drawer and looked at the black smudges on the windowsill to his left. The window was still open. He was sure there were several windows in town that had been open that night that wouldn't be again for a long time. And doors, too—most of the doors in town were normally unlocked twenty-four hours a day. He'd bet there were a lot fewer now.

Surprisingly, there wasn't any blood on the cover of the bed. But there was a spray of stain on the wall under the windowsill. Spray, he thought, and visualized the arterial blood spurting out in a long jet after her throat had been slit. His stomach twisted. He stood silently a moment, then exhaled audibly and moved to the walk-in closet.

Inside it he saw nothing that would contain any names or telephone numbers. There was a book bound in gold leaf on a shelf at the back and he took it into his hands and opened the cover.

It was Trinity's wedding album. Her smiling face peered big-eyed from every page. He recalled the same look when they were in high school, and again when she looked up and saw him in the bar last year. He stared at her face for a moment longer, then closed the cover, replaced the album, and walked to the table on the far side of the bed.

Nothing containing names or numbers was in its drawer, either.

Moving back into the living room, the telephone on the table beside the easy chair caught his eye. He remembered that the night of the murder a directory had been lying there.

Paige walked from the dining room. "There's nothing in the kitchen, either," she said. "Nothing anywhere with any names or telephone numbers."

Two thoughts struck him almost simultaneously. "What did you mean when you told Dr. Felter you weren't into S and M *yet*?"

"Somehow I just feel I'm right about the killer being attracted by those kinds of women, Brett. If I thought it would do any good, I'd almost advertise in that magazine, see if I could draw him out. To heck with what Seales said."

He thought that was what she might have meant. "Well, forget it. We're cops, not spies."

"Oh, I'm just talking. You know I wouldn't really do it. But if he's after women like that, then there has to be a way he singles them out, and we know the pro in New Orleans was using ads."

"Paige, I never know what you might do, you're so damned impetuous. But let me tell you, if you *did* attract him, the first you would know of it would be when he followed you home and whacked your head off."

"I said I was just talking."

He verbalized the second thought that had occurred to him. "Somebody's already been here. I know there was another telephone directory, not just the one I saw in the bedroom. I remember one on the table when you called Seales."

Paige looked at the table and nodded her agreement. "Yeah, there was. You said there's a directory in the bedroom?"

He nodded.

"Just a minute," she said, and hurried toward the hallway.

In a few seconds, she walked back into the room. She had the directory open in her hands and held it out toward him.

"Look," she said. "Nothing written here on the inside page. When Information gave me the chief's number, I wrote it down so I wouldn't forget it while I was getting the sheriff's. This is where I wrote it. There has to be another directory."

He nodded. A lot of people write numbers they want to remember into their directories. And not only there; there should be some numbers written somewhere else, too, on a sheet taped to the back of a kitchen cabinet or else on a pad somewhere. On something— there wasn't such a thing as a house without telephone numbers written down anywhere.

"But where are they?" he said as much to himself as her. "The F.B.I., the sheriff—one of them would have to have them, wouldn't they?"

The thought that suddenly passed through his mind was frightening. It was also ridiculous. He brought a wry smile to his face and shook his head.

Paige's eyebrows bunched. "What?"

"My mind's starting to work like yours. Now I'm wondering something that *I* have to have an answer for."

He stepped to the telephone as she stared at him with a quizzical expression. He punched in the number for the police station. Seales had left and nobody knew where he had gone. He had left word he wouldn't be back until the next morning.

Brett rung the sheriff's office. Hastings was in. It took nearly five minutes for the secretary to locate him.

"Sorry to take so long, Brett. We got a rat in here you wouldn't believe—been trying to catch him for a week. At least the newspapers are not complaining about him being at large. What can I do for you?"

"I'm at the Anderson home. Paige and I came out here at Seales's suggestion to try to find some names or phone numbers to—"

"And there's nothing there," the sheriff said before he could finish. "That's my doing. Right after you left here, I called the F.B.I. and told them about your and Paige's idea. They told me they'd check out anything, for me to box up what names and addresses I could find and send them over to their office. I sent a couple of deputies out to the house. They said they got everything they could find that had a name or number on it. It's all on the way to Applewhite now. By the way, we uncovered a bag of coke, too. Looks like the feedback Seales got on Anderson being a dopehead was accurate."

When Brett replaced the receiver, he sat down in the easy chair. Leaning back in it, he smiled sheepishly.

"For a minute there, Paige, I started thinking somebody might have come in here and gotten the numbers to hide whose they were."

"You mean the killer? He'd have to have a lot of guts to come back here."

"Not if he were a cop."

"A cop?"

"Yeah. Cops have been coming and going over here. He wouldn't have stood out."

"The killer a cop?"

"Why not? Psychopaths have come from the ranks of bums and they've been guys with doctorates. If it had turned out that the deputies hadn't picked up the telephone numbers, that everything that had a name or number on it was just suddenly missing—yeah, I'd be thinking a cop. Like the one in a uniform down by the pool house.''

Paige wasn't smiling now. "God, Brett, that would be something, wouldn't it? That the serial killer was not only from around here but maybe was one of us?''

Her forehead wrinkled in thought. "Gosh, Brett, how would you like to know that was the case and then receive a call late at night from an officer wanting you to come out to a secluded area—something he had discovered and wanted you to take a look at? I'd be scared to go even if it was Arnie calling.'' She shuddered.

CHAPTER 18

After leaving the Andersons', Brett and Paige stopped by their own house and dressed in their blue uniforms, retrieved the judge's order, drove to the telephone company's main office, and were shown to a record room where they went through the last three months of the Andersons' long-distance telephone calls.

There weren't very many, and only three of them to locations within a two-hundred-mile range of Pass Christian—two of them placing orders to a discount store outside Mobile and the other one, it turned out, a call to a bookie in Baton Rouge. When they left the telephone company, Paige had Brett stop at a small convenience store. There she purchased a copy of an adult magazine.

When she came back outside she was walking slowly, holding the publication up in front of her and thumbing through it. The cover featured a naked couple, entwined in glorious living color.

Two men walking by her on their way to the store turned and smiled after she had passed them. Brett smiled, too.

As they drove back toward the police station, she studied the personals.

"What's water sports?" she asked.

"Huh?"

"Water sports. It says here, ready and willing for about everything except S and M and water sports."

He smiled again.

The radio crackled and the dispatcher's voice came across the two-way radio, asking for him. He lifted the mike to his mouth, responded, and waited for her message.

"Lieutenant, I've had a telephone call for you. Lady making it said she'd call back in fifteen minutes. Said she had something she thought you oughta know about the Anderson case."

Bobby, carrying the black bowling-ball bag containing his hunting equipment, trudged along the edge of the pavement bordering the white sand beaches fronting the Mississippi Sound. He cursed the hot sun bearing down on the back of his neck, and cursed the noisy traffic moving bumper to bumper along the street as cars jockeyed for position to turn into the lot of the huge, several-tiered, multicolored Grand Casino to his left. At times the cars honked at him to move over more so they could pass him safely, and each honk had caused his neck muscles to bulge more noticeably—it now almost looked like someone had inserted an air hose and blew up the back of his neck.

But he kept smiling, a big smile. He had learned to do that when he was at the hospital. "Show them you're happy," the sympathetic nurse had said, "and always do what anyone in authority tells you—but especially smile. It's a sign of control, and satisfaction."

He had not understood the logic in that, what it really had to do with his mental condition, but had started flashing big smiles every time he met up with one of the psychiatrists or an orderly or a nurse, anybody with authority, anybody who would have a say in his being released.

Surprisingly, it had worked. He had been released within a year of the nurse's advice, so it must have worked. Remembering that, he forced his smile bigger, but another horn sounding behind him made it difficult to hold his pose, and so he transferred over to the other side of the highway.

There the honking became less frequent, and he began to relax when another loud blast came close behind him causing him to flinch. A vehicle slowed beside him.

He slowly revolved his head to face the pickup.

"Hop in and I'll give you a ride," a soft voice said from inside the cab.

Bobby peered inside the window at the smiling, red-cheeked

man, then at the long rifle hung across the top of the cab's back window. Bobby didn't want a ride, but a rifle was certainly a symbol of authority no matter how meek the little red-cheeked man driving the pickup looked, and he had said, "Hop in." Bobby decided to take no chance, opened the door and slid inside the cab, carefully retaining in his lap the bowling-ball bag containing his hunting equipment. He smiled at the red-cheeked man.

"How far are you going?" the man asked, glad that he was getting to do a good deed so soon after leaving the talk with his preacher. He had gone in for the talk because his married life was beginning to give him so much trouble, his wife constantly nagging, and his kids into one problem after the other.

The preacher had said that maybe if he would start doing a good deed each day, he would find that his life was more rewarding. Such advice didn't really seem to have a whole hell of a lot to do with his immediate problem, but he was willing to do anything that might help.

He looked back across the seat. There had been no answer given when he had asked the broad-shouldered man how far he was going, and now the man just sat there, his bowling-ball bag in his lap, smiling broadly.

Maybe I got me a deaf mute, the red-cheeked man thought. That would be an especially good deed, giving one of them a ride. He returned the broad smile and guided his pickup back out into the flow of traffic.

The driver of the eighteen wheeler he cut in front of held down on his horn and the red-cheeked man thrust his arm out the window and flashed an obscene gesture.

The truck driver pressed down on the horn again.

The red-cheeked man jabbed his finger repeatedly into the air.

Bobby kept smiling, though the muscles still bulged at the back of his neck, and his cheek twitched.

CHAPTER 19

Brett reached the police station less than fifteen minutes after receiving the call about the woman who had something to tell him concerning the Anderson case. He held the door open for Paige, then stepped quickly inside the building and walked to the glass partition where Quitty Corning, Seales's secretary, looked up through the glass from her desk cluttered with paperwork and notes.

"Quitty, has she called back yet?"

She shook her head no as she scratched at something on the back of her thick neck. "Said she would, though, Brett, in fifteen minutes. Been about that long now. By the way, your father called from Miami earlier. He said he's boarding the cruise ship tonight and that he probably won't call until he gets to Puerto Rico. I sulled up some kind of bad after that—him off on a cruise and me setting here in this heat and humidity. I'm going to take me one of those someday."

There was a faint crackling over the radio off to her side. She pressed the button at the base of the short mike.

"Go ahead," she said before anything had come over the speaker.

"How do you do that?" came Arnie Hatcher's voice back over the radio.

"Go on, Arnie."

"You promised me you'd tell me."

111

"You got a funny squeak in your radio," she answered.

"Well, I thought so. I knew you weren't psychic like you said. And another thing, you probably oughta be more professional like with your calls, Quitty."

"Is that so, Arnie?"

"I don't mean no disrespect. I'm just saying it's more professional, you know."

"Yeah, Arnie, okay. Go ahead, unit seven. How's that?"

"Yeah, uh, well I ... It's not a cat up a tree, Quitty. It's a raccoon."

"How was I to know what it was?" she replied. "Kids just called in to say they needed some help getting their pet down out of a tree. Knew it couldn't be no dog up a tree. Nobody I know of in town owns a monkey."

"Well, it's a coon, and I'm not going up after it, not even getting close to it. I just looked up in the tree and the thing showed its teeth."

"Arnie, those kids, you gotta do something for them."

"I ain't going up no tree after a coon that's showing its teeth—might be rabid."

The telephone on her desk rang.

"Hold on a minute," she said as she reached for the receiver. After answering she said, "Yes, he is. Just a second, please."

She pressed a button on the phone. "I think this is her—line three."

She buzzed him and Paige through the door off to the side of her desk and they walked into the next area and the nearest phone.

"Hello."

"Is this Brett Dunnigan?"

"Yes, who is this?"

"I'm sorry, but I don't want to give my name."

His brow wrinkled. When Paige saw that, hers did, too. He shrugged and shook his head.

"I don't know how to start," the caller said, "but I think there's a man you need to know about. The one Trinity went to see that night."

He gathered the receiver close to his ear. "She went to see?"

"That night. The night she was killed."

"Who?"

"Brett, maybe I'm just being silly, but I wanted you all to know about him."

"Who?"

"I'm not sure. He's married and Trinity didn't want to say. I went to high school with her—"

Then she had to have been in school with him, too. The woman's voice sounded strangely familiar, or was he just guessing it did?

"—When she moved back here I ran into her over in Biloxi one day and we ate lunch together. She told me about meeting him when she lived in Jackson. She had gone down to New Orleans one night and met him in a bar and they spent the night together.

"The next weekend, when they met again, she found out he was from Mississippi. I think she saw some kind of card he had. He had told her he was from Texas.

"He totally panicked, saying that he was some kind of big shot from Gulfport and he would be ruined if it got back there that he was stepping out on his wife. Trinity said she wouldn't have said anything about him to anybody, done anything to cause him a problem. But he refused to see her again.

"She called Gulfport Information, but his name wasn't listed. After that she was always looking through *The Sun Herald* trying to see his picture. But she never did.

"She said that when she moved here the first thing she did was run into him. She told me he wasn't from Biloxi, but from right here in town, and that the name he had given her was a bunch of bull.

"She said he turned pale when he saw her. He asked her please not ever to speak to him again and hurried off while she was still trying to talk to him.

"A couple of days later she saw him in his car and followed him and saw him stop at a house that wasn't his. She knew it wasn't; she had followed him there before. She told me when he went up to the door that a woman stepped out and hugged him. It really made her angry. I think her pride was hurt more than anything else—to be shot down by another woman. I don't know if that had ever happened to her before.

"That morning—the morning before she was killed—she came

over to see me before I left and said she was going to go confront him that night. I told her that was silly, to just forget about it, but she was insistent. I really think that she was reaching the point where she couldn't stand anything else negative happening to her; she was wanting to fight back.

"About everything, Brett, you just don't know. Her husband was so into drugs. She would find them and throw them away and come back and find him spaced out again. She told me once she found him crawling around on the bedroom floor. He looked under the bed, felt along the carpet. He must have been so far out of it, he couldn't remember where he had put his stuff. And all their money was going to his habit. It was just horrible for her. She . . . Ah, that doesn't matter now. What does matter is catching her killer. I don't know what she had in mind about confronting the guy, don't . . . She was probably still hung up on him, and hurting the way he'd treated her. Ah, hell, I don't know. I just don't know. But that night when I got in, I had a message on my answering machine. I wanted you to hear it."

His attention was suddenly drawn to a loud sound in the background behind the caller's voice. A train whistle. He glanced at his watch. Westbound, he had sat in his patrol car and waited for it to pass often enough. He hadn't heard it pass the station yet, so it was back to the east of town.

"The tape's broken up some," the woman continued. "I rerecorded it to take out my name whenever Trinity mentioned it. There will be some blanks in it where I did that, but you can understand it."

In the background he heard the sound of a passing vehicle, and then began to hear the train rumbling on the track. The sound of the passing vehicle, it had sounded like a big truck, had been clear. The woman was on an outside phone.

He grabbed the pencil which was lying next to a pad on the desk.

"I'll play it now," the woman said.

He quickly scribbled a note, then held it up for Paige to see.

WOMAN ON PAY PHONE CLOSE TO TRAIN TRACKS EAST OF TOWN—FIND HER!

Paige dashed for the front of the station.

The recording began:

"—went to see him tonight like I told you I was going to—"

Trinity's voice was easily recognizable even with the poor quality of the redubbing. He closed his eyes as he continued to listen.

"—He couldn't believe it when I walked in. He was so shocked. The bitch was there, too. She went crazy, slapped me. Turns out it was his sister. That's what he said, anyway. Can you believe she slapped me, ————? He said if I ever mentioned anything about him to anybody he'd take care of me good."

A choked sob was clear on the tape.

"He said that, ————; he really said it just like that. But he's not going to scare me off, though. Not after her slapping me, he's not. I'll show both of them. I'm going to get him. I told him I had friends, too, cops, too. We'll see who takes care of who."

There was an unusual sound, like Trinity was crying and laughing at the same time.

"—You'd been proud of me for how strong I was. I scared them; I know I did."

A few seconds passed without any sound, then her last words.

"Well, I'm going now ... Love."

The tape ended.

Said he'd take care of me for good. The killer? A man she knew? Had gone to see? And a sister? But that made no sense. The F.B.I. had said there was no doubt Trinity had been murdered by a psychopath.

The caller was back on the line. She spoke slowly, a catch in her voice.

"I don't know, Brett. I know everybody is saying it was the serial killer. But couldn't somebody have tried to make it look like it was him? Or is that possible? All I know is I'm scared. I hope she didn't say anything to him about me—about her talking to me about him."

Paige ought to be close to the tracks now. "Was there anything she said that might have given you a hint who he might be?"

"No, nothing, Brett. All I know is, he's married. I know the way you two felt about each other you'd be the one to call. I'm aware that you two—" The telephone receiver was suddenly slammed down hard. A moment later he heard the dial tone. Paige.

The woman saw her coming. *Get her, Paige.* Or did he really want her to? Just before she had slammed the receiver down, she had said *I'm aware that you two . . .*

What did she know?

Did anybody else know?

The telephone began to beep.

Paige stared out the car window at the gaunt old black man on an outside phone at a service station near the train tracks. Brett had said a woman. Where? Just on the east side of town, that's all. Pass Christian wasn't *that* damn small.

Across the street from the service station, an attractive redhead in her late twenties looked out the open window of the restaurant where she worked. She was watching Paige—and then the patrol car drove off. She opened her tape recorder, slipped the cassette out and placed it inside her pocket, then turned and smiled at a couple entering the restaurant.

By the time Paige returned to the police station, Brett had regained control. As much as he could. They went in to see Chief Seales together.

"I'd probably lay it to coincidence that she went out to see this character before she was murdered," Seales said. "It almost has to be. If it isn't, then that would have to mean he's the psycho—living over here. What're the odds of that being the case?"

"We thought he did at first," Paige said. "When we thought it was her husband."

Seales nodded. "Just because it's not likely doesn't mean we won't play it safe—do what checking we can. If she was as hung up on this character as the caller said, then she probably mentioned him to someone else. Good chance of that, anyway. Tell everyone to start asking around about who her girlfriends were. Go talk to them. I'll get the word about the call over to Applewhite. His boys can check out those people she worked with."

Vic was dubious, too, when Brett called him. "The killer being someone she knew," Vic questioned, "a psycho who's hit from Memphis to New Orleans to Mobile just happens to live over there—What kind of odds would you give that?"

"Vic, he has to live somewhere. And this town is almost the bottom of a triangle between the places he's hit. It would be easy for him to go each way and still get back the same night."

"The same night?"

"Yeah, like if he had a daytime job he didn't want to cause any suspicion by missing. I never believed Paige was onto something that would end up putting Trinity into some S and M deal. But this—she went to see this guy and was killed right afterward. The F.B.I. says that only the psycho. . . . There could be a chance they're wrong, that whatever he does has gotten out."

"Anything's possible—I guess."

"Vic, the caller said a big shot. Even if it is somebody trying to make it look like him, who in the hell is a big shot around here, and with a sister?"

There was silence for a moment, then a low chuckle came across the line. "Christ, Brett, this is crazy. Now you're getting me to wonder. Let me digest it a little while. I'll call you tonight. Your shift over at eleven?"

"We've got Armont and Arnie catching the last few hours for us. It's Paige's parents' anniversary. We're going to dinner with them. We should be in by ten or a little after."

He replaced the receiver and looked at Paige. "And then I've got to get some sleep," he said.

She smiled and nodded. "I promise I won't think of anything else."

The red-cheeked man braked his pickup to a stop at a red light on 90. He had driven quite a distance without his passenger saying anything. But of course he *couldn't;* he was a deaf mute.

He turned in his seat and faced the man, spoke slowly, carefully forming his words so they could be easily read.

"How far is it you're going? Just point when you want to get out is good enough."

"You passed it," Bobby said.

The man's brow wrinkled. "I—uh—why didn't you say?"

Bobby just smiled.

The light turned green. Somebody behind them honked. It was the eighteen wheeler again. The red-cheeked man jabbed his mid-

dle finger out the window of his pickup and then drove through
the light and pulled to the side of the pavement.

"Pushy bastard," he growled as the truck driver held down on
his horn while he drove past. *Just like my damn wife. Always
raising hell about something.*

When he looked back toward the passenger seat, the door stood
open and the stocky man, a broad smile across his face, was
walking back down the highway in the direction they had just
come.

CHAPTER 20

Antonio's, located in Ocean Springs, just south of the long bridge across Old Fort Bayou, overlooks the wide band of water leading into Biloxi Bay. Paige, in a soft yellow dress hanging to the midthigh mark of her bare legs, and Brett, in khakis, an open-necked beige dress shirt and a blue sports coat had arrived at the restaurant before her parents had and awaited them next to the cash register.

"Well, what are you two up to?" Dr. Felter asked, and they turned around to face him.

In a white suit, white tie, and white shoes, he was almost a blur, the only contrast being his light-brown hair falling against his shoulders and his AOA key hanging by a black strap from the breast pocket of his coat.

Paige had to hold back her smile. "We're meeting my parents here for their anniversary," she said.

"Ah, family," Felter replied. "A pleasure denied me by my predilection to a constant variety of damsels. A Casanova—that is what that noted newspaper termed me, wasn't it?"

"What *are* you doing alone? That's not like you."

"Oh, a temporary inconvenience I must suffer. I'm on a probation of sorts at the direction of those who are going to give me my new employment. I must not become involved in any further dallying with married women or their offer will be withdrawn."

"You could take out a single woman."

"And spoil a reputation I have taken years building? But, if the truth must be known, I believe that waiting for me inside the dining area is a perfectly exquisite divorcee. I view her as somewhat of a compromise between a woman kept pleasantly satisfied by the ongoing conjugal relationship she shares with her husband and the often opportunistic single types whose frenetic attempts at love I so deplore."

Paige smiled and shook her head in amusement as the doctor bid them good-bye and walked on into the dining area.

Bobby stood in the pitch-black area under a widespread, thick-limbed oak, hidden from sight. But he had a clear view of the apartment-complex entrance that the woman he awaited would have to pass through before driving on to her apartment. His bowling-ball bag sat at his feet.

He looked at the sky, watching the scattered dark clouds coming in from the Gulf. The storm front was rapidly approaching the area, and he liked that. He had always felt an affinity with storms, especially at night. Dark clouds rolling in quickly, the light of the moon cut off, darkness taking over light—the devil over God. He knew that was what it signified and how it would be for always on end.

His mother had not liked such thoughts coming from an eleven-year-old. But then he had not had to listen to her any more after the time the sleeve of her sweater had been caught in the washer, the material winding quickly around the spindle.

Or at least that's what the police had thought when in answer to his hysterical call they arrived to find her pale body, her sweater pulled from her arms and up her back before catching around her neck and bending her backward over the cold mechanical monster.

He had encountered the most trouble in lifting her deadweight and holding her across the machine while he had wrapped the sweater around the spindle after strangling her.

His grandparents had been the next to object to his thoughts and had counterattacked viciously by forcing him endlessly to church, each Sunday morning, each Wednesday, every holiday, every time a revival came along, every chance they got—incessantly. And they weren't weak and soft like his mother had been, but strong and raw-boned. He knew right from the beginning that they were going to be more trouble than she had been.

Then one night a twister had been reported coming toward their small farmhouse outside Kennett, a small town in the bootheel section of Southeast Missouri. His grandparents had hurried him around to their storm cellar, but, excited at the storm's ominous approach, he broke loose and ran to the big barn a few hundred feet behind the house.

Going up through the loft, he climbed to the very peak of the roof and sat there, staring to the west.

There in the sky was the darkest cloudbank he had ever seen. It ranged to the south as far as he could see and back to the north until it disappeared from view. The devil was coming, he had realized at that moment.

That thought had been suddenly punctuated by several simultaneous bolts of lightning racing through the sky. The great pulsating streaks of energy hung much longer than normal, illuminating the center of the cloud mass. And he saw the face then. It *was* the devil's, his great horns in a pair of clouds twisting above the bank into the sky, his narrow face coming to a rounded point where the very bottom of the cloudbank drooped its twirling tentacles, almost as if they were tendons and strips of flesh hanging from just under the neck.

Lightning had erupted again. And curling back before the leading edge of the cloud bank, the wide funnel, angled twisting to the ground, moved directly toward the barn.

For a moment he had gripped the tin ridge under him, his body stiffening. Then his momentary lapse of faith passed and he relaxed.

As his reward for his trust, the point of the funnel touching the ground suddenly rose, swung, whipped far to the south and back again, and leaped soaring over the top of the barn. The fringe winds had caught him, lifted him, and sent him first backwards, and then sideways, finally setting him gently to the ground.

The tip of the funnel had barely missed his grandparents' house when it crashed back to the ground in an explosion of dust, leaves, and tree limbs, and then continued on its way.

That was the first night he had ever prayed, actually got down on his knees beside his bed. If his grandparents' God received that much from his adherents, then it was the very least he could do for his devil.

But there had to be more, something special, more than just eliminating his devil's enemies, more than just killing them—his devil surely deserved much more.

As he had lain there in his bed after his grandparents had finally gone back to sleep, he had thought and thought, tossed and turned, asked for the devil's help and guidance. What would be appropriate to prove his worthiness to the devil?

Then, suddenly recalling the likeness of the severed head in the cloudbank, he sat straight up in bed. He had been answered. He knew what would be appropriate. *An offering.*

Excited, he had wanted to do it right away. But, again, his grandparents weren't the weaklings his mother had been, and he was only twelve, skinny and not strong at all. How would he go about making them dead first so he could remove their heads?

He knew it had to be in a way he wasn't suspected. He certainly couldn't serve the devil from that awful vision of an insane asylum with which his grandparents had threatened him.

It really bothered him what to do, how? He had finally gone into the kitchen for a glass of milk. And he had seen it. The little pilot light glowing blue on the stove.

Excited anew, he quickly extinguished the light but left the gas running, then ran to his room for his bow and arrows in his closet. Still in his pajamas, he had hurried outside the house.

In the barn he found some old gunny sacks and soaked them with kerosene, then wrapped them around the heads of his arrows.

Coming back to the kitchen door, he cracked it open to find the house filled with fumes. Smiling, he walked a good hundred and fifty feet away and lit one of the arrows.

Pulling the bowstring back as far as he could, he said a quick prayer to the devil and let the arrow go toward a kitchen window.

It stuck in the ground short of the house.

He moved closer, lit another and let the flaming object fly at the window.

It stuck in the wall a good five feet from the side of the window.

He moved closer, lit a third arrow, and shot it toward the house.

The windowpane shattered and a great explosion took place, mimicking the force he witnessed when the tornado's tail had crashed back to the ground. A cloud of flames, dust, boards, glass, and shingles erupted with a resounding roar.

He had been blown backward hard to the ground but unhurt, as he had known he would be. He had picked himself up and walked slowly back to the house, on his face a small smile, his only concern being that the detonation might have been so violent he might not find enough of his grandparents to make his offering.

But they were there, suddenly stumbling out of the black cloud of smoke enveloping what was left of their home. They were coughing, their pajamas singed; his grandmother was crying and holding her shoulder. But that was all that had happened to them. He had never before or since experienced such a deep disappointment.

Within three days, he was on his way to the mental hospital in Fulton, Missouri, first to be studied, then to be kept under observation, finally committed there as hopelessly insane.

The explosion had snuffed out the fire on the kerosene-soaked sack wrapped around the end of the arrow entering the house, leaving the arrow, along with his presence outside when the explosion took place, as obvious evidence of what he had done.

CHAPTER 21

Paige and Brett sat at a table in Antonio's. Dr. Little had called and said he had to stop by the hospital first and that he and Paige's mother were going to be a little late.

"I hate that Daddy never has any time of his own," Paige said, and frowned.

"He's doing what he wants to do. You've said that yourself."

"Yeah," she said. She stared across the table for a moment. "Brett, the way you treated the wrecker truck driver today was out of character for you."

He didn't reply and she stared a moment longer. She couldn't bring herself to say what was really bothering her, that she thought he had reacted that way because of Trinity; he had been acting differently ever since her death. But, again, how did she say that without sounding awful—express that she was feeling jealous over a woman who was dead? What kind of a person was she?

Bobby remembered growing from a skinny child into a stocky man with wide shoulders by the time he had been released from the Fulton, Missouri, mental institution, ten long years after being committed there.

An aunt of particular compassion had been the one to meet the final requirement for his release—someone to take him in during his first year of difficult adjustment back to the world of the sane. Most particularly, the psychiatrists had said, someone who could create a happy environment. For it was clear that his newfound happiness, as evidenced by his always-smiling face, had been a big part of his cure.

And his aunt was indeed a happy type. After taking him back to her home in Boston, she would often joke during the frequent parties she gave that he was the only one present who was definitely sane. He had a certificate from a mental hospital to prove it, she would say, and then laugh loudly. Everybody always roared. Remembering those times, Bobby's hands clenched and unclenched and his cheek twitched.

He was suddenly pulled from his thoughts by a car entering the complex. He stared as it passed by. *It was her.* He smiled his hate and his overwhelming urge, and watched her drive on toward her apartment.

"Look," Paige said, nodding across the floor in Antonio's where Vic McIntyre stood next to a table occupied by a young, long-haired blonde. "If I was Peggy, I'd kill him—would've already killed him"

Brett smiled.

Vic came on across the floor to their table. "Hey," he said, and smiled at Paige. "Didn't know you two were coming over here. Where's Dr. Little and your mother?"

"Daddy was called to the hospital," Paige answered, then gestured with a nod toward the blonde he had been talking to. "Your sister?"

"As a matter of fact, she's my cousin," Vic said as he slid into a chair at the side of the table.

"Uh huh. I hope I'm around when Peggy catches you one of these times."

"Well, since you're pressing it, I'll tell you, Paige, she did once. And so I slept on the couch for a few days. I can handle that again. Interested in any other facts about my private life? Be sure now before you decide, you might get embarrassed."

Brett smiled.

Paige stared.

"And now if that's settled," Vic added, "I wanted to tell Brett that the more I thought about the possibility of someone having found out the killer's trademark and using it to cover Trinity's murder, the more it seemed plausible. The F.B.I.'s known the trademark for months. There would also be the medical examiner who first noticed it. And probably the heads of the homicide departments in Memphis, Mobile, and New Orleans—and God only knows who else. People do talk; even when they shouldn't, they do.''

Brett nodded. "Yeah, Paige had hardly gotten out of the pool house that night and a waiter was telling her about it at lunch the next morning.''

"And later at the Hook, Line & Sinker," Paige added, "the waitress had already heard that James was strangled.''

Vic nodded. "Talk happens. A hundred cops could know what the F.B.I. has. Maybe a hundred more who aren't cops.''

"Yeah," Paige said, "maybe including the guy she went to meet—a 'big-shot,' one with a sister.''

"I wouldn't put much credence in him being a big shot, Paige. He could've been just trying to impress Trinity when he told her that. Hell, no telling what he really is, what he does. He might not have a sister, either. He could have told Trinity something like that trying to calm her down after she discovered the woman with him. What's Seales doing about the call?''

Brett spread his hands in a "who knows" gesture. "I heard him talking on the phone to Applewhite. They're not putting much stock in whoever she met being the psycho, but Seales isn't totally discounting it. He told me to get everyone asking around, see if Trinity might have had another friend she talked with, someone who might know who the man is.''

Vic nodded. "Can't hurt anything. Trinity's funeral at two?''

"Two-thirty.''

Paige stared off to the side of their table. "My God," she said, "half of the town's showing up here tonight.''

Being led by a waitress toward one of the tables at the center of the restaurant were Seales and Sheriff Hastings, both dressed in dark brown suits. Accompanying them and wearing a navy sports coat and lighter blue slacks was the newly hired Gulfport police chief, Rayburn Whitehead, a tall, distinguished-looking middle-aged black man who had been born and raised in the area, then moved in his twenties to Chicago, where he had fashioned a noteworthy career with the police department there. Applewhite, drab in a rumpled brown suit, brought up the rear.

Coming through the tables was Paige's mother. She was wearing a high-neck dress in a floral print, her slightly gray, brown hair stuffed up under a hat with a drooping wide brim. Brett and Vic stood when she reached the table. She shook her head.

"He's not coming," she said. "I went ahead and got a taxi. If your father wasn't on vacation, Brett, we'd just call him and have him come and eat with us, show Roger."

Though her words sounded like she was irritated, her tone was sad.

Brett glanced at Paige and back to Vic. "Vic, you got a minute?" He felt Paige's eyes come around to his.

Vic nodded. "Sure."

Bobby, his wide face inches from the windowpane, his thick hands clasping the brick ledge, watched the young blonde standing naked by the tub. Her breasts were small and firm, set high. Her hips were boyish and she had long, slender legs, everything he liked—what the devil had told him he liked.

She also had no shame. Just like the others, parading around in front of his eyes like she was. He felt a mixture of desire and revulsion, like he always did, like he had felt ever since that first time with his aunt.

She had come into his room one night when her husband was on a business trip. She wore a thin nightgown no more concealing than a plastic bag, her very intimate part there to witness, only slightly blurred.

She had sat on the bed and immediately began caressing him. "I'm sorry," she had said. "I'm sorry," and caressed him even more frantically.

He had immediately become filled with emotion—how was a twenty-two-year-old young man supposed to resist an advance like that? She had hiked up her gown and moved his hand to her, immediately begun moaning, gone crazy, slobbering. Her foul liquor-soaked breath had suffocated him, her hand rapidly moving his—and then the quick pain he would never forget. Twisting his hand in her ecstasy, she had caught his little finger and bent it sideways, snapping the tendon.

CHAPTER 22

Inside Antonio's, Brett and Vic stood near the cash register. Brett finally came to the point. "I was with her the night after she moved to Biloxi last year, before she moved back to here."

Vic's eyes knitted questioningly. "Trinity?"

Brett nodded.

Vic stared for a moment, then a faint smile crossed his face. "I never would have believed it. And now you're worried that with everyone asking around, it's going to get out—get back to Paige?"

"It's not going to have to get out. I don't have much choice but to tell Seales. I'm supposed to be the one setting up the asking around about men she's been with. And I've been out with her and don't say anything . . ."

"You been out with her since then?"

"Just that one time."

"Then who's there to even remember that far back? Forget about it. Conscience, Brett, old buddy, conscience; that's what's really eating at you." He smiled again. "For me, the only rule I got is I stay away from the ones dating my buddies. The rest of them are fair game—married or not."

Dr. Felter's all-white form passed them on the way from the dining area. He smiled at them.

Vic stared after him and the willowy blonde accompanying him. "That's my hero," he said. "I want to grow up to be just like him."

Brett smiled a little and they started back to their table.

As he took his seat, he leaned to the side for the waitress to refill his glass with iced tea. She asked them if everything was okay, then moved on to the next table. The restaurant manager came by next, inquired as to how their food was, then continued on.

Paige looked over her shoulder. Vic was on his way to an attractive brunette's table.

"I'd kill him," she said as she reached for her water glass. "I really would."

Mrs. Little stood. "Excuse me," she said. "You want to go to the ladies' room, Paige?"

Paige shook her head. As her mother made her way away from them, Paige looked back across the table.

"What were you talking to Vic about?"

"Vic had told me he knew a couple of private investigators up in Jackson. He was going to have them check around on what kind of reputation Trinity might've had. I just wanted to see if he'd heard anything yet."

Her forehead wrinkled. "And you couldn't have asked him that in front of me?"

"With your mother here? And I imagine you're getting tired of hearing me speak about her, too."

"Brett, she's who we were talking about at the time."

"I just didn't want to keep digging into it in front of you."

"Brett, that's your job—and mine." She set the water glass back on the table. "Besides, I told you I wouldn't be jealous. I couldn't be, not with what happened to her. I can't believe you would think something like that."

He shrugged.

She stared a moment longer. "Well," she asked. "What did he say?"

"They said they were unable to find out anything—one way or the other."

At one of the tables in the center of the restaurant, Applewhite watched Vic talking to the young brunette. "He's married, isn't he?"

Seales stopped a forkload of linguini halfway to his mouth and glanced across his shoulder to see who the agent was talking about. "Oh, Vic—yeah."

"Figures," Applewhite snorted. "He used to work on the force in New Orleans, didn't he?"

Seales nodded. "Yeah, several years."

"Quit to be a big-time investigator, huh?"

"No, doesn't do much of that, almost none, in fact. He told me that he only took the Lloyd case because the widow's loaded and paying him a hell of a fee to see what he can find out about the psycho. On top of that, she's offered a reward of a hundred thousand bucks to anyone who can uncover the nut. He says he's getting paid while he's trying to make a hundred thousand."

Applewhite snorted. "She'd be a lot better off if she'd leave it up to us—for free. I can imagine what he's charging her."

"She came to him, Jerry. It's a free market."

Applewhite watched Vic as he pulled out a chair and sat down with the brunette.

"What's the big friendship deal between him and Dunnigan—there's the age difference?"

"Brett's uncle and Vic were friends in the service. Lee was his name. He was killed in a car accident right after they were discharged. Vic was driving—rumor had it he was drunk. He felt guilty, I guess. He and Brett developed a friendship of sorts."

Bobby experienced a mixture of desire, revulsion, and anger as he stared through the window at the blonde stepping into her bathtub. The desire was for her body. The revulsion was, too. He was always confused by that. The anger was because of his aunt and her snapping the tendon in his little finger.

But he had to wait a while for his revenge. He had known that to act too soon might lead to another trip back to the hospital, and might again interrupt his work for the devil.

After moving from his aunt's house when his year of intermediate care was up, he lived in St. Louis where he strangled a prostitute in the backseat of his car.

Six months later he returned to Boston. He had waited until a Monday when he knew his aunt's husband would be out of town, then visited her after she had fallen into a drunken sleep.

It had been so perfect, coming into her bedroom naked, sitting on the side of her bed and gently waking her.

"Look what I've got for you, Auntie," he said into her shocked face, and pulled her hand toward him, made her caress him once more before strangling her.

When he was through he carefully curled her little finger down on itself and squeezed hard until he heard the faint click as the tendon snapped.

Since then there had been how many? The next one had been in Chicago. The one after that in West Des Moines, Iowa. The first prostitute came from Columbia, Missouri, a cute little University of Missouri student making tuition on the side. Each time he snapped the tendon of their little finger, enjoyed the revenge, had a good time.

But something, he soon sadly realized, continued to be lacking, and in his prayers he nightly voiced to the devil he begged for guidance.

Finally, he was answered, and it was so obvious. The ten years of drug treatment in the mental institution had caused him to forget his first vision, the one the devil had shown to him during the approaching storm—the severed head. He could hardly wait.

And it wasn't long, his next victim coming soon after he had moved to the warmer climate of the Gulf Coast. He found her in New Orleans—and fulfilled the vision. And it felt right, really right. Finally, he was doing the devil's work as it had been intended all along. He knew his reward would be great.

The second head he removed was the prostitute's in Mobile. He had settled on prostitutes after deciding they would be the most experienced ones to serve his master in hell. The third head had come from the prostitute in Memphis.

He was sure the devil didn't mind him extracting his personal revenge by snapping the tendon in his victim's little finger. What did his enjoying a tiny bit of personal pleasure hurt so long as he collected the offering for his beloved master, and sent him a servant, too? How many had he already sent?

Let's see, he thought, and hunched his thick shoulders forward, counting on his fingers, eagerly running over the list again, savoring each memory. He added the second time in New Orleans and the last one in the very area he was now—what was her name?

Trinity, that was it. He mustn't ever forget her. She reminded him
a lot of a picture he had seen of his aunt when she was younger.
He smiled when he ran out of fingers. Eleven women in all. He
and the devil made quite a team.

Suddenly, his thoughts were brought back to the present as a
second figure moved before his eyes into the bathroom. It was the
woman's husband. She did nothing to cover herself, just continued
lying back in the tub, the water crystal clear, revealing everything.

The shameless bitch. He grabbed the brick window ledge harder
with his big hands, feeling his loins stir with pleasure, hating the
sensation—hating her.

He looked at her husband now at the sink next to the window,
beginning to brush his teeth. His shoulder-length, thin blond hair
framed his narrow face and skinny neck, only inches away.

He felt the yearning, gripped and released the brick ledge.
Gripped and released. Gripped and released. His little finger began
to hurt.

His anger grew. He couldn't stand the shameless display any
longer. He turned away from the window and moved toward the
front door of the house.

The scrawny runt of a husband would be no problem when he
answered the knock. Then into the bathroom. He'd sit on the side
of the tub like he had done on the side of his aunt's bed. Tell her
to be quiet and let him guide her hand where he wished. Then
the tub would fill with blood, the water turning red and finally
concealing her shame. He wondered if the head would float.

Inside the apartment, the slim female in the tub glanced at her
long-haired boyfriend as he turned away from the sink. "Turn the
switch to about fifteen minutes, honey," she said.

He stopped at the door and turned the Jaccuzi dial to fifteen.

The water began rushing through the jets in the tub and against
her back and sides.

"Oh," she sighed. "That feels so good." She looked at her
boyfriend smiling at the door.

"Don't get any ideas," she said. "I got a John gonna be showing up here in an hour and he's a killer. I won't be able to
move afterward."

A soft smile crossed her face. "Maybe, though, if you'll rub my back when I get back from his motel, maybe I'll do *somethin'* for you.''

She sank lower in the warm water as he stepped smiling from the bathroom and closed the door behind him, muffling the loud sound of the Jaccuzi motor.

He moved to the dresser, opened a drawer, and lifted out a set of yellow nylon pajamas festooned with big red cartoon characters.

CHAPTER 23

At the front door, his black bowling-ball bag sitting on the ground off to the side, Bobby heard the lock starting to turn, but the cycle didn't complete—there was no click of the bolt retracting. A second passed and the lock was again turned.

This time there was the satisfying sound of the bolt sliding back into the door and he felt his heart begin to pound.

The doorknob turned halfway and stopped. Then it turned again and the door cracked open, then swung wider.

Looking up at him was a dark-haired boy no more than six. He was dressed in blue cotton pajamas that clothed his body as tightly as a pair of long underwear.

He stared at the unexpected child. There had been no children any of the other times he had observed the prostitute.

It was God's meddling. Some trick meant to stop him.

It would not work. The first man he had killed, in Memphis, had been unexpected, too. Not only had that man's presence been no problem, his killing had added a certain tingly warmup to the main event, the collecting of the offering.

He looked into the eyes of the smiling boy, feeling pleasure in the realization he could snap the small neck using no more than just a little pressure. He wondered if it would sound like a tendon snapping.

"Momma is taking a bath," the boy said, and smiled again, trying to be nice to the big man.

Bobby smiled coldly, stepped inside, and pulled the door toward him, closing it behind him. *Almost no pressure,* he thought.

He reached for the boy's neck, but hesitated when the husband, clad in yellow nylon pajamas covered with cartoon characters, stepped from the hallway into the living room, stopping suddenly when he looked that way.

"Bobby, what are you doing?" he said, startling Bobby. *How did he know his name?*

The man started boldly toward him, stopped, and caught the little boy's shoulder to turn him around. He stared down into his eyes.

"Bobby, you never, never, never open the door to strangers. You understand? Now get into your bedroom, pronto!"

The man smiled and shook his head as he raised his face after pushing the boy toward the hallway. "It's Carol's kid. We're going to have him for a two-week visitation. He's from a farm; what does he know?"

He glanced at his watch. "You're a bit early. Let me tell Carol you're— Aaaarrgg!" His eyes bulged at the force of the sudden steellike grip of the hand that grasped his neck.

Bobby's other hand balled into a tight fist and he struck the man hard on his chin, then a second time, and then quickly a third.

The man's hands, clawing at the gripping fingers, fell back to his side, his eyes closed, his knees buckled. But he didn't fall— Bobby's grip held his limp, thin body where it hung.

The boy, wide-eyed, ran down the hallway.

Bobby quickly finished his work, stepped outside and retrieved his bag, then followed the boy. From the earlier position outside the window, he knew that the bedroom and bath he had been peering into were at the end of the hall.

Nearing the doorway, he stopped long enough to set his bag on the floor and open it. A rotting stench came from the bag as he rummaged through it, his fingers brushing against crusted black stains and an occasional bit of fetid flesh.

Finally, he found the executioner's hood he had painstakingly crafted and was so proud of. He slipped it down over his head, and in his pride immediately felt like he was an inch taller. He slipped the thick-bladed knife out of the bag.

Then he heard the bumping sound—from back up the hall in the empty bedroom he had passed.

He moved back to the doorway, saw a suitcase open on the carpet at the foot of the bed, and the little boy in his tight blue pajamas, his back to the doorway, quickly going through the bag's contents. It had been lying on the bed when Bobby first went by, the boy nowhere in sight. He had been hiding.

The boy found what he was looking for and spun around. Both his hands clasped around the butt of a heavy automatic.

"You little bastard," Bobby growled, and stepped forward.

The boy shut his eyes and fired. Bobby flinched, his eyes widening behind the hood's viewing slits. "You—"

The boy fired again.

The bullet caught Bobby in his shoulder and spun him around, knocking him back against the door facing, and he dropped his knife. He tried to smile, but the pain in his shoulder was such he could only grimace, and that scared him. He didn't want to lose his power.

The boy fired again.

Bobby pushed off the door facing into the hallway, and leaned back against the wall.

The boy fired the nine millimeter again and Bobby heard the bullet rip into a two-by-four in the wall behind his head.

The boy fired again, the bullet passing through the wall this time without hitting a stud, burying into the wall on the far side of the hall.

The boy fired again.

Bobby, growling, pushed off the wall and, holding his hand to his bleeding shoulder, stumbled down the corridor toward the living room.

The woman screamed at the sight of him. Holding her towel around her slim body, she hurried to the bedroom and looked inside at the trembling wide-eyed boy and the gun he held far out in front of him.

She hurried to him and grabbed the automatic, then ran back through the hall and after the hooded figure she had seen leaving.

She squealed when she saw her boyfriend's body on its back near the open front door. But she didn't stop running, hurdling the body and moving out into the night.

The hooded figure was sprinting down the middle of the tree-lined road toward the exit from the apartments.

She held the automatic in both hands, raised it, and fired; several birds fluttered up out of the shrubs in front of her apartment at the loud sound.

Before her second shot she took careful aim and then squeezed the trigger slowly.

At the report, the pistol jumping again in her hands, the hooded figure threw his arms back, arched up on his tiptoes, and pitched forward onto his stomach in the middle of the hard pavement.

In Antonio's, Brett stood near the cash register with Paige and her mother, Chief Seales, and Sheriff Hastings. Vic had left with the brunette. Hastings was holding a pinch of tobacco in his fingers waiting to get outside. The Gulfport chief of police, Rayburn Whitehead, had gone a few minutes before to answer a telephone call and Applewhite had accompanied him. Now, his narrow, dark face tight, the chief hurried back into the alcove.

He spoke rapidly. "A man in a hood came after a woman in her apartment—strangled her boyfriend. Left a bowling-ball bag behind that had a piece of cardboard in it with an O written on it. She shot him. Maybe it's over."

Everyone hurried toward the door except Paige's startled mother, who stood stunned as her daughter flipped her car keys back into the restaurant just before following the men out the exit.

In little more than thirty minutes they were at the scene, Chief Whitehead, Chief Seales, Applewhite, and Sheriff Hastings in one car, and Brett and Paige in her Maxima.

The man's body wasn't there.

Where he had lain on the pavement there was only a faint pink smear.

The sergeant in a Gulfport officer's uniform stepped out of the cluster of officers standing around the spot.

"Chief," he said, talking to Whitehead, "he ran east. We're searching in that direction and have men all around the area. He can't get away in any direction."

Whitehead looked up at the sound of the helicopter approaching the area. Its brilliant searchlight swept back and forth across the buildings beneath it.

"Highway patrol," the sergeant said. "Another one's coming."

At the approaching helicopter, Bobby, his shoulder throbbing from the two closely spaced bullet wounds, bolted from the woods into the big yards of a subdivision not far from the apartments.

A police officer turned and raised his revolver but held his fire. He was at such an angle to the fleeing man that, if he missed his shot, it would travel on toward the several teenagers standing near the rear of the next yard over.

A second officer fired from the back of that yard but missed and hoped his bullet didn't hit any of the onlookers standing at the edge of the street.

Both officers started running after the man.

Bobby ran between two widely spaced houses, saw on the street before him police officers coming in a run from his left. More were coming from the right. Directly across the street, a woman holding her young daughter's hand stood in her front yard staring at him. He made for her.

She froze for an instant, then jerked her daughter around and pulled her toward the front door of the house.

When Bobby, in a dead sprint, crossed the pavement, officers to both sides raised their weapons but didn't fire for fear of hitting each other. He went in the front door of the house at the same time as the woman and her daughter did. The police stopped and stared at one another.

CHAPTER 24

A hundred officers from every jurisdiction imaginable surrounded the house where the serial killer held the mother and daughter hostage. A pair of helicopters hovered under the dark clouds overhead, the craft's searchlights bathing the house in a brilliant white glow.

Applewhite, in his car parked up on the sidewalk a hundred feet from the north side of the house, was trying to get his radio patched to the telephone inside the home.

Down the street in the opposite direction, Brett, Paige, and half a dozen officers watched from behind a deputy sheriff's car turned sideway in the middle of the pavement.

Sheriff Hastings, Chief Whitehead, and Chief Seales leaned over the hood of a highway patrol car driven up in the front yard directly across the street from the house.

Brett half expected to see a head roll out the still-open front door at any minute. Then a second head. Then as everybody charged, maybe a shot by the maniac into his own skull, or his body found with his throat or wrists slit.

However the night ended, there would be no more serial killer to contend with, that was a given. But was there any way morning could come without two more innocent lives being lost? The officers who had witnessed the mother and daughter said the girl couldn't have been more than six.

Brett glanced toward the highway patrol car where Seales, stripped of his suit coat, leaned over the hood. In his hands he held a scope mounted Mini-Ruger 14.

If he could only get a few seconds' clear glimpse of the man through a window, Brett thought, get a clear shot, then the night might end without any more blood shed. In Seales's earlier tenure as a New Orleans police officer, he had twice been the top shot on the city's police rifle team. In a shootoff only a few years prior, he had completed the only perfect score ever posted by a contestant.

Inside the house, the woman lay on her face on the carpet. Her hands were bound tightly behind her with an electrical cord ripped from a lamp. Bobby, his black hood still in place, stood a few feet away. He held the little girl by the hand and, ignoring his shoulder dripping blood, stared down at her. Her face was blank, pale.

The woman swallowed, tried to keep her voice from breaking. "Please don't hurt her."

Bobby raised his hand and touched his palm gently to the child's head, then wound his fingers softly in her hair. She made a movement to pull her head away, but stopped when his fingers tightened.

"Pleeease!" the mother begged.

Bobby smiled down at the girl, but she couldn't see his gesture. A tear ran from her eye. His hand slipped from her hair and he caught her arm and started across the carpet with her.

"WHERE ARE YOU TAKING HER!"

Bobby led the child to the table at the far end of the couch. There he reached to the lamp on the table and yanked it, jerking the cord out of its socket.

In a moment he had ripped the cord from the lamp and began tying the child's hands behind her back, leaving the long ends of the cord to hang toward the floor.

When he finished, he leaned and caught her around the waist with his good arm, lifted her and deposited her on the couch, forcing her over onto her side.

The mother's head started back and forth.

He began unbuckling his belt.

"OH, NO! GOD, NOOO!"

The little girl started crying.

The telephone rang.

Brett stared at Applewhite speaking over his car radio. The buzz had gone through the officers that he was in contact with the killer inside the house. A moment later, Applewhite handed the mike back to an agent sitting inside the car.

Brett looked back at Seales. Another helicopter swept low over the house. There was a sudden murmur of voices and Brett looked toward the house. In the brilliant light from the helicopter, the killer stood in the open doorway, the woman held in front of him, a kitchen knife to her throat with her body pulled tight back against his and only part of his dark hood visible around the back of her head

"THAT CRAZY SON OF A BITCH!" came Applewhite's megaphone-amplified exclamation. "I TOLD HIM TO GIVE ME FIVE MINUTES. EVERYBODY HOLD YOUR FIRE. HE'S COMING OUT TO HER CAR—LET HIM!"

Then a collective gasp filled the heavy night air. As the killer stepped from the doorway, those assembled had seen the young girl, her back strapped to his by a cord tied around her waist and his chest. He had cinched his belt under his chin after looping it up and around her neck. When he leaned his head forward, it pulled hers back. Only her legs were unfettered and they hung limp as if the motions of his head had already strangled her.

He moved slowly off the steps onto the sidewalk and began sidestepping toward the Oldsmobile parked in the short driveway.

Brett knew he wouldn't get away. They couldn't allow that no matter what the consequences. They would allow him to leave in the car and drive until he ran out of gas. But the helicopters and dozens of cops would follow every mile of the way. If he wished, he could then sit in the stranded car for hours.

But when it finally dawned on him there was no way he could escape, would he kill his hostages or simply himself? Brett feared he knew the answer and didn't want to be around when it came down to the final minutes.

At a raised voice behind him, he turned his face and looked in that direction. It was the same anchorwoman he and Paige had

seen on television the day they had eaten lunch at the small
beachside restaurant. She stood beside a van, shouting instructions
up to a camera crew who stood on the top of the vehicle.

The van's telescoping antenna was raised to its limit and pointed
back toward their station. The populace along the coast was getting
a live view of a tragedy Brett was sure would cause some of them
to vomit before it was over.

He looked back to the house. Out of the corner of his eye he
saw Chief Seales aiming the Mini-Ruger 14 across the top of the
highway patrol car hood.

Nobody was noticing. Everyone present, even Sheriff Hastings
standing a few feet from Seales, had their eyes riveted on the
maniac and the two females.

Brett looked toward the house. From his angle he had a better
view of the hooded head than Seales did—and even it was not
enough for a shot. The black material of the hood was pressed
against the back of the woman's head, the slits of the eyes lost
behind her long red hair gently whipping in the warm breeze.
Even with a miracle, there was still the young girl's head close
to the rear of the hood. Any shot through the brain would more
than likely pierce hers, too.

He looked back at Seales, saw the chief's fingers clasp the stock
directly behind the trigger, the fingers lift and clamp again. He
was going to shoot. *No!*

The hood turned slightly toward the Oldsmobile.

The sharp crack of the Mini-Ruger 14 caused a hundred men
and women to flinch.

But not the maniac. Releasing the woman, he settled backward
toward the lawn, was stopped momentarily when the young girl's
feet touched the ground. Then he fell back on top of the child.

She screamed and buckled like a wild horse, actually lifting the
big limp body strapped to her back. She screamed and bucked
again. The mother was screaming hysterically. Officers were running toward the spot.

CHAPTER 25

In Gulfport, the older man and woman leaned forward on the edge of their couch as they watched their television set.

"My God!" the woman exclaimed at the shot. She watched the child kicking hysterically as the officers rolled the man over and tried to unbind her from his back.

Her husband stared as the TV camera came in for a close-up of the hooded face.

"I don't want to see his face," the woman said, and turned away.

The man's eyes were wide, staring. A hand reached down toward the mask. It was pulled back from the face.

"MY GOD!" the man exclaimed.

The woman looked quickly.

"MY GOD!" she exclaimed. *"BOBBY!"*

Brett stared down at the wide face of the psycho lying on his back off the edge of the sidewalk. He didn't look any different from any other stocky, partly bald man you would pass on the street in any town. There was certainly nothing about him that gave any indication of the horror that had swirled inside his mind. In fact, even in death there was a pleasant look about him, a slight upturning of his lips, almost a smile.

How many victims had smiled softly in return, only to realize too late that they should have been warned by the look in his wide-open eyes. For there was something about them, a hollow, vacant look. And not only because they were now fixated in death, but almost like they were entrances to a deep cave, a passageway into a demented hell.

There was no indication that either Trinity or her husband had struggled before they died. A soft knock on the door, a pleasant look on the face of the man who stood there when they opened it? Did he have a pleasant voice, too?

Surely they wouldn't have voluntarily let a stranger into their house at that time of night, no matter what his explanation.

The window was open. Had they opened it, or had the psycho come in that way instead of through the front door?

But still, no struggle? Brett knew that was one of the main reasons he had thought so much about the man Trinity had gone to see that night. That particular man could have been known to both her and her husband. He might have been invited inside after he knocked. There would be no struggle if someone like that, there to talk something over, suddenly attacked without warning.

But this was no man that he had ever seen in the area—certainly no big shot well known to everyone. Who was he, and where was he from? That was all that was now left to know. An officer stepping in front of Brett blocked his view of the face.

In a moment, a body bag was laid beside the psycho and the officers began working with his limp form.

"Brett," a voice called behind him.

It was Seales. "Gulfport P.D. just received a call. We know where he lived now."

Twenty minutes later, the group of officers, F.B.I. agent Applewhite, Brett, Paige, and both police chiefs included, met the nervous apartment manager and his wife in front of their small office.

"This way," the man said in a shaky voice. The woman didn't want to go and remained in the office. She and her husband had been managing these same apartments for twenty years and thought they had seen every kind of tenant.

My God, she thought, *and I talked to him nearly every day.* A cold chill swept her whole body and she trembled violently.

The man led them to the apartment door and unlocked it, stepping back as the officers led by Chief Whitehead walked inside.

They entered a small living room. An antique chifforobe was to the right of the door and a white couch was against the far wall. A coffee table sat in front of the couch and there was an easy chair nearer the door; a television was off to the left.

Off the right of the room they passed through a small dining area, a narrow kitchen back to its right and a hall to its left.

Down the hall, they encountered a bath on the right and, at the very back of the hall, a bedroom. There was nothing out of the ordinary in any of the rooms.

There was one more door on the left of the hall. It was locked.

"See if the manager has a key to this," Chief Whitehead said over his shoulder to an officer.

"Wait a second," Seales intoned, squatting almost to his knees as he looked at the knob and lock.

"It's nothing," he said. He reached into his hip pocket, pulled out his billfold, and took out a piece of metal about the size of a credit card.

He worked at the door only an instant before the lock sprung.

They all stared silently into a shrine. Directly in front of them against the back wall was the altar. Hanging on the wall above it was the devil-worshiping symbol of a defeated Christ, an upside-down cross with the arms broken, sloping downward at a forty-five-degree angle. The whole symbol was enclosed in a circle—the peace symbol of the 1960's, seventies, and eighties, but now recognized by law-enforcement officers everywhere as having taken on quite a different meaning among those into black magic and devil-worshiping.

That was all there was, nothing grisly; not a drop of blood anywhere, no vases or jars, only the altar and the symbol behind it. There was a thick book on the single shelf in the middle of the altar.

Whitehead lifted the volume, laid it on top of the altar, and opened it.

"What is it?" Seales asked, his forehead wrinkling as he stepped up beside him. Applewhite moved to Whitehead's other side.

It was a simple cheap scrapbook. On the first page was a newspaper article and a faded picture of a middle-aged woman. The picture had a dark X drawn across it with a magic marker.

Tragic Washing Machine Accident was the small headline above the article.

The clipping on the next page was from a St. Louis paper and headlined *Unidentified Woman Found Strangled.* There wasn't a picture. The article had an X drawn across it.

Taped to the next page was an article about a prominent woman in Boston, found strangled in her bed. The picture, an X drawn across it, was an attractive middle-aged woman.

Whitehead continued to turn the pages, past articles from a Chicago paper, from one in Des Moines, Iowa, and one in Columbia, Missouri. All the stories had pictures accompanying them and all had the big dark X's drawn across them with a Magic Marker.

Then there were the recognizable articles. New Orleans first, followed by Mobile and Memphis, and then New Orleans again. And, the last one, *The Sun Herald*'s account of the attack on Trinity along with the picture that had been used with the story.

Seales nodded, a cold smile crossing his face. "We got the son of a bitch," he mumbled. "We got him for the ones we knew about and more. May the bastard rot in hell."

Brett looked a second longer, then turned away.

Paige watched him walk toward the door. Trinity's murder had bothered Brett deeply. She knew it wasn't from any romantic attachment; she knew that without any doubt. But he did care about Trinity's death. He wouldn't have been human if he hadn't. So why did it still bother her?

She shook her head in disgust at her feelings, glanced at the scrapbook, then followed him down the hall. Catching up to him, she took his forearm and gently squeezed it just before they passed out of the apartment and into the fresh night air.

He stood at the edge of the sidewalk for a moment, staring out into the lights of the buildings across the street.

"It's good it's over before they even buried her," he said. "That's good."

The apartment manager walked up to them. "Officer," he said.

Brett raised his eyes to the man's.

"Officer, I think there's something you all oughta be knowing." Brett nodded without speaking.

"Well," the man said, "this woman killed over y'all's way—he couldn't have done that."

Brett stared at the man. "What did you say?"

"He couldn't have killed that one," the manager repeated. "That Anderson woman. He was in jail."

"What are you saying?"

"He was in jail when she was killed. He didn't have the money to get out until the next morning. I know, I loaned him the last hundred dollars myself. He'd been locked up on an assault charge for over a week; didn't have the money to get out."

CHAPTER 26

Paige had awakened early and was in the shower. Brett still lay in bed and stared at the ceiling as he thought. Trinity hadn't been killed by someone trying to cover up a sex crime—she hadn't been raped. Nothing had been stolen from the house, so it wasn't the burglar. Or was it? She could have surprised him in the act. But how would a burglar know what the serial killer always did to his victims? How would anybody know outside of someone with connections to the police force, someone with the kind of power to have those connections—a big shot. Any way he looked at it, the investigation was now dramatically shifted to the big shot she had gone to meet. That person now had to be the number-one suspect.

But that made no sense in a way. You don't follow someone to their house and nearly decapitate them because they told you off, because they're jealous—even because they might ruin you. And that's what the caller had said the man told Trinity—that the man said he would be ruined.

Ruined how? Politically? Some other way? He moved his thoughts back to the print left on the bathhouse door. It had been smeared by someone who had to have been among the officers and others combing the yards that night—and done between the time Paige and Armont had seen it and Seales went to look at it. Smeared. Accidentally or intentionally?

The telephone rang and he reached for the receiver.

Mrs. Lloyd's voice was low and soft. "I'm sorry, Lieutenant, but I couldn't wait any longer to call you. Mr. McIntyre was by here earlier and told me about the killer being shot. But he really only knew the barest details. I just now heard on the news that there was a book of some kind with the details of the murders. I want to know everything, Lieutenant. I have to know."

"It was only a scrapbook with old newspaper clippings."

"Oh." She was silent for a moment. "I thought there was some writing in it—like a diary. It might have said something about my husband."

"No, ma'am." If it had, she wouldn't have needed to read it.

There was a few more seconds of silence. He didn't know what to say.

"Lieutenant, I also heard that the woman over there wasn't one of his victims."

"No."

"Do you have any idea who it was?"

"We'll catch him."

"I hope so. Mr. McIntyre told me the day after it happened that you knew her. I'm sorry. Believe me, I know how you feel."

"Thank you, but it was a long time ago. She was a high school classmate."

"Oh, I thought—" There was another moment of silence and Brett felt himself becoming uneasy. His conscience, Vic had said. *She wouldn't know.*

"I guess then Vic had been friends with her since you had," Mrs. Lloyd added.

His eyes widened. "Excuse me, what did you say?" He swung his feet off the bed to the floor.

"He told me the day after she was murdered that being friends with her didn't make it any worse for him, but I could tell it did. You can't have personal contact with somebody like that and not feel badly about her being killed. I mean, feel more than normal. Then this morning—he was upset again. I didn't know what to say to him."

Dr. Felter glanced from his bathroom back into his bedroom. She lay on her face with her long hair down her back and a bare leg outside the sheet. Much younger than most marrieds he had been out with, her youth alone had smitten him when she had walked into his office the day before. She had more or less stated that she was frustrated and wanted to be bedded. He smiled. Politicians liked to claim that bad publicity was better than no publicity at all. They might be right. That's how she had heard of him—the famous Dr. Casanova, in article after article in the little independent paper. He smiled again. In a way it reminded him of his youth. Not so heavy then, but still not the type that girls flocked to, and frustrated because he hadn't yet scored, at sixteen he'd tried a different tact. He simply told every girl that appealed to him that he would like to take them to bed. He got his face slapped a lot, and was thrashed once by an angry boyfriend, but he got a lot, too.

He raised his face to the window over the bed when he heard the sound of a high-powered boat passing by on the Wolf River behind the cabin. He would hate to give up this little hide-a-way; women seemed especially enthralled by a place overlooking water. But Fort Lauderdale, where he had his next job, had water, too, water everywhere, running through it and around it, and was also metropolitan enough that he shouldn't have any more problems with little local papers, with nosy people he had to keep an eye out for. He smiled again. Life just got better and better.

By the time the church service for Trinity had ended and Brett had driven to the cemetery, the sky had become heavily overcast, the dark clouds lending an even more solemn note to the pallbearers carrying the casket slowly from the hearse toward the tent erected over the open grave. Paige stood beside him. He glanced at her. He hadn't said anything to her about what Mrs. Lloyd had told him.

He glanced at Vic, standing with Seales and Sheriff Hastings. A big shot, the caller had said. That wouldn't be a private investigator barely making enough to feed himself and his wife. Vic had said often enough how he was doing worse now than before he quit the New Orleans force; he had laughed sarcastically about it. "Quit being a cop," he had said, "to make some money, and I'm damn near starving now." That's why the possibility of a reward from Mrs. Lloyd had gotten him so excited.

But discount the talk of a big shot—Vic himself had said that

could have been a lie. Yet the caller also said that Trinity had
followed the man to his house, that it was in this very town. Vic
lived in Gulfport now and had for months. And he had no sister,
either. But Vic had also been the one to say maybe there really
wasn't a sister. But why, if Vic really did have anything to hide,
why would he have mentioned his relationship with Trinity to
Mrs. Lloyd in the first place?

Brett shook his head in frustration at his swirling thoughts. They
were crazy; if Vic was a suspect based on the fact that he had
admitted to having been out with Trinity, then Brett knew he was
also in the same boat, as far as anybody else looking at it.

But, then again, he had told Vic about his relationship. Why
hadn't Vic taken that opportunity to tell about *his* relationship?
Jesus, he couldn't stop his wondering.

He saw Seales whisper something to Vic. Sergeant Green stood
a few feet away from them. He had come despite missing his shift
because of the flu. Arnie had his eyes toward the ground.
Applewhite was also in attendance, but only to see who else came.
He had said that sometimes a murderer showed up at his victim's
funeral to get his final kicks, like an arsonist often came back to
join a crowd watching a fire.

Brett looked back to Vic, forced his thoughts away from him,
and looked out to the gravel road where an old blue van sat in
the shade of a big oak. There was an F.B.I. camera crew inside
the vehicle. He looked back at the faces in the small gathering.
None of Trinity's family were there; her mother had been a single
parent and had died years before after a short illness. Among the
dozen or so women in attendance was an older woman who used
to teach psychology at the high school. She wasn't the woman
who had spoken to him on the telephone, the voice had been much
younger. Was it one of the other women at the funeral?

Brett looked back at Vic. He couldn't keep his eyes off him.
Been friends with her is how Mrs. Lloyd had put it. But so had
probably half of all the males that had ever given it a try. Still,
why hadn't Vic said anything?

The preacher started his prayer and Brett dropped his eyes.
The last thing he noticed was Applewhite studying the faces of
the mourners.

CHAPTER 27

When Brett arrived back at the police station after the funeral services, Applewhite and the two agents who had been in the van were waiting with Seales. The few women who had been at the service had been no trouble to identify; Seales, Hastings, and one or more of the other officers attending the burial had known them all. Applewhite handed the women's telephone numbers to Brett.

Thirty minutes later, he hung up after speaking to the last one. He shook his head. "I didn't recognize any of the voices. Whoever called me, she didn't come to the services. She knew we'd be checking on who was there."

Hastings nodded. Brett noticed Applewhite glance at Chief Seales and hold his stare for a moment.

"Brett," Seales said, "I've got to go in the back and speak with Jerry, then we're going to want to be talking to you. You, too, Paige."

As Seales and the F.B.I. agent walked toward the rear hallway, Brett glanced at Sergeant Green and Arnie standing a few feet away. They had been asked to wait, too. It was obvious what was going on. Applewhite was now thinking about the possibility of a cop, too. They would all be questioned. Good. Then every so-called big shot in the area needed to be talked to, whether he had a sister or not. And who else?

"Brett," Quitty said, walking up to him and holding out a sheet of paper. "A Mrs. Lloyd called. She said you would know what this was about."

He took the sheet in his hand. Written on it was the name of a woman and an address.

"What is it?" Paige asked.

"Must be the friend of her maid's she was talking about."

"Not much help now, is it, Brett? If the killer is the person she went to see that night, whoever it was, then my idea about some kind of games, group sex, that couldn't be, could it? If he's the type to have been all that worried about somebody finding out he'd been with Trinity, then he certainly wouldn't be engaging in something like that."

Seales called from the back of the area. "Sergeant Green, could I see you for a moment?"

Brett moved to the telephone on Quitty's desk and punched in Information. The name on the piece of paper was listed, and he called it. The woman answered his ring promptly.

Arnie was called to the back of the station next. Brett finished his conversation with the woman and replaced the receiver. Paige looked at him. He shook his head.

"She doesn't know anything."

A few minutes later, Paige was called to the rear of the building. Only a little while after that, Seales appeared in the back again.

"Brett."

There was nothing said as they walked down the hall. Paige, Arnie, and Armont were in conversation at the far end of the corridor. Paige glanced his way and smiled.

When Seales turned in the doorway of the conference room, Applewhite was seated at the right end of the old wooden table that took up most of the space in the small area. The two agents who had been in the van were standing against the wall behind his chair.

Seales took his seat at the end of the table opposite Applewhite and nodded Brett toward the chair at the middle of the table, then leaded forward in his seat.

"The governor and both our senators have requested that the F.B.I. stay on here for a few days," he said. "Officially they're typing up loose ends regarding the psychopath, but actually they're lending us their assistance in trying to solve the Andersons' murders. As you know, they've had some of their people over here ever since the night it happened, going door to door. They've come up with a couple of things they need you to clarify."

Brett looked down the table at Applewhite. The blocky agent leaned forward on the table and took over. "Let's start with the night of the murder, Lieutenant. I believe you were on duty until eleven."

"Yes."

"The night dispatcher said she called you about a reported drunk and you didn't answer. She said that a few minutes later she called you about the first sighting of the prowler and you didn't answer then, either. Both those calls were a little after ten."

"I knew about the one call. It was about the same time I was checking an open window at the back of a restaurant. I guess the other one was, too."

"I see. Did you report it when your shift ended—the open window?"

"No."

"Why not?"

"Something like an open window wasn't on my mind then."

"I see. By the way, why did you answer a call when you didn't have to? I understand Sergeant Armont Green told you he could handle it."

"I thought it might be the burglar who's been hitting us hard. I didn't want Sergeant Green to have to check the house without a backup."

"Wasn't this officer we just spoke with . . ." Applewhite glanced at a notepad on the table by his arms. "Arnie Hatcher. Wasn't he on duty then and available as a backup?"

"He was. I made the decision I needed to be there."

Seales spoke then. "Brett did what he should have. Arnie's new to his job."

Applewhite nodded. "Did you drive through the victim's area that night?"

"A couple of times."

"When was the last time, Lieutenant—the approximate time?"

"I don't know, maybe eight-fifteen, eight-thirty. I checked on a house where the owners were on vacation—the Kellums. I called into the dispatcher then. She keeps logs on the times we do that kind of checking. She could give you the exact time."

"The reason I'm asking, Lieutenant, is because a little after nine a car that looked a lot like yours drove into the area. It ended up parking a few blocks away down a dead-end street. A resident noticed it and wondered what it was doing there and walked down to see. He was going to get the license and call the police. Before he reached it, he heard a police radio. Thinking it was the town's unmarked car, he came on back."

Brett shook his head. "It wasn't me. The only place I parked was in front of the Kellums' when I went to check their doors. I wasn't there that late, either. What about the license? You said he looked at it."

"He was going to but didn't after he heard the radio. He did say it was a dark-colored Ford, like the town's—like the unmarked car you drive. But he was fairly certain it was an older model."

Brett looked toward the other end of the table. "The burglar?" he said to Seales. "Maybe that's when he hit the Kellums. He could've gotten his hands on an old radio or a scanner, maybe using it to keep up with us."

Seales nodded. "Could be. Or the murderer."

Applewhite spoke again. "Lieutenant, this woman who called you to tell you about the victim going to see a man that night shortly before her death—you have any idea why she singled you out to call?"

"I guess because she knew me. If she went to school with Trinity, then she had to have been there when I was."

"You told the chief her voice sounded familiar."

"There was something about it, but I haven't been able to place her."

"Had the victim phoned you since moving back here?"

"No."

"The reason I asked is that there was a page torn out of one of the telephone directories; the inside page next to the front cover. We had the lab check the following page to see if they could pick up indentations from anything that might have been written on the missing page. It's really a simple technique. I remember when I was a kid and we were playing spy games, we used to send secret messages that way. You write on any soft sheet of paper and, if you press down at all, it leaves an indentation on the page underneath it. As a kid, we'd shade the page with the side of a pencil and the indentations would show up white on a dark background. The lab's a little more refined than that, but that's basically the process. Your number came up."

Brett was caught off guard. "She hadn't called me. I don't know why my number would—" All at once he didn't like the way Applewhite was staring at him, or the way the agent had played with the last question instead of asking right out about the number. It was almost as if the agent had been trying to lull him to sleep, then suddenly said it was his number to see what kind of reaction it prompted.

"The way you asked that, it's almost like you're wondering if I—"

"Mine was, too," Seales said, and Brett looked back down the table to him.

"My number was on the page, too," Seales repeated. "My home number. I don't know why, either. And Jerry's not *wondering* anything about you. He's only trying to get a handle on some things that have turned up."

Brett suddenly remembered. "Paige wrote it."

"Paige?" Applewhite said.

"Yeah." Brett looked back toward Seales. "Chief, remember when she called your wife right after we discovered the body? She got your number from Information and wrote it on the inside page of the directory while she was waiting for the sheriff's number."

Seales rose, walked to the door, and called for Paige. In a few seconds, she stood next to Brett's chair.

Applewhite asked the question of her. "The night of the murder you wrote Chief Seales's number inside a telephone directory?"

She nodded.

The agent looked down the table toward Seales. "There was something on the page the killer didn't want us to see, Chief, his phone number, his name, *something*. There had to be. And with your number not having been written down until after the body was discovered, whoever tore the page out had to have come back later that night, at least come back sometime between the body being discovered and the next day when the deputies picked up the directory."

Paige had a puzzled expression on her face.

"The page that you wrote my number on," Seales said to her. "It was missing by the time the deputies took the directories. Did you notice any other numbers or a name?"

She shook her head. "I just reached to the bottom of the page. The flashlight wasn't directly on it. I didn't notice."

"Brett's number was at the top of the page," Applewhite said. "She might not have noticed."

Paige's brow wrinkled questioningly. Brett didn't look at her.

"Chief," Applewhite started, "a killer doesn't simply walk back into a house to look around. He had to have had a reason to go back. And the reason wasn't because he knew there was something on the page he didn't want us to see. If he'd already known that, then he wouldn't've torn the page out when he killed her. He had to have come back for some other reason, then noticed whatever it was. Nobody would have a reason to have been in there but . . . How many people were in the house after the murder? Officers, technicians from the lab, the ambulance attendants . . ."

"You and me for starters," Seales said, "and Dr. Felter. There was Brett and Paige and Sergeant Green. There were the deputies Hastings sent over to search the house for names and numbers. In the period from the murder until the directories were picked up, no telling who else was in there."

"But somebody connected to the investigation, right?" Applewhite thought a moment. He glanced at Paige and back down the table to Seales. "I'm through with her, Chief, but I still have a question I want to ask Lieutenant Dunnigan."

After Paige had left, shutting the door behind her, Applewhite looked back at Brett.

"You said the victim hadn't called you. Had you talked to her at all?"

"No, I—" He nodded. "Yeah, once. In a grocery store in town last week. We talked somewhere around three or four minutes, maybe a little longer."

Applewhite was silent for a moment, then nodded. "Okay, Lieutenant, that's all I have."

"Tell the others they're free to go," Seales said.

As Brett walked from the conference room, Applewhite looked

down the table. "Well, he didn't deny talking to her," he said to Seales.

"What did you expect?"

"He told his wife he hadn't, according to her."

"What would you have told your wife?"

"The truth, Chief, if that was all there was to it. But then, every marriage is different. I don't know how jealous his wife is of other women, especially women he used to date."

He held his hand back over his shoulder and one of the agents pulled a sheet of paper from his inside coat pocket and handed it over.

It was a photocopy of a page out of Trinity's diary, found hidden in her bedroom. Kept only intermittently with gaps of weeks between entries, there had been only one entry since she had moved back to the area. It was dated three days before her death.

Ran into Brett in the grocery store. Only got to talk to him for a few minutes, but touched his arm and my fingers tingled. His eyes showed me he tingled, too. Maybe later.

CHAPTER 28

"She never called you, did she?" Paige asked as they walked up the hall from the conference room.

He shook his head.

She didn't say any more. After they had emerged into the front of the station, she walked over to Arnie, who had summoned her. She was one of the few people who didn't make fun of him.

In a moment she laughed at something he said. Brett stared at her. She was easygoing, open—what she appeared to be, and nothing except that. He dropped his eyes and stared at the floor. It was nothing, what he had done. But if it *was* nothing, then why hadn't he told her?

Then his eyes narrowed at the thought that kept nagging at him. Why hadn't Vic told him about being out with Trinity? *If it was nothing.*

Seales still sat in the small conference room. He looked again at the newspaper with his story—a story of a man run off the New Orleans force for administering an excessive beating to a prisoner in his custody, a story of a man who had only lasted a month on the Mobile force before running afoul of another internal investigation, a story of a police chief in a small town with a force hopelessly lost in an investigation over their head, and, finally, a story of a man who had the same as sexually assaulted the woman reporter who had interviewed him by constantly staring at her body.

He read the last line again and crumpled the paper in his hands. "Bitch!"

A light rain started falling as Brett drove away from the station, adding to his depression. Applewhite had talked to Paige for several minutes before he had been called in and questioned. What had the agent said to her that might make her start thinking? He obviously hadn't told her about the conversation with Trinity in the grocery store or she would have said something about it. But the telephone number— Had the roles been reversed, Brett knew he would have asked her more about that. She had to be wondering. She had to be wondering about something.

Paige, the windshield wipers of her patrol car moving slowly back and forth, drove along the main street through town, her mind swirling with her thoughts. Somebody came back to the house and tore the page from the directory.

Somebody. A big shot. Big shot with a sister. Big shot with no sister. Not a big shot—a cop? A cop who deliberately smeared the fingerprint? There was a brown Ford, a couple of years older than Brett's. Big shot in old Ford? Burglar in old Ford? Killer in old Ford?

The woman caller had told Brett that the man trying to avoid Trinity had said he would be ruined if it got back to the area that he was stepping out on his wife. How could a cop be ruined by something like that? An elected official could be, though; the news could turn the voters off. Look what had happened to Dr. Felter.

An elected official, one who would have been concerned about voters' reaction to his affair—was that it? An elected official with a sister. Big-shot elected official in old Ford. Her mind continued to swirl. She saw Brett's car coming from the other direction. She waved as he passed and then glanced in her rearview mirror.

The phone number in the directory.

After Applewhite and Seales found out about the number, they were probably wondering if Trinity had been in contact with Brett. They would be. But she knew better. If Trinity had called, he would have told her, she was certain of that.

But Trinity had to have been planning on calling or she wouldn't have written the number there. Had she written it down because she had something she needed to tell Brett but never got a chance to, something about somebody—the big shot maybe? That could have been it.

An older agent drove Applewhite through the rain on their way back toward Gulfport. Another agent sat in the back.

Young and dark-haired, he opened a folder in his lap.

"The psychopath's name was Robert Joyner," he said. "Moved down to this area just before his first attack. Made pottery and sold most of his works in flea markets. That was his only source of income as far as we know."

"How is tying him to the victims going?" Applewhite asked.

"No word any different from this morning. His mother's death, of course, we know he's responsible for that. He admitted to it while he was in the hospital at Fulton. And the University of Missouri student, the only one where the Bureau had a print on record. It came off the pew where he left her body at a backwoods church in a place called Millersburg, part way between Columbia and Fulton. But that's still all we can tie to him, at least the one's who can be tied back for absolute certain."

Applewhite nodded. "Psychopaths are all driven to exaggerate the number of their victims. The bigger the body count, the bigger they think it makes them look. They collect as much information as possible on all the unsolved cases they can. They can sound quite convincing even when you know there's no way they could be the killer. That would explain the Anderson woman being in his scrapbook. If Seales hadn't shot the bastard, we could've worked most of the names out of him by playing to his ego. Now we're never going to know for sure who he killed and who he didn't, at least not all of them."

He shook his head at his next thought. "Seales was out of his mind taking that shot. It's only luck that he didn't get the girl, too—only luck. Everybody in this part of the country thinks they're some kind of Wyatt Earp. You see kids riding around with rifles in the back of their pickups. You want crazy—hell, everybody down here's crazy."

"We're up to over ten confessions now," the young agent said.

"That's one thing that's the same here as back in New Jersey—loonies come out of the woodwork after these kinds of killings."

The older agent driving had been in the bureau as long as Applewhite. It was his personality to not speak much, but when he did he usually drew attention. "This Lieutenant Dunnigan's number being on that page doesn't bother you, does it, Jerry?" he asked of Applewhite.

"It makes me curious. If she wasn't going to call him, why did she write it down?"

Paige stepped into the drugstore to buy a pack of gum, and saw them—old lady Champlin and Susan Collins. Susan had earned a reputation as a law-enforcement groupie with all the deputies she had dated—three in the short time that Paige had worked on the force. And Mrs. Champlin, she had been one of the coast's Republican power brokers for years. Between them they knew a lot of cops and big shots.

When she stopped in front of them, they quit talking and faced her, smiling.

"Mrs. Dunnigan," Mrs. Champlin said.

"Mrs. Champlin, Susan."

The older woman twisted her face into a partial frown. "They found out any more about that poor woman's murderer?"

"No, ma'am."

Mrs. Champlin shook her head. "It was just terrible."

"Yes, ma'am. You don't know anyone who might have dated her, do you?"

A questioning expression crossed the woman's face. "Why in the world would I know something like that?"

"We're asking everyone that. So we might question any of her old boyfriends."

"Well, I certainly don't know anybody she dated. The people I work with don't associa—" As she caught herself, the woman smiled feebly. "No, I certainly don't, Paige."

Paige looked at the younger woman. "You haven't heard any of the deputies talking about her, have you, Susan?"

"You mean, have any of them dated her?"

"That, too. But I thought maybe one of them might have said

something about her. She was very attractive. Maybe one of them might have seen her around with somebody.''

"If they did, Paige, I'm sure they would have already told the sheriff. Especially since everyone is looking for any man she might have been out with. That's what I hear, anyway.''

Now Paige felt a little foolish at asking, though when she had seen the two women the question had quickly jumped into her mind. Impetuous, Brett called it.

Shortly after ten P.M., during a break in the rain, Brett guided his car off into a beachfront parking area to the right of a U.S. 90 and parked facing east.

He turned off his ignition, looked out across the choppy Sound toward the lights of an ocean tug in the distance, then leaned back in his seat and began watching for drunks coming back from a Saturday night of partying in Gulfport and Biloxi.

Catherine Maddox had trailed Brett through Pass Christian and out to the highway, slowing her car when he guided his off to the side of the pavement and parked. Driving past him, she watched in her rearview mirror, then slowed and made a U-turn at the next crossover on 90.

When the car stopped behind him, Brett stared into his rearview mirror. In a moment, a young woman stepped out of the vehicle and came toward his window. His hand started toward the butt of his pistol, then he recognized her. It was Catherine Maddox. She worked at a local restaurant. He had been in there to eat less than a month before. What was she . . .

Her voice. He suddenly connected her face to it. The voice of the woman who had called and played the answering-machine tape.

He opened his door and stepped outside as she came up to him.

"Brett," she said, "I was the one who called you.''

He nodded.

Her face was tight with her nervousness. "All the newscasts are saying the serial killer didn't kill Trinity,'' she continued. "It was the man she went to see, wasn't it? He killed her.''

"I don't know, Catherine, maybe.''

"Brett, would the police make me tell them about you and her if I went to them? I mean, I don't know what they'll ask and I don't want to get you in any trouble, but I have to go to them."

"What did she tell you?"

"The night you spent with her; when you went out to Back Bay with her."

He was silent for a moment. "She had to tell you there wasn't anything to it. We just talked."

"I assumed . . ." she started, her brow wrinkling. "She said that you were the only one she had ever really cared about."

"Nothing, Catherine. Nothing happened. Just take the tape to Chief Seales. You don't have to say anything about Trinity and me."

"Brett, what if Trinity mentioned to the killer that she talked to me? I'm scared. I want to go to Chief Seales and tell him everything I know so the killer will know I'm not aware of any more. I want that to be out in the open—that I told him everything."

Brett stood silent for a moment. "You mean, tell him about me, too?"

She nodded. He felt a twinge in his stomach.

"Brett, they were asking about you when they came by the restaurant."

"Who?"

"The F.B.I."

"What did they ask?"

"Just talked about you and her dating when you were in high school. They asked if I knew whether you two had been seeing each other since she moved back here."

"What did you tell them?"

"I told them I hadn't talked to you or her since she had come back, that I'd only seen her in passing. But now I'm scared. I want to tell them the truth."

The twinge in his stomach had turned into a twisting feeling. "Catherine, we don't even know for sure that the man she went to see is the killer. Even if he is, if he knew she had talked to you and was worried she'd told you who he was, he would've already come after you. Why would he wait until you had time to tell somebody his name? Maybe it would be best for you to just give them the tape and leave the rest alone. That way the killer will never know you talked to her about me or anybody else.''

She stared at him for a moment. "Brett, I don't want to hurt you, but I don't want to get hurt, either. You wouldn't just be telling me I shouldn't say anything because you're worried about Paige finding out?''

She kept staring. She wanted him to say for sure. Her cheek twitched.

He took a deep breath and nodded. "Okay, Catherine. Let me talk to Paige—tell her myself. Then I'll come by the restaurant and get you Monday and we'll go talk to Seales.''

She nodded, smiled feebly, and started back to her car.

The well-built young man in the blue Chevy parked a half mile farther west up 90, watched Catherine as she guided her car out around Brett's and drove on down the pavement. Then he started his engine and steered his car out onto the highway and followed her. When he passed Brett's car, he averted his head to the side so that his face couldn't be seen.

CHAPTER 29

As the blue Chevy followed Catherine Maddox down 90 and onto a narrow road leading back into a moderate-income residential area in Pass Christian, another car, a brown Ford a couple of years older than the unmarked patrol car Brett drove, weaved its way slowly through the trees behind a newer luxury subdivision a couple of miles north of the beachfront.

It parked next to a grayed cedar fence. The driver's door opened and a thin figure with long hair dressed in jeans and a dark sweatshirt stepped out into the almost total blackness created by the heavy clouds blotting out the moon.

At the fence, he placed his hands on the one-by-six nailed flat to the top of the structure and jumped his waist up onto the top of the barrier, then threw his leg over the boards. He rolled to the ground on the other side and sunk behind the row of bushes there.

A bolt of lightning jumping between clouds outlined the back of the modern Colonial in quivering light.

He glanced to the left and then back to his right, pushed his hair back from the side of his face and cocked his head, listening for a moment.

Pursing his lips, he emitted a low, barely perceptible whistle. After a few seconds more, he reached behind him and tapped on the cedar fence.

His emaciated body tense, ready to climb back over the fence should a dog appear in answer to the noise he made, he moved his head from side to side.

After a moment, he moved his slightly trembling hands out in front of him and pushed aside the bushes, stepping between them. Moving silently across the lawn, he angled by the edge of a crescent-shaped pool and up to the back door off the sun porch.

There he peered through the big single glass pane in the center of the door. His nervous, heavy breathing formed a fogged spot on the glass.

Brett leaned against the wall in the police station as he talked with Sergeant Green and Arnie, who were about to start their shifts.

"Lieutenant," Green said, a serious expression across his face. "They think it's a cop, don't they?"

"They ask you about me?"

Green nodded. "Yeah. Asked if I'd ever seen a car around here that looked like your patrol car and if you'd ever said anything about the victim to one of us or if we'd ever seen you around her. I told them that until I saw her picture in the paper after the murder, I wouldn't have known who she was. Also told them that I hadn't ever seen you around any other women other than just talking. I know they had to ask, but it rubs you the wrong way—did me, anyway."

The long-haired figure inside the Colonial turned on his small penlight and moved quickly out of the kitchen and through the living room to the closed door leading into the master bedroom.

He reached for the doorknob, slowly turned it and peered inside, then pushed the door the rest of the way open.

The king-size bed against the far wall was empty.

He moved to the mirrored dresser on the wall to his right. Opening a drawer, he quickly rummaged through it. After a moment, he shut it and reached to the other side of the dresser.

As he did, his elbow caught a tall bottle of cologne sitting on the glass top of the dresser and the container tipped over. He grabbed for it, his forearm hitting the small lamp there and toppling it into the line of bottles, and they all turned over, a large one smashing into pieces.

He froze, cursed under his breath, and remained motionless.

*   *   *

In an upstairs bedroom, the dark-haired boy sat up straight in bed.

"What?" the young blonde asked.

"Shhhh."

She was quiet for a moment, her eyes narrowing as she glanced at the closed bedroom door. She looked back at him.

"What?" she repeated.

He slipped his feet from under the sheet to the floor and hurried in his underwear to the door where he locked and bolted it.

"What, Joey?" the girl asked again, a tinge of nervousness now in her voice. She began replacing her bra. "What is it?"

"There's somebody downstairs."

"Ohhhh."

"Shhhh," he said as he reached for the telephone.

The 911 telephone on the dispatcher's desk in the police station rang. Martha was in the bathroom. Brett lifted the receiver.

"Police department."

A low voice whispered, "There's somebody downstairs."

"What?"

"There's somebody in the damn house." The voice sounded young.

"What's the address?"

The voice gave the address in a still lower voice and then said, "Hurry, please."

"Where are you now?"

"Damn, mister, in the house."

"Where in the house?"

"In a bedroom. Upstairs."

"Lock your door."

"You think I'm crazy? It is. Will you please come on!"

Brett replaced the receiver and gestured for the sergeant and Arnie to follow him as he started toward the door.

"It's some kid saying someone's broken in on him. The address he gave is Dr. Hankins's house."

Green shook his head. "He's out of town on vacation."

"Yeah," Brett said, "and he doesn't have any children, either."

* * *

The doorbell startled Catherine Maddox. She glanced from the late-night movie on television toward the front door.

The doorbell rang again. Whoever it was shouted something. A cold chill ran up her back and she looked at the small revolver she had placed beside her telephone.

The doorbell rang again.

She clasped the pistol, rose slowly from her chair, and walked to the edge of the foyer, peering around it. She could see through the leaded glass panel in the door that there were three men, all in dark suits.

One of them tried the doorknob.

CHAPTER 30

Brett slowed his unmarked car, his brakes vibrating, and extinguished the headlights as he turned into a cul-de-sac. A hundred feet farther he pulled off to the side of the street and parked in front of a French provincial house. A hundred feet ahead on the left of the end of the cul-de-sac was the Colonial with a columned, drive-through portico. It was completely dark.

As Brett opened his door and moved outside, Green stepped from the other side of the car and Arnie climbed from the backseat.

Brett nodded toward Arnie and gestured up the blacktop with his flashlight. "You go around to the back."

Arnie glanced toward the house, swallowed, nodded, and started across the yard of the house to the left.

"Deputies," Green said, glancing down the street behind them.

The darkened car parked behind Brett's car and three uniformed men hurried to them.

The chief deputy, Bo Carswell, looked at the house. "Said there was a kid in the house."

Brett nodded. "Yeah, in an upstairs bedroom. If you can get your deputies to each side, we'll go on in. Arnie's already on his way to the back."

Without Carswell speaking, the two deputies quickly started toward the house. A light rain started falling.

Suddenly, there was the faint sound of a window raising, followed by a high-pitched voice shouting at them from behind the columns.

"He's out in the damn hall!"

Brett sprinted forward, unholstering his automatic as he ran. "Whoever's in there knows we're here now. Be careful."

They ran across the shallow front yard of the Colonial and under the portico to the sides of the front door.

He tried the doorknob but the house was locked.

"Hurry!" came the loud shout from above.

Brett shined his flashlight up toward the open window. The boy, bare-chested, leaned out, looking down at them.

"Hurry, please!" he begged. "He tried to open the door."

Brett gauged the distance from the window to the ground. "Son, I want you to hang by your hands and drop. We'll break your fall."

A young, long-haired blonde in a T-shirt leaned out the window next to the boy. Wide-eyed, she was staring at the ground and shaking her head no.

"Come on, honey!" Brett shouted. "You have to."

"Oh, God," the girl moaned, and bit her hand.

"Come on. It's not much of a drop; we'll catch you."

The boy said something to the girl. A moment later her bare legs backed out the window.

Carswell stepped up beside Brett. The boy was holding the girl by her arms and then he let go. She shrieked. But the fall was only a short one and they were able to catch her easily.

Brett nodded up the street. "Get down by our car and stay there."

"Watch it!" Carswell warned. The boy plummeted downward, his body slamming into theirs, knocking Carswell to the ground.

"Shit," the deputy said, and reached for his ankle.

The boy dashed in the direction the girl was running.

"I'm not big on just walking in there," Carswell said as he hobbled back to a side of the door.

Brett looked toward the street. "Get the car up here and turn the headlights on the house."

Carswell limped toward the blacktop.

In a couple of minutes he drove up onto the slightly elevated yard, setting the headlights on high and directing the spotlight at the second floor, illuminating the window the boy had jumped from as well as the light rain, little more than a mist, drifting slowly down through the bright beams.

Brett, crouching, moved to the nearest window on his right, raised his automatic, and smashed it into the pane.

Leaning his face forward where it was nearly even with the side of the window, he shouted at whomever was inside to come out.

After a few seconds with no response, and Carswell hurrying back to the front door, Brett shouted again, and again received no response. He moved back to the door.

"What in hell do we do now?" Carswell asked.

A marked patrol car, its lights flashing, came speeding up the cul-de-sac and turned into the Colonial's yard to stop next to the car already there. Right behind the patrol car came a pickup. It stopped in the street. Two more of the town's officers—Franks, uniformed, and an older man in his civilian clothes—hurried toward the house's front door.

Seales arrived next. He stopped his car in the street and walked past the cars on the lawn, his stocky figure dark and seemingly even wider than normal in the glare of the headlights behind him.

"Where's the kid?" he asked.

"There were two. They're down the street."

Seales tried the doorknob, then simply rang the bell. After a moment, he rang it again.

Sergeant Green and Carswell glanced at each other.

Seales pulled a thin piece of metal from his pocket and knelt in front of the doorknob. In a moment, there was a click and the door opened slightly.

They stood back as he pushed the door hard and it swung open with a bang against an inside wall. Snaking his arm around the door facing, he flicked a switch on the wall panel just inside the house, lighting a brilliant chandelier in the foyer.

There was a small sitting room off to the right, a dining-room entrance back to the left. Directly in front of them, white-carpeted steps led up toward the second story.

Without saying anything, Seales drew a snub-nosed .38 from inside his coat and, holding it out in front of him, quickly stepped inside, and crouched next to the dining-room door.

Brett stepped to his right into the sitting room. Leaning back against the wall, he flicked on the switch next to his head.

Past the sitting room, the living room now glowed with light, revealing a wide room, white-carpeted, with an off-white couch and green armchairs. There was a marble fireplace built into the back wall.

He stepped cautiously through the sitting room to the living room. Off to his right he could see the open door to a bedroom, also white-carpeted with a king-size bed against the far wall.

Green and Carswell moved up the stairway, slowly leap-frogging each other, their pistols pointing up toward the second floor.

Seales stepped from the kitchen entrance at the far side of the living room.

Brett, keeping his eyes on the door to a narrow sun room behind the fireplace, moved quickly to the bedroom door. He peered inside.

On the left wall were French doors leading to a covered patio. Back to his right was the entrance to a bathroom. He saw the broken pieces of glass on the dresser. He moved to the bathroom and glanced inside.

When he stepped back into the living room, Seales was emerging from the sun room and nodded back over his shoulder toward the kitchen.

"He came in through a window in there."

When they returned to the front door, two more officers arrived. Green and Carswell were now on their way down the stairs. The house was ablaze in lights.

"The bed in the room the kids came out of has its covers messed up," Carswell said. "No other sign of anybody being here."

"Sergeant," Seales said to Green, "go see what in the hell those kids were doing here. Carswell, get the deputies in here. With a partner, I want all of you to go through every closet, look in every nook and cranny in the house. Start on this floor first." He glanced up the stairs. "Let's you and me start up there, Brett."

In a few minutes, lightning occasionally erupting outside the house as they worked, they had thoroughly checked every possible hiding place, except the attic.

Seales looked up at the trapdoor in the hallway ceiling. He

reached and caught the cord and pulled down on it, a dark void opening above them.

There was a light switch to the left side of the wall and he flicked it on.

Paige, in blue jeans and a white blouse, her service revolver in her hand, appeared at the front door and quickly hurried up the stairs.

Seales pulled the folding stairs down. Brett stepped on the bottom step and started toward the attic. The steps gave slightly and squeaked.

"Be careful," Paige said. Seales glanced at her.

Nearing the top of the stairs, Brett thought he heard a barely perceptible sound and stopped.

He heard it again, coming from above him.

Then, again.

Rhythmic.

Breathing.

Loud enough to be heard all the way across the attic floor from a wall on its far side. He unholstered his automatic. Hesitantly, he raised his eyes slowly above the attic-floor level and stared in the direction of the sound.

There was a pile of boxes against a far wall. He grasped the butt of his automatic with both hands and pointed the weapon in their direction. He had to clear his throat before he could speak.

"Come out of there or I'm going to shoot."

He felt the ladder move as Seales started up it. In a moment, the chief's wide shoulders pressed against his.

Brett nodded toward the boxes and Seales lowered his weapon in that direction.

The breathing was faster and deeper now, clearer. Brett felt the hair rise on his forearms.

"You've got five seconds and we're going to shoot," Seales said, but shook his head as he glanced at Brett.

"Five-four-three-two—"

The boxes moved. A large one slid a foot forward.

Seconds passed, nothing more happened.

"Come on!" Seales commanded.

After a few more seconds, without taking his eyes off the boxes, he talked across his shoulder to Brett. "Get some tear gas and a couple of masks."

One of the boxes moved again. The top of a head bobbed above the edge of one, disappeared, and rose once more.

For a long moment, all that could be seen was thin brown hair.

As the sound of thunder reverberated through the attic, a pale, narrow forehead slowly rose. The gaunt face came into view—the wide eyes, the long-beaked nose and hollow cheeks.

"Come on!" Seales commanded.

The man rose the rest of the way, though he was more boy than man, not over nineteen or twenty at the most.

"Raise your hands above your head!" Seales said.

The man glanced nervously to his left and back to his right, as if he were looking for a way out.

"Your hands, dammit!" Seales shouted. "Get them up!"

The man stepped forward. There was nothing in his trembling hands, but he still hadn't raised them.

Brett came up the last two steps. Keeping his automatic leveled, he said, "Turn around."

The man's eyes seemed to focus on him. A quizzical expression crossed the narrow face. The eyes slitted.

"Watch out, Brett," Seales cautioned in a low voice. The man screamed and charged.

Brett met him with a lunge and they crashed to the floor, a cloud of dust rising from the boards at the impact.

Seales was quickly beside them, grabbing the man's left arm and twisting the hand down while he brought the bony elbow forward. With him screaming, they forced him over to his stomach as Paige joined them, helping.

Brett jammed his knee into the small of the man's back and reached to handcuff him. In a moment, except for his deep gasping, he was still.

When they stepped out the front door of the Colonial, the trembling young man in front of them, Carswell nodded back across his shoulder toward the two teenagers in one of the patrol cars.

"The boy's Dr. Hankins's nephew," Carswell said. "He figured that with his uncle out of town, this was a good spot for him and his girlfriend not to be disturbed.''

Arnie, his uniform damp from the rain, came across from behind the house. He smiled broadly.

"On the other side of the fence," he said. "Guess what's there? A car that looks just like yours, Brett, only a couple years older. It's got a scanner in it. That was what the guy who talked to the F.B.I. thought was a police radio. We just caught our burglar.''

CHAPTER 31

With his dark hair thick and wavy, his body slim and erect in a well-fitting orange jumpsuit, H. Wayne Warren could pass for someone much younger than his fifty years. He had, in fact, successfully conned innumerable women into believing he was much younger—but once too often. He replaced the telephone receiver and sank back in his chair.

"It was the burglar," he said. "They finally caught him." He shook his head. "It's just a matter of time and they're going to know who we are, too."

His sister, broad and stocky, her brown hair cut short around a square, hard face, shook her head. "How? How are they gonna find out?"

"They're going to. I'm telling you, they're going to."

"Nobody saw her talking to you, Wayne, nobody knows anything about it. How could they?"

"How do we know someone didn't see?"

"Because the F.B.I. would've already come for you if they had."

His hand was already trembling. He swallowed at that. She stared at him and found it hard to conceal her disgust. There was no way he was going to hold up. It was going to be the end for both of them.

* * *

Applewhite stepped into the booking room of the police station and made straight for Seales. Brett looked at the agent and back to the door as Vic came through it.

"What have you found out so far?" Applewhite asked.

"It's Bradey's doing," Seales said, scowling. "Him and his damn politics." He glanced over at Brett.

"Brett, you remember when I had you all start calling in every time you checked a house when somebody was out of town? We'd always kept an eye on the houses as a courtesy to people on vacation, but we never kept a formal record of it. That was Bradey's big idea—our politician alderman. He wanted each time we checked called into the station and logged. He wanted to be given the information so when people got back in town he could personally call them and tell them about our diligence. Politics. Nothing but a way to kiss people's ass for votes. Well, this kid, he picks up a scanner and starts monitoring y'all's calls. We're not only telling him each time a certain house is deserted, but that it's already been checked and won't be looked at again for hours."

Applewhite wasn't interested in that. "What's the chance of him being the killer?"

Seales shook his head. "Not one. He's spaced out like you wouldn't believe. He might have killed anybody who got in his way. But to kill someone and try to make it look like someone else did it—his brain's scrambled too bad to ever think of that. And how's he going to know about snapping the tendon? He's saying he'll take a lie detector test. As soon as his system clears out, we'll give him one—make sure." He shook his head again. "That is, if he doesn't kick over on us; something bad's wrong with his breathing. The drugs, I guess, something he's done to his system; sounds like an old steam engine. We have a doctor on the way over."

"I don't give a shit what's wrong with him," Applewhite said. "I only want to know for sure whether the bastard might be the killer or not."

Seales nodded. "Brett," he said.

"Yes, sir."

Seales nodded him toward a corner of the area.

"Brett, this guy's not going to be the one. The psycho didn't kill Trinity, and *he* didn't. I can't see the guy she went to see doing it, either, but we have to turn the burners up until we find him—and anybody else she slipped out with. And that might take some doing; I don't see how she had any time left for her husband. We know of a half dozen already." He pulled a sheet from his pocket and handed it over.

"This is an ad that I want you to get in the papers along with her picture," he added. *"The Sun Herald* and the smaller papers, too. It asks for anyone who has ever been out with her to call us."

Brett didn't understand the point.

Seales noticed his questioning look. "The killer's not going to call us, Brett—that's a given. Some of the others she dated might, though. Maybe they know names of other people she's been out with. If nothing else, that'll allow us to eliminate the ones who do come in if their names turn up later. Maybe someone will recognize her and maybe remember seeing her out with somebody."

Brett nodded. "Yeah." He looked at the ad, then raised his face again. "You said you knew of a half dozen already?"

"No cops yet, unless you consider Vic a cop."

Brett stared his surprise.

"Don't look so shocked, Brett, he can smell out a woman like that from a hundred miles away. He said he met her in a bar one night. He's got a few minutes of time unaccounted for but not long enough. He flew back in from Memphis early the night she was murdered, then carried a report on over to Mrs. Lloyd at her house in New Orleans. She's not absolutely sure of the time he arrived there, but she did remember it was around an hour after he had called her from his office, that when he arrived, the local news was only ten or fifteen minutes from coming on. She paid him some expenses she had promised him and he left. So that would put him arriving there shortly before ten, only a little while before the prowler was being seen the first time. And she was dead by eleven when you got there. He couldn't have possibly made it back from New Orleans in the time he had, especially not and have the time to make the attack."

Brett nodded. "Yes, sir."

Seales's eyes narrowed. "You look blank, Brett. He did end up back here that night. In fact, he was already there when I arrived. He was talking to you. If the print was smeared on purpose, he had as much access to it as anybody. Didn't you expect us to check out his alibi?''

"Yes, sir, of course. You said you knew about a half dozen?''

"The others you don't know, I don't imagine. All of them from Gulfport or Biloxi, and all but one of them with an alibi.''

"What did you do about him?''

"He bears some more thought. Told us where he was. At a night club by himself. Applewhite's checking to see if anyone remembers seeing him there. If we can't come up with something in a little while, we'll see if he wants to take a polygraph.''

"What's his name?''

"Jack Burns. Young guy. His dad left him a big dairy farm north of the coast.''

"A big shot?''

"He's got a little money, but he doesn't live in this county, much less this town—and how could Trinity have ruined him, even hurt him? He's not married—not to mention he doesn't have a sister.''

Brett nodded. "Yeah.''

"Other than that, I can't tell you much about him. Applewhite hasn't told me any more.''

There was nothing in the tone of Seales's voice, but rather his look that said he didn't like being left in the dark.

Paige turned off the highway and followed the narrow blacktop where it turned into the gravel driveway. She stepped from the car and hurried through the now-heavy rain to the front door of the small one-story house. She fumbled for a moment with the stubborn lock, stepped inside, and flipped on the living-room light.

In a few minutes, she was down to her bikini panties and bra and stood in front of her dresser.

She turned sideways. Her stomach was still perfectly flat. Twenty-six, she thought, how would it be at thirty-six? What about after her first child? Three, if Brett had his way. *Gosh.* She looked at her stomach again. Maybe she ought to have some photographs taken in a bathing suit. See, she would say; look, children, that's how Mommy used to look before you came along.

Smiling, she walked toward the bathroom, heard the front door open and shut as she did.

"Want to take a shower together?" she called back over her shoulder.

In the bathroom, she opened the shower door and turned on the water, held her hand under it until the temperature was right, then stepped inside the stall.

She looked up into the water, wetting her face, and began to soap it.

Her eyes closed, she heard the shower door when it opened rather than saw it. Suddenly, his hands grabbed her.

She squealed. "Brett, have you gone crazy?"

He had stepped inside the stall with his full uniform on, even his shoes.

She squealed again, then was suddenly silenced by his lips pressing against hers.

After a long kiss, she leaned her face back from his. "Gosh," she exclaimed, "I'll have to remember to ask you to take a shower with me again."

He reached his arms under her legs and behind her back.

"No!" she laughed. "You'll fall."

He ignored her, lifting her as if she didn't weigh anything and backing out of the shower.

"At least let me dry off."

He moved to the bed, laid her on it, and moved on top of her, his hair dripping water into her face.

She laughed again and wiped at the water, then noticed him staring deeply into her eyes.

"Gosh," she said, "what *has* got into you?"

He stared a moment longer, then moved his lips to hers, and she returned his kiss eagerly, like she always did. Her first gasp was lost in the thunder outside the house, and then her soft murmurs of pleasure joined with his.

He would tell her in the morning.

Applewhite stood in a hall in the police station as he looked at the traffic ticket found in the glove compartment of the Ford belonging to the burglar.

"So he couldn't be the one who murdered the Andersons," Seales explained. "Speeding ticket is marked 10:10 P.M., nearly forty miles away from here. Couldn't have been him. But we're still going to give him a polygraph as soon as he's flushed out.''

"Are you happy?'' the sheriff's wife asked him.

Hastings turned his head on the pillow and looked at his wife propped against the headboard. She had her magazine on her lap and stared at him in a funny way.

"What do you ask something like that for?''

"I don't know, honey,'' she said. "It's just that sometimes I get to thinking about how boring our lives are.''

"What you're saying is, you're not happy.''

"Oh, no. I am. But you wanted to stay in the Navy and make it a career. You loved the water so. Just sitting here on the same coast all the time, I know you have regrets. And it was me who talked you into quitting.''

He smiled and looked back at the television as he answered her. "I'm perfectly happy. Never been happier. Love being a sheriff, love the coast, and love you.''

His wife sighed and shook her head. "I certainly hope you're not just saying that, Richard.''

"I'm not . . . And now let me go back to watching TV.''

But she wouldn't. "Richard, it doesn't bother you all the politicking you have to do? I mean, putting up with all the phone calls and all?''

"Everything's perfect, Ann, okay?''

She sighed, lifted her magazine, and went back to reading it.

"I certainly hope so,'' she said without looking back at him.

At the next commercial, he looked out of the corner of his eyes. It was her that was wondering what she had done with her life—regretting it, he believed. She had been showing more and more signs of that over the last few months.

Even though he hated the thought, he realized he was going to have to start keeping an eye on her. The signs were there.

CHAPTER 32

They had stayed in bed, skipping breakfast, finally rising to dress and go to church. Paige had fixed them sandwiches for lunch and they sat around the house watching television until it was almost time for his shift to begin. When Brett moved into the bedroom to put on his uniform, she followed him inside and sat on the end of the bed.

"There must be a few dozen F.B.I. agents in town," she said. "I half expected to see one in church. They're all over the place, talking to everyone. I thought they were going to be assisting us. What are we supposed to be doing?"

"Doesn't look like they want us to do anything," he said as he slipped on his uniform shirt. "From what Seales said and the look I caught from him, I'm not even sure they're telling him more than they have to."

"It's because they're thinking it could be a cop—one of us over here? They don't trust anybody."

"Can you blame them?" He sat on the side of the bed and slipped on his shoes, began tying the laces.

"What about Hastings?" she asked. "They're keeping him informed, aren't they?"

"Him being the county's chief law-enforcement officer, probably—if he's bothered to ask. As laid back as he is, he might just be letting things ride. Seales has too much pride to ask him if they're keeping him up."

"You know what they ought to do, they ought to slip in everybody's houses without them knowing it—all the big shots in the area. They might just stumble onto something—if they kept their arrival secret."

"Paige."

"They might." She glanced at her watch. "I really hate it when I'm off and you have to work."

He smiled. "You're out of vacation days almost. It'll be my turn."

"Yeah, and then I won't see you. You'll always be fishing. At least I stay around when you're not on your shift."

"Meeting your mother?"

"Yeah, a little later. I told her I'd meet her at four. We're going shopping over at the Edgewater Mall, but I'll be back in time to fix dinner. I'll call the dispatcher when I get it ready and you can slip over here and eat."

He decided he would wait until then to tell her. He looked at his watch. "I'd really like a po'boy."

Her eyes narrowed. "Brett, you're going to get fat."

"You want to drive down and get one with me? I can drop you back here before I go on my shift."

"You want me to get fat, too."

He called the little beachside restaurant and the sandwiches were ready when he arrived, his soft shell crab and hers shrimp. The delicious smell of crawfish boiling made him want to change his mind, but he had already ordered the sandwich and so he didn't say anything. They ate on the way back toward their house, washing the sandwiches down with old fashioned Barq's Root Beer, distributed in cans nationally but still served on the coast in the same kind of glass bottles it had been served in when a Biloxi family had come up with the secret formula nearly a century before. As they passed the home of the town's mayor, Paige lowered her po'boy from her mouth and looked out the passenger window.

"Who are they?" she asked.

Brett looked at the pickup backed up to the side door of the one-story brick house. Two men were loading a sofa into the truck bed. "I don't have the slightest."

"Mayor's car isn't there."

Brett put his foot on the brake. His car vibrated as it slowed, and he made a U-turn in the street.

When they walked up the driveway the two men glanced at them and then went back inside the house. Brett was cautious as he peered around the side of the doorway into a kitchen. And he saw that one of the men was J. B. Browning. The thin black man peered back at him.

"Hey, Mr. Brett, Miss Paige."

"J. B.," Brett acknowledged as he stepped into the house. "Mayor getting rid of some old furniture?"

"Mayor's too tight for that, you know that. He don't cotton to spending nuthin' he don't have to. Found a man who said he'd re-cover it dirt cheap—old couch and a couple of chairs. Was me I'd throw them away."

"Where is he?"

"Went to get a tarpaulin in case the rain starts again. Just as the work got heavy, too."

Two oversize easy chairs were already moved to the kitchen. Browning and the other man leaned and caught each side of one and, their sleek muscles straining, lifted it and started toward the door. Paige walked around them and peered into the living room. A second later, she disappeared inside it.

"Paige!" He hurried after her.

She was going into a hallway on the far side of the room. "Paige." She looked back at him and smiled, then continued down the hall to a doorway off to its right. She stepped through it. He shook his head and walked toward the hall.

By the time he reached the doorway, she stepped back out of a small bedroom and made her way on down the hall.

"Paige, come on."

"What's wrong with looking around?"

"Come on, dammit."

"Just a minute," she answered, and turned and walked toward the next doorway, disappeared through it.

Brett shook his head in disgust.

"Brett!" came a heavy voice behind him—the mayor!

He turned around to face the tall, dark-skinned man.

"Brett, what are you doing?"

Brett forced a smile. "Hey, Mayor. Saw these guys carrying off a sofa and stopped to check what was going on."

"Yeah?" The mayor's brow was wrinkled questioningly.

Brett started back toward him. "Just checking to see that nothing else was disturbed; make sure of what was going on."

"Brett, that's old man J. B. Browning and his friend. I'd trust J. B. in my house before anyone else I know. I thought you knew him."

Brett nodded. "Yeah. Just wanted to be absolutely certain, though."

The mayor's eyes went past him, and Brett turned to see Paige emerge from the far doorway. He spoke quickly. "Paige, the mayor's back, so I guess we can quit checking around to see if anything's been disturbed. I told you that when J. B. told you something, you can take it as fact."

Paige came on down the hall and passed them. He turned and followed her. She looked back over her shoulder toward the mayor and said, "You never can be too careful nowadays."

Back inside their house, Brett finished his po'boy and threw the wrapper in the garbage can, then placed the extra bottles of Barq's they had bought in the refrigerator.

Paige looked at her watch. "I have to be going if I'm not going to keep Mother waiting," she said. "I'll call you when I get back over here with your food."

When Paige's Maxima pulled out of the short driveway with only her in the vehicle and, instead of turning toward downtown and the police station, headed in the direction of the highway, Catherine Maddox's brow wrinkled and she glanced at her watch.

Looking back over her shoulder, she searched for a car parked where someone could be observing her, but didn't see one. She made a quick decision and drove toward the driveway.

Brett was in the bathroom combing his hair when the doorbell rang.

When he opened the door, he was startled to see Catherine.

"They know, Brett. The F.B.I. They came to my house last night. They said I'd be obstructing justice if I didn't tell them why I drove out to see you. I could have called you and told you, but I wanted to tell you face-to-face. I'm sorry."

He glanced past her and looked up and down the street. "Come on in."

After shutting the door, he turned back toward her.

"They were watching me, Catherine, weren't they? That's how they saw you, wasn't it?"

"They wouldn't say anything, just wanted to know why I came out there to meet you."

They had to have been watching him. There was no reason they would have been following her. That bastard Applewhite. "Come on into the living room. I have to make a phone call."

"Brett, they told me not to say anything to you. But there's nothing they can do to me for coming here, is there?"

"No."

In the living room, he sank down in the chair next to the telephone and lifted the receiver as she watched him.

The chief answered on the second ring.

"Seales here."

"Chief, I need to come over and see you. I have the woman with me who called and played the tape."

An hour later, the rain began to fall again. Applewhite switched off the speaker phone after talking to Chief Seales and leaned back in his chair.

"Dunnigan would have really had to squeeze the time," he said. "I can't see him killing the woman, then making it back to the house and picking his wife up as quick as he did." He shook his head. "No, no way."

The muscled young agent sitting in the chair across the desk nodded his agreement.

The older agent standing at one of the office windows wasn't as positive. "I don't know. It's not absolutely impossible. And what keeps standing out in my mind is there was no sign at all of a struggle. There wasn't a thing out of place in the house, not an article of her clothing torn, nothing under her fingernails—she didn't resist at all. Neither did her husband. He was hit one time in the head; no sign of a struggle. They either knew the killer or the bastard was able to catch them both totally unawares in their own home. What's the likelihood of that happening? And there's what Dunnigan would lose if his wife found out he had been with the Anderson woman—assuming she'd leave him.''

The younger agent nodded. ''A few million bucks.''

''To be exact, two point seven million and accumulating interest,'' the older agent said. ''And the trust is irrevocable, hers for keeps—and her husband's, as long as he's married to her. Be hell to have that in the palm of your hand and then realize you might lose it. Wonder how far I'd go to prevent that?''

Applewhite nodded. ''I want everybody over there who knows him questioned. And where was it he went to college?''

''Up at Hattiesburg—University of Southern Mississippi,'' the younger agent said.

''Yeah. See if you can locate anybody who knew him then. I want to know all I can about his background, how he acted back then, whether he had a temper—everything that can be found out about him.''

CHAPTER 33

The rain was letting up as Brett's car vibrated off the blacktop onto the spot where old man Pennebaker had stopped at the swamp after trying to outrun Sergeant Green. He lowered his window and stared out across the brown water spotted with patches of green algae.

He remembered back to the two times he had taken Paige frogging and he smiled. Why in hell had he ever left the casino with Trinity? After he told Paige about it, no matter how much she might want to believe nothing happened, deep down she was going to wonder, never be sure; especially since he also told her he hadn't talked to Trinity in the grocery store. He had lied twice. Before he met Paige he had often wondered if he would ever meet somebody he felt like he could trust deeply enough to marry. And now *he* had been the one to betray that trust.

Thinking that, he became irritated for another reason. He was beginning to sound like a whiner. Beginning, hell, he *was* whining, like a whipped pup. Why in hell didn't he just go to her and say, Listen I've got something to tell you. I met Trinity one night and we drove out to Back Bay to talk over old times. Why not, Paige? She was a good friend, and of course that's what it was all about— just old friends talking. What other reason would I have to have been with her? What are you, crazy? Thinking something like that? Hell, if that's all the trust you have in me, I must have married the wrong woman. I'll be back when you're ready to apologize for that.

Was he crazy?

He shook his head and raised his face back to the swamp. Out a hundred feet from the bank he noticed a ripple, and an ever so slight movement. He looked closer. An alligator was gliding slowly toward a stand of swamp grass, the creature's mostly submerged blunt snout slowly parting the algae.

Brett noticed the deer then, a doe and her young fawn. The mother was standing in water up to her knees, her baby, close beside her, was submerged to the stomach.

Had it been winter and deer season, the doe would have been more sensitive to noises and been gone before he had ever stopped his car. He looked at the alligator gradually closing on the unsuspecting deer.

Nature's way, he thought, the hunter and the hunted. As terrible as it was, it was also comfortingly simple, not like humans with all their complicated worries, the decisions they had to make— their consciences, their whining. He looked at the alligator and pressed down hard on his horn.

The doe started, whirled, and bolted back through the marsh, her baby following close behind her. In minutes, they had disappeared into a clump of tall underbrush. The alligator slowly submerged.

A large water moccasin swam out of the swamp grass and passed over the spot where the alligator disappeared. Brett waited for the snake to be suddenly engulfed.

But nothing happened, the thick, gliding body finally disappearing into another patch of grass.

He shifted into reverse and backed out in a half circle where he was headed back into town.

All he did was sit in the bar at the casino and talk to her. But how was he to explain why they ended up driving to Back Bay?

But nothing happened. That was the key—nothing, not a damn thing happened. He hadn't meant for anything to happen. He had gone there because he—

He shook his head. What was he trying to convince himself of? Of course something happened. He went with her. And for just a little he would've made love to her. It had certainly done more than pass through his mind. Just because he didn't, didn't make it right—and Paige wasn't going to think it right, either. He shook his head again and pressed down on the accelerator.

A quarter mile later, he saw the old Chevy sitting off to a side of the narrow pavement. His jaw tightened. Bastards, he thought, still following him.

As he drove past the car, he stared at the face behind the steering wheel, and the man looked away.

Yeah, Brett thought sarcastically, *tell Applewhite I was doing something down at the swamp. Maybe it's where I threw the murder weapon.*

A few hundred feet farther, he glanced into his rearview mirror. A pulpwood truck coming down the highway had to pull over near the edge of the pavement to safely clear the old Chevy, which was barely off on the shoulder. His jaw tightened again and suddenly he swung a U-turn and headed back to the spot.

He stopped his car bumper to bumper directly in front of the Chevy and opened his door.

The dark-haired young man looked to Brett to be no more than in his early twenties. Probably not long out of the F.B.I. Academy. As the man lowered his window, there was a smile on his face.

Brett didn't return the look. "You think you can park any damn place you want?"

A puzzled expression swept the young man's face. "What, Officer?"

"Get out of the car."

The man hesitated a moment, then moved the papers he had been working with out of his lap, opened the door, and stepped outside.

"Turn around and put your hands on your car."

"I'm sorry, what is—"

"I said, turn around and put your hands on your car."

As the man did, glancing back over his shoulder, Brett added, "What I should do is whip your ass."

The man's eyes widened.

Welcome to Mississippi, you bastard. Bad, isn't it? He wondered how far he would have to press the agent before the man would reveal his identity? He intended to do just that, and then later smile as he thought how Applewhite would look when the agent tried to explain how he was found out. He patted the man's hip pocket and pulled out a wallet.

Opening it, he saw the business card:

J. Paul Toney—Insurance, Laurel, Mississippi.

Brett closed his eyes and shook his head. It was a moment before he spoke. "I'm sorry," he said.

"What?" the young man asked, nervously glancing over his shoulder.

"I'm sorry; you can go on."

The man opened his door and quickly slipped inside.

Brett handed the wallet through the window. "I'm sorry," he said again. "Just had a bad day. You shouldn't park so close to the edge of the pavement. It's dangerous."

He noticed how wet the man's face was and only then realized it had started raining hard again. He shook his head and walked to his car, climbed inside, and made a sweeping turn out onto the road and back toward town.

The two men in coveralls in the old pickup a quarter mile up the road stared as Brett's car went past, then guided the rented truck out onto the pavement.

When they reached the Chevy, the man driving stopped long enough for his partner to step outside. Then the pickup started up again.

The young insurance salesman from Laurel had raised his window and wasn't about to let it down again as the man in faded coveralls walked toward him. Instead, he dropped the gear into drive and started to press on the accelerator.

The agent held his badge up to the rain-splattered window. "F.B.I.," he said. "Will you step out of your car, please?"

CHAPTER 34

It was raining hard as Paige's Maxima flashed by on the dark highway, the vehicle's tires throwing a spray of water to the sides of the pavement. Brett, parked on the frontage road above the beach, stared after her for a moment, then reached for his microphone and called the station.

In a moment, Martha answered.

"Martha, I'm not feeling so hot. Don't know what it is, but I was wondering if you could get anybody to take over the rest of my shift?"

"You younguns never take care of yourself. Just like Sergeant Green. This keeps up and we can shut down the force. Let me see if I can pull somebody outta bed. I'll check back with you in a minute."

He was halfway to his house when her voice came back over the radio.

"Franks said he'd catch your spot, Brett. Chief said if you're not feeling any better in the morning to let him know in plenty of time for him to get somebody else to take your shift. You think you can remember that, or do I gotta call you and remind you?"

A few minutes later, he drove into the short gravel driveway at his house. Paige's car wasn't there.

In the house, he sat back on the living-room couch, his mind swirling with a mixture of guilt, real fear at how Paige was going to react, and thoughts of the "big shot" Trinity had gone to see.

* * *

The rain had stopped, but Arnie's uniform was soaked as he knelt on the side of the fence where the killer had fallen into the azaleas. He shined his flashlight along the ground and used his fingers to separate the straw around the slight depression in the bed. His lips drew in a tight line when he couldn't find anything. Overhead, a pair of sea gulls wound their way through the night toward the beach.

Paige parked in the driveway behind the red MG. She sat in her car for a moment, the lights shining on the house.

Trinity didn't hide what she was. To a man passing her house, knowing how beautiful she was, knowing *how* she was, it would've been like a sailor passing the rocks where the Sirens sat singing their songs of temptation. Who might not have resisted other than the man she had met in New Orleans?

Paige opened her door and stepped outside. She turned on her flashlight and shined it ahead of her as she walked to the front door. It was locked. The back door was, too. She began trying the windows around the house.

The one she found unlocked was the same one that had been open the night of the murder, the window into the bedroom. The screen was still off and leaning against the house.

She stood a moment, steeling her nerves to deal with the smell and the bloodstains again. Then she pushed the window up, gritted her teeth, bounced, and jumped her head and shoulders through the opening.

Pulling herself on inside, she leaned over and placed her hands against the carpet and tumbled awkwardly over onto the floor.

She rose to her feet, tried to keep her gaze as much as possible on the sides of the walls rather than the floor. But it did no good; there was no way to look without viewing the stain. She quit trying.

What was she doing there? She didn't know. It was only that while she had been shopping with her mother, a thought had kept running through her mind. Another one of her crazy ideas. She would have thought the house would have given up all its secrets the night of the murder. But then somewhere later a page had been torn from the telephone directories. What had been on it other than their telephone number, and was there anything else the house had yet to give up?

It was crazy, she thought again. There couldn't be. But the thought kept coming back and so she had decided to stop by to satisfy her curiosity. *So where did she look first, and for what?*

She walked to the doorway leading into the hall. A light switch was there and she flicked it on. The odor of death seemed even stronger in the hallway.

Stopping at the edge of the living room, she turned on the light switch there and looked around the area.

After a moment, she walked slowly through the dining room into the kitchen. The ceiling tile was rain-stained and drooped in places, but didn't seem to be wet now.

Through the back door window she saw in the moonlight the figure of the German shepherd and a man standing just inside the fence at the rear of the yard. The man started toward the house.

When he drew closer she saw that it was Arnie. In a few seconds, the back door opened.

Arnie's mouth fell open as he stared at her. "What are you doing here?" he asked.

"How did you open the door?"

He held up a key. "It was under the mat at the front door. I got it earlier. What are you doing?"

"What are *you* doing, Arnie?"

He shrugged. "Nothing."

"Nothing?"

He dropped his eyes to the floor. "I was hoping I'd find something else. You know—" He raised his face. "Something that might help."

His uniform was soaked. He obviously had been out in the open when the heavy rain had passed over, probably down toward the pool and hedges again. His earlier finding of the piece of rubber glove had earned him more than the snickers and funny looks he usually received from others on the force, even from the people who lived in town and had heard about how easily he frightened. In the middle of the night, still with his shift to work, and he was out looking for something again. She couldn't help but feel sorry for him.

"Well," she said, "I guess I'm doing the same, but I don't

know what it is I'm looking for." She smiled. "Sounds like we're both crazy, doesn't it?"

He didn't respond.

"Come on," she said. "We're here, might as well look."

Passing back down the hallway, she again noticed the odor. It *was* stronger than inside the bedroom. And it was not only stronger, it was different. More pungent.

Something rotting?

She glanced at the trapdoor in the ceiling over the hall, and her mind moved to how the burglar had been hiding in the attic of the Colonial home.

Hiding? Hidden? *Something hidden and now rotting?*

Arnie stared curiously at her. "What?" he asked.

"I don't know, Arnie."

She reached to the wall and flipped on the switch there. Pulling on the string, she lowered the trapdoor. The odor washed down over her.

Arnie sniffed, glancing up toward the attic. His brow wrinkled. "You think he could've brought something in . . ."

"That's what I'm wondering," she said, and pulled down the folding stairs, then started up them.

Just before reaching the top, she took a deep breath, then stuck her head up and looked into the attic.

It was floored. Nothing but the dusty boards could be seen in each direction. She stared back into the farthest, shadowy, cobwebbed recesses where the rafters ran down to meet the joists.

"Go on," Arnie said.

"What?"

"Go on."

She looked back across her shoulder. He was on the bottom step. He was staring at her, his lips in a tight line. Then he pulled his revolver from his holster.

"Go on," he said again.

Her blood froze. She thought back to Brett saying the print might have been smeared deliberately—by a cop. She had commented that if it was a cop and then one of the men on the force had called her and asked her to meet him out at some secluded place— *Even if it was Arnie*, she had said. And then she remembered that the night of Trinity's murder the dispatcher had not been able to get him on the radio. Her throat was suddenly so tight, she could barely speak.

"What, Arnie?"

"Christ almighty, Paige! Are you scared or something? Get down and I'll look. People talk about me being nervous. It's probably only a dead rat, anyway."

She closed her eyes. Her knees were so weak she had to sit on a step as he moved past her up into the attic, her heart only then beginning to slow its pounding. Maybe it wouldn't have been such a bad idea to have listened to her father and gone into the health-care field.

Jesus! she thought. *What am I going to pull next?*

"What did I tell you, Paige," Arnie said from above her. She looked up to see him holding the peeling, bloated body of a raccoon by its tail.

"God, Arnie," she said, and hurried out of his way as he started down the steps.

At the kitchen door she watched him drop the raccoon's body into a garbage can on the porch and replace the lid, then wipe his hands on the side of his pants.

She looked at him for a moment. "Where were you the night Trinity was killed—when the dispatcher couldn't get you on the radio?"

"Nowhere."

"I heard her trying. You didn't answer."

"Oh, then. Yeah, I thought you knew. That F.B.I. agent asked that. I was taking a lea—I was going to the bathroom. I was outside my car down by the edge of a bayou, stepped up on a log. Thought I did, anyway. Then the thing moved—damn alligator. I fell back in the mud. Ran home and changed my uniform. I called the dispatcher as soon as I got back in the car."

Paige shook her head in amusement. Nobody but Arnie. She stepped past him. "I'll see you later, Arnie."

"Paige," he said as she reached the screen door.

She looked back at him.

"I need to ask you something, Paige, sorta confidential like."

She nodded and faced back toward him.

He raised his hand and nervously smoothed his hair back from his forehead. "That night down at the pool house, I was the one Sergeant Green saw."

She couldn't believe what she heard. "You smeared the print?"

He shook his head. "I didn't touch the doorknob. Do you think I'm the type to be going in someplace like that by myself?"

He wasn't. "Why didn't you tell Seales?"

"Because I know he's already wanting to fire me. He wouldn't have believed I didn't go inside. He would've thought I smeared the print and then didn't tell him."

"Why are you telling me now?"

"Because I want to know what to do. With Sergeant Green seeing an officer down there, everybody's thinking one of us smeared it accidentally. But after Green said he came back out of the house right after I walked off, I got to thinking it wouldn't have been an officer."

"I don't follow you."

"Paige, whoever did it had to do it quickly. I think it was the killer, and I don't think he was a cop."

"You said that, but why?"

"I saw the sergeant and the others up at the house when they came outside. I started to go up there but heard a couple of deputies in the next yard, and I went on over there. With me walking in that direction, Sergeant Green up at the house, and the chief coming from the other direction, how could any other officer get to the pool house without one of us noticing him? I didn't, Green didn't, the chief didn't. It had to be somebody who did it in just a few seconds and was gone. And to not be seen he had to hide. An officer wouldn't have hidden. Why would he? No one would have thought anything about seeing another officer—even if he had smeared it on purpose."

Brett, still in his uniform, glanced at his watch when he heard a car drive up in front of the house. He went to the front door. It was Paige.

She lifted a bag of groceries out of the car and hurried through the rain toward the house. He stepped outside to meet her.

"What are you doing home?" she asked.

"Where have you been?" he asked as he took the bag of groceries. "I saw you pass on the highway over an hour ago."

She told him about her experience with Arnie as they walked toward the kitchen.

"It was dark," he said as he set the bag on the counter. "Some cop could have walked off at an angle and no one saw him. The backyards over there are big, and there's a lot of shrubs. We can't be sure. And then he might not have wanted it known he screwed up—smeared it. He could have made sure he wasn't seen and still be innocent. What did Seales say?"

"Surprisingly, not much, other than since the cop Armont saw—Arnie—didn't smear it, there's now obviously a better chance that it *was* the killer—that it was smeared on purpose. But he admitted he's just guessing, too. He doesn't have a real feeling either way." She stepped past him to the counter and began lifting the groceries from the bag.

Brett stared at her for a moment. "Did he mention anything about me?"

She looked back over her shoulder. "About you?"

"Paige, I talked to Trinity in the grocery store that day I ran into her."

Her brow wrinkled as she turned to face him. "Why did you tell me you hadn't?"

"I don't know. I just did."

Her forehead remained wrinkled. "What difference would it have made to tell me? You think I would've been jealous over that?"

"Paige, right after we were engaged, I was over in Biloxi at a casino and Trinity came in ... We ended up driving to Back Bay and sat a while talking."

"Drove to—"

"We didn't do anything, Paige, just talked."

"Just?" She shook her head. "Why are you telling me this now?"

"Trinity told one of her friends—Catherine Maddox. She's the one who called and played the tape."

"So you had to tell me." Her jaw tightened and she shook her head. "I ..." She stepped past him toward the living room.

She stopped in front of the couch as if she were going to sit down, and shook her head again.

"All this time," she said, "I sensed something about the way you were acting. I was telling myself how terrible I was to be thinking that way.''

"Paige, I—''

"I don't want to hear any more," she snapped angrily.

"Paige, I swear to God that nothing happened. I don't know what else to tell you.''

"Nothing happened! You went, didn't you?''

"We just talked.''

"Talked, huh? That's nice.''

"About high school, Paige, that's what we talked about, the things that went on back then. Not about us.''

A bitter smile crossed her face. "You have anything else to tell me? About any other times—her or anybody else? Or is it you haven't been found out about those times? Yeah, that's it. You don't *have* to tell me about those times.''

"Come on, Paige. You know there weren't any other times.''

She glared hard at him. "Oh, I know that, huh? How do I know that? How do I know anything about you? I thought I did.'' She wheeled and walked rapidly toward the bedroom.

He followed her to the door. She sat on the end of the bed.

"I told you all that happened, Paige. That's all, I swear.''

"You're lying.'' Her face was twisted into an expression he had never seen before.

"Paige, I swear.''

"Does Seales know?''

"Yeah.''

"What did he say?''

"I'd already told him about talking to her in the store. He wasn't happy I hadn't said anything about the time I was with her, but he understood why I hadn't—that it was months ago and that I was worried about your reaction. I'm sure Applewhite's not going to shrug it off that easily, but I don't care. Whatever he wants me to do is fine. Like I told Seales— polygraph, whatever.''

She continued to stare. "Just get on out of here. I don't want . . .'' As she paused, she shook her head again. "Damn, Brett, right after we were engaged. If you were still thinking about her, why did you marry me?''

"Come on, Paige. I wasn't thinking anything. I told you, she came up to the bar and—"

"I don't want to hear any more, okay?" she suddenly snapped. "Just shut the door and leave me alone."

"Paige—"

"Shut the door!"

CHAPTER 35

The alarm went off at eight in the morning. As Brett reached to turn the clock off, Paige slipped from the other side of the bed, pulling the sheet with her and wrapping it around her slim body.

He stared at her as she walked toward the bathroom. The night before, there had been nothing more said after he had shut the door. She had either been asleep or pretending sleep when, an hour later, he had come back inside the room and began undressing. When he slid onto the bed, she had risen and gone into the living room where she had spent most of the rest of the night. He had not said anything when she finally came back into the room.

Vic had said not to worry about it—that it was only his conscience bothering him. No, it wasn't his conscience, it was his fear, and now he was scared to death. Not that Paige would leave him. She wouldn't do that over what he had done; she wouldn't do that over almost *anything* he did, no matter how wrong. He had that much faith in how much she loved him. When he was worrying about her leaving him it was just his imagining the worst possible. But not much worse than the fact he might have taken a trust away that would never come back, ruined the faith that she had in him. And that's what scared him to death.

Slept on the couch is all that happened, Vic said, when he talked about his wife catching him. Just shrugged it off like it didn't matter. But then Vic looked on marriage in a lot different way than he did, than most anybody else did. A woman to cook and have sex with, maybe even companionship— There was no question he cared about Peggy. But care didn't equal love, not Vic's kind of care anyway. It couldn't. It was more like a buddy than a wife. It was— Brett narrowed his eyes.

Buddy, Vic was always calling him.

And buddies don't date their buddies' girlfriends.

Damn. That's why Vic hadn't said anything about going out with Trinity. To Vic, Trinity had once been his buddy's girlfriend, there might still be feelings there, and buddies don't ... Christ, what a warped mind. Hell, he bet Vic actually wondered if he was still dating her. Christ! Glad Vic and Applewhite weren't buddies.

Shaking his head, he slipped from the bed and put on his robe, then walked into the living room.

Thirty minutes later, when Paige, now dressed in dark slacks and white blouse, stepped from the bedroom, she asked him if he wanted any breakfast. He shook his head.

"I'm going shopping again with Mother," she said. Her voice was matter-of-fact, monotone. "Then Daddy wanted us to eat with him to make up for his missing dinner with her on their anniversary. He wanted you to come, too, but I told him you wouldn't be able to get off work. I'll bring you something back, if you want."

He nodded.

A reflective look crossed her face. "You know, I wish there was someway I could look in the houses. All of them, cops, elected officials—anybody else we could think of."

"Paige, they wouldn't have anything in their houses."

"I'd like to look anyway." She shook her head as he stared at her, and the first smile she had shown since he had told her about Trinity crossed her face.

"Don't worry," she said. "I wouldn't do something like that. I'm just thinking out loud."

"You make me nervous, Paige. You really do. I never know what you might be capable of."

The smile freezing on her face told him that his comment had sparked the same thought in her—what he was capable of. She turned and moved across the living room toward the door.

As she stepped outside, he could hear the rain starting to fall again.

*   *   *

Applewhite watched the rain pelting against his office window in Gulfport. He looked back toward the door when the young, dark-suited agent carrying a section of poster paper came into the room and walked toward the desk.

"This is it," the agent said, laying the section on the desktop. "It's as near as we can place everybody."

Applewhite leaned forward to look at the names.

"The first line lists all of the people we could come up with who might have been down near the pool house that night," the young agent said. "Basically everybody who was on the scene—highway patrolmen, deputies, police officers, the doctor, that private detective, and, for that matter, any of the neighbors there watching—how do we know?

"But if you eliminate the names down to only the ones who could have been in both places, inside the home where they could have torn the page out of the directory, and also down at the pool house where they could've smeared the print—that's the second line—you can see it narrows the names down considerably. "The Dunnigans, the doctor, the lab technicians, the sergeant, and a few more."

Applewhite stared at the poster before he spoke. "The only problem is that one of those people who was down by the pool could have come back to the house the next day or even the next night and torn the page out. It doesn't have to be somebody who was in the house that night. In fact, it could be somebody that's not on either line."

"Yes, sir, but you asked me for a start to name the most obvious ones who could have been both places. There they are—except for you, of course." He smiled.

Vic stood in a precinct station in New Orleans. The gray-haired homicide detective he had been speaking with shook his head. "I just don't know any more than that, Vic. The F.B.I. doesn't, either—no real leads. Other than that stuff about the guy she went over to see that night."

Vic shook his head. "There's got to be something, something everybody's missing. I felt it the first night—everybody jumping to the conclusion her husband was the psycho. But it stayed with me even after they found his body. They were still jumping in the wrong direction.''

''What do you mean?''

''I don't know. It's just a feeling. If you look at it logically, it's narrowing down. She wasn't killed by her husband. The psycho didn't do it. The possibility of the burglar is out now. This guy they're all looking for—the one she went to see—it seems to be narrowing down to him. But I just don't know. I have a feeling that that's too simple, too.'' He dropped his eyes as he thought for a moment then raised his face again. ''Did you find out anything about what I asked you?''

''You mean who other than the F.B.I. knew about what the psycho did? That's anybody's guess the way people talk. But, officially, a couple of medical examiners and the sheriff in each of the affected counties.''

CHAPTER 36

Paige's steps echoed ahead of her down the tiled hallway. No one was at the reception desk in the alcove off to the right of the corridor and she went on past the desk to the next door.

Her father sat at the metal desk in his compact office, the room's only other furnishing a narrow, two-seat couch against the wall directly across from him. A short, slightly built man, his thin brown hair dropping across his forehead as he studied a folder open before him, he was dressed in a gray suit. He looked up when she stepped inside. "Hi, honey," he said.

"Daddy, you have a moment?"

He nodded, removing his glasses and closing the folder. "Sure."

She moved to the couch and sat on it, was silent a moment.

"Daddy, Brett used to date the woman who was murdered."

"Uh-huh. You told me."

She didn't remember when. Not since the murder. It could have been anytime in the past she was so jealous of Trinity. And now more so than ever. Of a dead woman. She took a deep breath and went on.

"Daddy, last night he told me that after we were engaged, she ran into him in a place over here. He said that they talked for a while and then drove out to Back Bay and parked."

She looked, but there was only the slightest tensing of her father's eyes. She should have expected so little of a reaction—at least right at first. That was the way he was. As impetuous as she was, he was fanatically the other way. He didn't do anything without thinking, and thinking for a long time. She could remember once when he was angry at a company he was doing business with and he wrote them a nasty letter. Even then, as upset with them as he was, he filed the letter in his drawer overnight—to think about what it said. Then he never sent it. She looked at him. He had said something as she had reflected. "What?"

"Go ahead, I'm listening," he repeated.

She nodded. "Yeah. Brett said that they didn't do any more than talk after they were there. But whether or not they did or didn't, it's making me feel terrible that he went out there with her."

Her father sat forward, propping his elbows on his desk and steepling his hands off to a side of his face as he began speaking.

"If he did more than just talk, what would you want to do?"

"I don't want to do anything, Daddy. I want to trust him."

"Then trust him."

"I'm just supposed to forget about it?"

"That won't happen. But if you make it a point to not dwell on it, it'll eventually fade away."

"What about later, when he's out somewhere and tells me something came up and he couldn't get back to the house when he was supposed to? Then I'm going to wonder again—not just accept it like I used to."

"He made a mistake, Paige. But he's a good person. I told you that when you first said you wanted to marry him, and I still believe he is. Whatever did or didn't happen, he loves you deeply. You have the kind of marriage that doesn't come along all that often. You want to keep it that way, then you'll let what he did, whatever it was, fade away. If you don't, if you let it keep eating at you, then you might as well divorce Brett now. There isn't such a thing as a happy marriage without trust. It's not possible."

"I know. But how do I forget—let it fade away?"

"It'll come. You just have to let it."

She had hoped he would have been able to magically reassure her like he had done when she came to him with a problem as a child, relieve her mind in a way where she could go away happy. But he hadn't. How do you trust someone who lied to you? Forgive—yes. Go on to other things—yes. But forget, *how*? And how was she to purge from her mind the thought that Brett still hadn't told her the whole truth—all that had gone on that night? *Just to drive out there to talk*. She shook her head.

"It'll come, baby," her father said. "Over time it'll come. You just have to let it."

Applewhite leaned back in his chair, thinking.

"It doesn't mean anything that Dunnigan brought the woman in to Seales," the older agent standing in front of the desk said. "He knew we were aware of her. What else could he do?"

The younger agent was standing near the door. "He did tell the chief he'd take a polygraph," he said.

Applewhite shook his head. "The bottom line is I still don't think he had the time," he said. He picked up the time log and looked at it again. "According to the dispatcher, he wasn't out of pocket for more than a half hour or so any way you stretch it. I can't see that being enough time to kill her, carry her husband to the pool, get cleaned up, and meet his wife at their house. But we'll take him up on his offer, anyway. Tell Seales to set the polygraph for tomorrow. And then get back to me with the time. I want to be there."

After Paige and her mother finished shopping they joined her father for dinner at Antonio's. "Better late than never," he had said when he insisted they go to the spot where the celebration was originally scheduled. Paige looked out of the windows at the lights of small boats moving on the water. Though it was night, it was finally clear and the storm front that had produced the rains of the last couple of days now moved on inland.

Her mother quit picking at her plate and laid her fork down. "Doesn't it just scare you to death," she asked, "knowing there's a murderer out there?"

"Mother, there's somebody murdered every day somewhere."

"Not by that kind of person, Paige, and not where you live. Working where you do is the only thing I liked about you being a cop—a policewoman."

"Honey," her father said, removing his glasses as he looked across the table at her. "Whoever the killer is, he went to a lot of thought in trying to make it look like the psychopath. He might be crazy, but he's cunning, too. I want you to be careful. I know how you are when you get something on your mind."

"Daddy, you sound like Brett. I told him that since the man Trinity met said he would be ruined if his stepping out got back to the area, that maybe we should be thinking about an elected official. Who but somebody like that, a person who would have to face the voters, could be ruined? I told Brett I wished there was some way I could look inside each of their houses."

"Lord, honey," her mother said. "What do you think you would find?"

"Nothing, possibly. I'd just like to look. We got a chance yesterday to go inside the mayor's house."

When she noticed her father's brow wrinkle, she smiled. "Legally, Daddy. There were some men moving furniture there and we checked to make sure they were supposed to be there . . . Your look reminded me of Brett. He thinks I'm so wild I might try and do something like that on my own."

"Well, that's not a very supportive husband," her mother said, "to not give you any more credit than that. . . . You wouldn't, would you?"

Paige smiled. "And you wonder why Brett might think something like that? No, I'm not that crazy, Mother."

The waiter set the carry-out box containing the shrimp she had ordered for Brett's dinner in front of her, and she smiled her thanks.

Her mother rose from the table. "You need to freshen up?" she asked.

Paige shook her head.

As her mother moved away from the table, her father laid his fork in his plate and spoke.

"You thought any more about it, honey?"

"I believe Brett, Daddy. At least about nothing happening. I did before I came over to talk to you today. It just made me so angry—so jealous."

He smiled. "I didn't say you shouldn't make his life miserable for a little while."

She smiled.

*   *   *

An hour later she had taken her parents home and was nearly back to her house. As she passed through the center of town, she saw no sign of Brett's car. She recalled its vibrating brakes and reminded herself to make sure he got them fixed—they could go all the way out on him. She thought about stopping and having Martha call him about the shrimp she had brought, but it was only an hour until his shift ended and she decided to wait.

Once home, she went to the kitchen where she placed the shrimp in the refrigerator, then stood there a moment staring at the box, thinking of him. *Forget about it. How?*

Lost in her thought, she didn't really hear, but rather sensed the movement behind her. She whirled around.

The ceiling light glinted off the heavy lead pipe as it flashed down hard into her forehead. She crumpled backward to the floor. The figure moved over her, straddling her with his feet and staring down at her.

CHAPTER 37

Brett's car vibrated to a stop behind Paige's and he walked to the front door. The lock was contrary again and it took him a few seconds before he could get it to work.

Inside, he shut the door and engaged the deadbolt, something he had started doing since Trinity's murder. He walked into the living room.

"Paige," he called.

There was no answer.

"Paige."

He stood a moment, listening, then walked toward the hall off the right of the living room.

At their bedroom door, he glanced inside. The ceiling light was off and the bathroom on the right was dark.

Going back through the living room, he moved to the rear door and looked out into the small fenced backyard. The tool shed where Paige sometimes stored things was dark. Sitting next to it was the old, rusted swing set she had bought from a family moving out of town. She was going to fix it up like new, she said, after they had children. He smiled, shut the door, leaned against it for a few seconds, then walked to the wall telephone in the kitchen and punched in a number.

There were three rings before a sleepy voice answered.

"Waymon, this is Brett. Paige didn't walk over there, did she?"

"No, Brett."

"Sorry to bother you. I just got back to the house and she wasn't in. I was wondering if maybe she went next door."

"No, not in this direction, anyway. You all come up with any leads on the murderer yet?"

"Not yet. But we will. Sorry again to bother you."

He rang the Jacksons, the neighbors on the other side of the house. They were a much older couple, but Paige sometimes visited with them.

There were four rings before an answering machine came on. He replaced the receiver.

Somebody came by and she ran somewhere with them for a moment. He remembered the dinner she was going to bring him. He walked to the refrigerator, opened it, lifted out the carry-out carton, glanced at the shrimp, then took a bottle of the root beer from the refrigerator and moved to the microwave over the stove.

Out in the backyard, the door to the toolshed cracked open and a figure peered outside. Brett could be seen at the table in the kitchen. The figure stepped from the shed and hurried past the swing set toward the side of the house.

At the back of Brett's unmarked car, the figure worked with the trunk latch for a moment and it sprang open.

Fifteen minutes later and finished eating, Brett's concern had grown to the point where he had begun to be irritated. If she was going to be gone this long, she should have called so he wouldn't worry. He moved into the living room and began watching television.

Several minutes later, after glancing over his shoulder toward the front door for the twentieth time, he reached for the telephone next to his chair.

After two rings, the dispatcher answered.

"Martha, this is Brett. Has Paige called down there?"

"No, Brett, haven't heard from her."

He punched in Dr. Little's number. Paige's mother answered on the second ring.

"Sorry to bother you so late, but you haven't heard from Paige, have you?"

"She's not there?"

"No, ma'am, she—"

"Have you called the highway patrol?" Mrs. Little asked anxiously.

"No. Her car's in the garage. She's gone with somebody. I thought maybe she might have called over there and told you who."

"Be sure and let us know when she does come in, Brett; we'll be worrying."

"Yes, ma'am."

"Promise?"

"Yes, ma'am."

As he replaced the receiver he felt a nervous sensation in his stomach. She *would* have called by now. He quickly rang the police department again.

"Martha, contact the shift officers and tell them to get on over to my house."

"Paige?"

"She hasn't come back yet. It's starting to bother me."

By midnight, a dozen officers, half of them off duty and in their civilian clothes, had arrived at the house. Every door in the neighborhood had already had its door knocked on. Seales was standing by the telephone and answered it when it rang.

"Hello. No, this is Chief Seales . . . Just a minute." He held the phone toward Brett.

"What's going on, Brett?" Dr. Little said in a low voice.

"I don't know, sir. She's not back yet."

"Why is the police chief there?"

"I called the station and told them about Paige. It's going to embarrass me when she walks in, but—"

"I'll be there as soon as I can." The receiver was placed down hard.

Seales had opened the door and spoken to an officer standing just outside the house. In a moment he shut the door and came across the carpet.

"I told them to start searching the yards around the nearby houses, Brett."

By one, the search had expanded to a several-block circle around the house. Dr. Little and his wife sat nervously on the couch.

Applewhite walked through the front door and went toward Chief Seales, who was standing near a far wall as he talked to Arnie. A moment later, Vic entered the house. He came across the carpet.

"Don't worry about it, buddy," he said. "It's going to turn out that Paige—"

"I'm not in the mood for bullshit, Vic." Brett immediately regretted his words. "I'm sorry."

Vic patted him on his shoulder. In a moment, Applewhite walked to the front door and two agents standing there. The three of them moved out into the yard.

Vic nodded toward a chair off to the side of the couch. "Buddy, why don't you give your legs a rest."

"Vic, she found out something."

"No, that's not it, buddy. It couldn't be. When did she have the time? She just drove back here from eating with her parents."

"I don't know how, but she found out something."

"What did you say?" Dr. Little asked nervously from the couch. Mrs. Little's face was absolutely pale. "Oh, Lord help us," she exclaimed.

Her husband slipped his arms around her shoulders and spoke softly to her. She nodded.

"Brett," he said. "She would like to lie down."

Brett nodded. "Sure. It will be quieter in the back bedroom."

The couple stood and walked toward the hallway. Brett watched after them for a moment, then shook his head in exasperation. "Vic, I can't just sit here. I can't do that. I'm going to at least drive around—look."

"Sheriff Hastings has all his deputies out looking and the highway patrol's blocking all the roads. There's nothing else to do."

Nothing else to do. Brett wanted to yell out, curse, hit something, somebody. He was angry, full of hate for a person he didn't know—and scared worse than he'd ever been in his life.

Mrs. Little's scream came from the bedroom.

They rushed toward the door.

She had dropped the pillow and was staring at the bed. Where the pillow had lain across it was the cardboard sign, the word "surprise" written at its top and the number 2 in a big red numeral in its middle.

*   *   *

Seales stepped outside and walked to where Brett stood near the edge of the street in front of his house.

"We have everyone out looking," Seales said. "Hastings's deputies and the highway patrol have roadblocks everywhere." He shook his head helplessly. "I don't know what else to do."

Brett, scared that if he tried to speak his voice would break, nodded. Vic stepped up beside him.

Brett shook his head and forced his voice clear. "It's about who killed Trinity. Paige found out something—something."

"No, you would know if she had."

"Something, Vic. Or maybe he *thought* she found out something. She was always thinking out loud about it. We don't know who he is, she could have said something to him. He came after her to keep her quiet."

Applewhite and an agent with him were at the side of Paige's Maxima in the garage. They opened the doors and looked inside it. The young agent reached around the steering wheel and removed the keys. They moved to the trunk and opened it.

Brett's stomach suddenly tightened and he said a quick prayer.

The two men looked inside the trunk, then shut it. The young agent walked toward the street.

"Lieutenant Dunnigan," he said, "do you have your car keys?"

Brett glanced across his shoulder toward Applewhite, looked back at the agent for a moment, then reached into his pocket and produced them.

The agent moved back toward the rear of the unmarked Ford. In a moment, the trunk was open.

"Brett!" Applewhite called. "Could you come here for a moment?"

As Brett walked up to the rear of the car, the younger agent stepped away toward the house.

"I would never have believed it," Applewhite said and looked inside the still-opened trunk.

Brett leaned slightly to the side to see what he referred to.

Even in the dim illumination of the trunk light, the sheen off the dark spot in the corner was unmistakable. He felt his heart stop.

Applewhite said, "Lift your hands out away from your sides."

Still staring into the trunk, Brett shook his head in confused shock.

"That's impossible. It's—" He felt the cold steel of the younger agent's automatic against his back.

"I said, move your hands out, Brett," Applewhite repeated.

Brett looked at the agent. Almost in a daze, he spread his arms and slowly raised them over his head. His automatic was stripped from its holster by the agent behind him.

Vic's voice was sharp as he hurried up to them. "What in hell's going on?"

"Back out of this, McIntyre," Applewhite said sharply. He looked back at Brett. "You have anything to say?"

Brett only stared into the trunk.

"Read him his rights and take him to the car."

Brett looked back at the blocky man and forced his words through a constricted throat. "I want the blood typed. Paige is AB."

The agent behind Brett jabbed him with the barrel of his pistol. "Put your hands behind you."

When Brett did, a pair of handcuffs were quickly snapped into place.

"Somebody's set you up," Vic said. "You didn't hear anything, see anything out here?"

Brett could only shake his head.

Applewhite sneered in disgust. He had seen others go speechless when they were caught, go pale, get sick at their stomachs. Tough guys, murderers, drug pushers with no care about who they destroyed, and then they suddenly became weak-kneed and scared to tears when they finally had to face what they had done. They were all cowards when it really came down to it; he had never seen one who wasn't.

CHAPTER 38

Brett, absent his shoelaces and belt, stared straight ahead at the wall until the older officer in the booking room at the police station spoke for a second time.

"Brett, please, I have to do this."

Brett looked in the man's eyes and nodded. He lifted his hands and allowed his fingers, one at a time, to be rolled against the ink pad and moved to the card. He was handed a rag and he wiped his hands. The officer put the cuffs back on him.

"I not only want him in a cell by himself when you get him to the jail," Applewhite said to the officer, "I don't want anybody on either side of him."

"That's the sheriff's business," the officer said, not in a particularly friendly tone. He looked at Seales. "You want him in a holding cell until the deputies get here?"

Seales nodded.

The young F.B.I. agent beside Brett grasped him by the elbow and turned him toward the door of the small cement-block enclosure built into the wall. Seales and Applewhite moved down the hall. Arnie opened the door to the cell. Brett was pressured forward by the agent's hand at his back.

He looked at Arnie. Arnie dropped his eyes and looked at the floor.

Paige only had two days, just two days.

He glanced over his shoulder at the F.B.I. agent, then back at the older officer, then Arnie again.

Two days.

He knew he had only one chance, and only for a brief second at best. He suddenly turned sidewise into Arnie and grabbed quickly for the butt of his pistol, fumbling at the same time with the safety strap.

"What are—"

Brett jerked the weapon from its holster, jumped sidewise to avoid the agent's grasp—and cocked the revolver, pointing it out around his side.

The agent froze. Arnie, wide-eyed, was backing away. The older officer stared expressionless.

The agent shook his head. "You're a fool, Dunnigan," he said.

"Lift your hands out away from your coat and get them above your head."

The agent slowly raised his arms.

"Arnie, get his pistol."

Arnie started to reach under the agent's coat.

"Use your left hand, Arnie. And keep your back to me."

Arnie reached inside the agent's coat and pulled the automatic out of its holster.

"Lay it on the floor now, quietly."

Arnie bent and did as he was told.

Brett looked at the agent and the jailer. "Turn around."

As they did, he looked at Arnie. "Get the handcuff key."

Arnie faced toward the agent. "In my left pocket," the man said.

In a moment, Arnie held the key in his hand.

Brett glanced down the hallway, then stepped forward and awkwardly pushed the revolver out to his side, pressing the barrel into Arnie's stomach. "Reach around me—slowly—and undo the cuffs."

His hands trembling, his arms reaching, Arnie took a few seconds inserting the key, then turned it. A cuff fell away from Brett's wrist and he jerked his hands around in front of him. He took the key from Arnie and undid the other cuff. "Handcuff them back to back."

As Arnie used his handcuffs and the F.B.I. agent's to secure the men, Brett kept glancing down the hall in the direction Seales and Applewhite had walked.

"Hurry, dammit, Arnie."

When Arnie had finished handcuffing the two, Brett pointed them toward the floor. They bent their legs and sank awkwardly back to back toward the concrete, losing their balance and sitting down hard.

He stared coldly at them, hoping they would remain silent. There was a second hall leading toward the back of the station. He pushed Arnie toward it.

"When we go through the door, we're going fast, Arnie. If you can't keep up, you're in trouble."

Arnie nodded nervously, then said in a trembling voice, "I didn't think you did it."

"I didn't."

The young agent yelled for help. Brett pushed the door open. He grabbed Arnie by the shoulder and threw him toward the landing, then came behind him, pushing him down the stairs. He heard the F.B.I. agent yell again. Arnie stepped awkwardly, screamed and fell, and Brett tumbled over him.

He rolled and came to his feet. "Come on, dammit!"

Arnie was holding his ankle, his eyes wide as he stared up at Brett. "I can't."

Brett glanced at the front corner of the building and the street just beyond it, looked back at Arnie, then turned and ran toward the street fifty feet away. As he did, a faded gray pickup truck with one headlight came along the pavement. He dashed in front of it and waved his arms.

The truck skidded to a stop and he ran around the side and threw open the door. An old, slenderly built black man stared wide-eyed at the revolver.

Brett grabbed him by the shoulder of his coveralls and dragged him outside the vehicle.

The back door of the station house flew open and Applewhite lunged outside onto the landing and raised his automatic.

Brett ducked into the truck as the first bullet was fired. The old man dove toward the pavement.

Brett slammed the door, jamming his foot on the accelerator at the same time.

The wheels of the pickup shrieked, caught against the rough surface, and the vehicle jumped forward as Applewhite fired three more shots.

Brett sped down the street. Nearing an intersection a hundred and fifty yards away, he didn't slow, but jerked the wheel hard to the right and took the turn so sharp the pickup tilted up to the left, then slammed back down on the street. Its accelerator pressed to the floor, it roared loudly ahead.

A half mile farther, Brett made another screeching turn, and in seconds was heading toward the swamps to the north of town. He glanced into the rearview mirror and saw the first sign of blue flashing lights behind him, two sets, racing side by side, closing, gaining ground on the pickup.

The lowlands were just ahead. Brett waited until the last moment, jammed on the pickup's brakes, and cut the wheel hard to the right.

The vehicle momentarily tilted up on its wheels, then slammed back down and bounced to a stop.

He threw open the door, raced down the bank, and jumped wildly out into the swamp. Splashing water in front of him, he hurried as fast as he could into the swamp grass.

The two patrol cars, their lights flashing brilliantly, slid sideways on the road and stopped. The officers were outside of the cars immediately and running to the edge of the bank.

Applewhite lowered his automatic. He didn't have anything to shoot at. The sound of a night creature came shrill and high-pitched from the darkness.

CHAPTER 39

Brett sloshed through water only knee-deep, but was so exhausted he was unable to move much faster than he had when in the deeper water stretching out a quarter mile behind him. Gasping, he threw himself onto a partially submerged log. It was nearly a minute before he could slow his breathing enough to listen. There was no sound behind him.

He pushed up from the log and, still breathing deeply, looked around, trying to get his directions.

His knee ached. He reached to rub it and felt a gash. In the distance, he heard the faint thumping sound of a helicopter. He threw his remaining sock to the side, stepped over the log, and moved deeper into the swamp.

Applewhite drummed his fingers impatiently on his desk as he watched the sheriff talking on the telephone to the governor.

"Brett knows the swamp like the back of his hand," Hastings said into the receiver. "We have a huge area where he can come out at any spot. He gets to a car and he could be five, six states away from here in no time."

He was silent a moment, listening.

"Yes, sir. We've got roadblocks set up on every highway close to it."

He listened again. "Yes, sir. We'll have both men and dogs in there in a few minutes—at first light."

He glanced at Seales and shook his head, then spoke back into the telephone again.

"Yes, sir. I understand. . . . Yes, sir. I'll keep you informed."

He replaced the receiver. "Governor said he feels calling out a National Guard unit might be overdoing it a little—you know he isn't the serial killer. He said he'd think about it, though."

Applewhite slammed his palms against the desktop. "Think about it!" he exclaimed. "What in the hell's there to think about?"

Hastings stared at the agent for a moment. "Jerry, I told you I'd call the governor and suggest he give us some help, but I kind of agree with what he said. If Brett stays in the swamp, we're going to get him. If he comes out, I can't see him getting past the roadblocks."

Applewhite shook his head in irritation. "Hell, I could hide in there and you'd walk right past me. How many men do we have, fifty or sixty, to search it? Hell, we need the National Guard and anybody else we can muster. You people down here— Yes, sir, Governor sir, if you don't mind thinking about it, sir; we'd appreciate what help you could give us, sir. Crap!"

The thump, thump, thump, of the blades could be heard long before the slowly moving helicopter moved into view above the tops of the thick cottonwoods and willows. Brett crouched low in a clump of bushes as the brilliant light passed over him and moved slowly deeper into the swamp.

Rising to his feet, he stared up through the top of the trees toward the faint yellow glow in the sky. The sun was beginning to rise. They would be starting into the swamp now, the men and their dogs. And not F.B.I. agents from New Jersey, but bearded guys in camouflage jackets, men who by the time they had finished high school had been in the swamp a thousand times, fishing, deer hunting, trapping, and shooting ducks, men who knew the swamps as well as he did, who knew where the deep water was and where there were submerged ridges that could be walked on, who knew where a man should be after he had entered at a certain spot, and where he couldn't be. Under any other conditions he would be moving into the swamp with them, confident in the knowledge they were going to get who they were going in after. He took a deep breath and started sloshing toward the river whose back waters helped create the swamp.

Applewhite stepped out of his car before the agent driving it brought it to a complete stop. He hurried across the lawn and around the side of Brett's home.

Two agents walked toward him from the toolshed. The younger one held up a long plastic envelope containing a crowbar.

"You sure there's blood on it?" Applewhite asked.

"Ninety-nine percent certain," the agent said. "It's been wiped clean, but there's still traces. Only thing now, is it the Anderson woman's blood or his wife's?"

Sheriff Hastings parked his car and walked to them. He looked at the crowbar. "I'll have a deputy take it over to the lab," he said.

Applewhite glanced at the young deputy next to Hastings. He was about Brett's age, probably had known him all his life. He thought a moment and shook his head. "No, my agents can take it there."

Hastings's face tightened. "What did you say, Jerry?"

"I said I'd have one of my agents take it to the lab."

"No, Jerry. We'll do like I said."

"What?"

"Looks like we might be busy the next couple of days," Hastings said, "until we run Brett down. Meanwhile, I guess you're right, maybe it's time to be cutting out this yes, sir, and trying to keep everything on a polite level. Fact of the matter is, we're not in New Jersey and you're not running the show here. I am. I'll be the one who decides who takes what, where and when. If you've got a suggestion, I'll be glad to listen, but it'll be just that, a suggestion." He looked across his shoulder to the deputy. "Carswell, get the crowbar on over to the lab and tell them I want to know if it's blood for sure, and what type it is if it is blood."

He started back toward his car. Carswell stepped forward and took the plastic envelope from the young agent before following after the sheriff. Applewhite's cheeks flushed red.

Brett, shivering from the continued exposure to the water, stood submerged to his waist in the last stand of swamp grass before a clear expanse of the bayou. Through the tall oaks on the far bank, the sky was now a faint yellow, and brightening. Hours gone already. The cardboard sign that had been left under the pillow had a "2" on it. Please at least let her have that long. Don't let her already be—

His lip trembled and he stepped forward, looked a last time at the swift current racing before him, much stronger than usual due to the heavy rains of the last two days. A floating log swept down the center of the channel. An eddy strengthened into a several-foot-wide whirlpool and then was gone. A willow twisted before him, sunk from sight, and then jumped back into view. He stepped forward, was caught by the current and swept downstream as he breaststroked hard for the opposite bank.

Near the center of the bayou, the current ran against him like a fire hose, rolling him, moving him even faster downstream and toward a fishing camp on the far bank.

Beginning to gasp with his effort, he fought to make headway across the channel and drew closer to the other bank. The current began to lessen. He stroked harder, grabbed for the short dock of two-by-four planking supported by fifty-five-gallon drums, caught its edge, and hung on.

There were two small, aluminum, flat-bottom fishing boats there, tethered by short links of chain padlocked to the two-by-fours.

Still having to pull against the current, he moved alongside one of the craft taut against its chain. The links were looped through the carrying handle at the blunt bow of the boat, then threaded through an eyelet nailed into the side of a two-by-four lashed to the top of the drums.

He gripped the chain in front of the eyelet and pulled first in one direction and then the other. The nails gave ever so slightly and he tugged with all of his might.

The eyelet popped loose, his elbow flying back and hitting against the bow of the boat, making a booming sound. He froze, his gaze on the cabin at the foot of the docks as the boat slowly, then faster, glided away from the bank.

The front door of the cabin opened. A stocky, partially balding man, his stomach bulging over his boxer shorts, stepped outside.

He took a final drag off a glowing cigarette butt and flipped it out toward the water.

His eyes narrowed at the shadowy shape out in the center of the channel—a boat. He looked quickly back to his dock and saw the empty berth.

Brett lifted himself out of the water and rolled over into the boat.

A shout came from the bank and he looked back at the fat man in his underwear running toward the end of the dock.

Brett reached to the Evinrude motor and pulled the starter handle. The motor coughed. He pulled the handle again and the motor came to life.

He cut the steering handle to the left, straightened the boat in the middle of the channel, and opened the throttle wide. The man ran back toward his cabin.

CHAPTER 40

The Harrison County sheriff's department cruiser came to a sliding stop on the narrow bridge and a pair of deputies carrying shotguns hopped outside. They went to the rail and looked upstream.

"He hasn't had time to make it this far yet," the young deputy said.

The older deputy spat out into the water and leaned forward over the rail. "I've known him since he played football at the high school," he said. "I never would have figured him for this."

With the current's help, the Evinrude motor, though small, carried the light aluminum boat at nearly thirty miles an hour; Brett's dark hair whipped wildly in the wind.

He glanced into the brightening sky and back down the mist-shrouded channel, still enveloped in a shadowy darkness from the tall trees on the bank blocking the sunlight, and he didn't see the nearly completely submerged log.

The bow of the boat hit with force, bounced high, and tilted to the right. The motor roared as it left the water. The front of the boat, revolving to the right, crashed back into the bayou, the bow immediately submerging; Brett went flying through the air.

The older deputy on the bridge cocked his head. "Did you hear anything?"

The young deputy shook his head. "No, didn't."

"Thought I heard a motor," the older deputy said. He cocked his head to the other side for a moment, then relaxed and spat again out over the rail into the swift, swollen brown water below.

"No, don't guess so."

Brett, soaked and shivering, knelt in the bushes at the side of the dirt road not far from the bayou. He looked at the small, tin-roofed cabin on the slight rise just ahead. An old brown pickup was parked in front of the structure. Smoke came from the cabin's chimney. Whoever was there was cooking breakfast. Brett stepped out on the road and hurried toward the pickup, his bare feet leaving tracks in the damp soil.

The key was in the ignition. He released the emergency brake and moved the gears into neutral. He began pushing at the side of the truck.

Its deadweight held for a moment, then the wheels gradually began turning. He reached for the steering wheel and guided the truck out into the middle of the road.

Forty feet farther and the road dropped off in a gentle downward slope. The wheels of the truck began to turn faster, and Brett, still pushing, began to trot.

A hundred feet more and the road leveled out again. The truck began to slow. Finally, he was having to push once more. His feet kept slipping. Another gentle rise started and he could make it no farther.

He slipped into the cab, glanced back through the rear window at the cabin, and turned the key.

The motor coughed, then ran gently, quietly. He depressed the clutch and dropped the gearshift into low, slowly pressing down on the accelerator.

In minutes, he came to a bridge crossing the deep, rain-swollen bayou. He stopped the pickup, backed it a hundred feet down the road, and dropped the gear into drive again, leaving his door open as he slowly depressed the accelerator.

The pickup was traveling about twenty miles an hour when he pulled the steering wheel over hard and guided it past the side of the bridge, waited for the truck to almost reach the water, then jumped out and hit the ground, rolling.

The rear of the pickup barely cleared the edge of the bank before the nose of the vehicle tilted downward into the bayou with a great splash.

He walked to the edge of the bank and stared until the truck, moving downstream with the current, had sunk from view. He hurried into the thick pines on the opposite side of the road.

It was almost double the distance he had estimated to the narrow blacktop road on the far side of the pines, and he was breathing hard by the time he reached it. He looked down at the pants of his uniform, which were torn in places by the thorn thickets he had not taken time to go around. He had something stuck in the sole of his foot.

He looked up the road to the service station on the left. It was still deserted, though a sliver of the sun was now peeking above the tops of the pines across the road. He ran toward it.

In the telephone booth, uncomfortably exposed out near the blacktop and worried about the men who would soon be there to open the station, he quickly punched in a number. A rabbit stared at him for a moment, then went back to eating clover growing by the edge of the woods.

"Highway patrol."

"Uh, I got a—I got somethin' to report."

"Yes, sir."

"That Brett Dunnigan fella that 'scaped from jail."

"Yes, go ahead."

"Well, I, uh . . . I seen him a while ago."

"Who is this, please?"

"I gotta live 'round here and there's a bunch of folks not believin' this stuff 'bout him. Not gonna be givin' my name out."

"Where did you see him?"

"Out on 49. Just as bold as you please, gettin' gas at the fillin' station. He was in an old brown pickup. Went north."

"A brown pickup—what year?"

"I's in such a shock when I up and seen him, I'd be lyin' iffen I said I caught the year. Just an old one, right smart of rust on it. Got the license number, though—1FFS913."

"Would you repeat that, please?"

"1FFS913."

"You said he was going north?"

Brett replaced the receiver, waited a moment, and began punching in another number. He had no change and was having to use his credit card number each time, but who would know that for another month?

The telephone rang and Fred Adkins rose from the table and the stack of pancakes in front of him and walked to the telephone hanging on the wall in the kitchen.

"Yeah."

"Is this Mr. Adkins?"

"Yeah."

"This is the highway patrol. Do you have a Ford pickup registered to you, license plate number 1FFS913?"

"Yeah, do. Why?"

"We just received a report that it was stolen."

"Not none of mine it ain't, it's parked outside." He leaned to his side and glanced through the front kitchen window. His brow wrinkled.

"Wait a damn minute! Let me look here."

Letting the receiver dangle from the telephone, he walked to the window and stared out it. He looked to his left and to his right, then turned and hurried back to the telephone.

Applewhite stood at the window when the telephone on the sheriff's desk rang. Hastings answered it. In a few moments, he replaced the receiver and came to his feet.

"He stole a pickup and got out to 49, going north toward Hattiesburg."

Hastings walked to the door and leaned out into the hall, calling to the department dispatcher.

"Notify the men in the swamp that they can come on in. It's the highway patrol's baby now; Brett's headed north toward Hattiesburg. Call Seales and let him know about it, too. He might as well let all but his regular shift call it a day."

CHAPTER 41

"McIntyre Security."

"Vic."

"Brett. Where in the hell are you?"

"I'm going to need some help."

"What did you run for? In a couple of days, we'd been able to prove somebody set you up."

"I haven't got a couple of days; I have to find Paige now."

There was silence on the line.

"Vic?"

"Brett, how do you think you're going to find Paige? Buddy, you're going to have—"

"No, remember the other victim? They weren't killed until the days written on the cardboard ran out."

Vic spoke in a low voice. "Buddy, listen, this isn't the serial killer—he's dead, remember. You're not doing yourself any good being on the run."

"She found out something, Vic. She saw something. I have to find out what it was. I need your help." The sound of a motor came through the air. His muscles tensed and he stared down the blacktop.

He heard it again, the sound coming from deep in the woods. A bulldozer. A logging crew somewhere. He lifted the receiver back to his ear.

"Brett?" Vic was saying.

"Yeah, Vic."

"Brett, you're not thinking straight. Listen to me. Paige came straight from eating with her father and mother; when did she have time to see something?"

"Somebody thought she saw something."

"Brett, you need to—"

"Are you going to help me or not?"

"To do what?"

"You can get me a car. A nondescript one that won't draw any attention. Some clothes, sunglasses, whatever you think I need to get back into town and not be recognized."

"Brett, I . . . Damn, Brett, I'd laugh at that if it wasn't so crazy. Sunglasses! You wouldn't make it five minutes. What are you going to do back there, anyway?"

"I told you. She found something. I have to find out what."

"Okay, so if she did, you don't know what it is. How do you find something when you don't even know what it is you're looking for?"

"Dammit, Vic!"

"I can get you some money, get you to Mobile. You can stay there for a few days until we think what to do next. God, this is crazy, Brett. You really need to turn yourself in. You can take a polygraph. Seales told me he already had one scheduled about Trinity."

"Vic, they aren't going to give me a polygraph now. The prosecution wouldn't allow it, not where it would be admissible anyway. Not now, not with me charged with Paige's mur— Not with them thinking I'm responsible for Paige."

"We could get the judge to let you out on bail. Then you can look for whatever it is you're wanting to."

"No. Paige hasn't got that much time left. I've got to look now." He glanced back over his shoulder at a pickup coming slowly up the road. He hurried his words. "Vic, I'm asking you for the last—"

"Okay, buddy, where are you?"

Vic replaced the receiver and stood in thought for a moment then hurried from his office to his car.

Ten minutes later, he drove into the parking lot of the apartment complex where he lived. When he stepped inside the front door, he saw the ironing board and the pile of clothes in the small dining area off the living room. The television screen was angled in that direction and blaring. His wife was there. He shut his eyes in exasperation. *Damn!* "Peggy?"

She stepped from the hallway. "Hey, honey," she said.

"What are you doing back home?"

"My boss had to fly to Chicago. He said take the rest of the day off. Like I really should. He left me so much typing I'll never catch up." She glanced at the television. "I've been watching the news about Brett. I'm not believing it."

"It's a mistake, Peggy. It'll all straighten out."

"A mistake?"

He moved on toward the hallway. "I haven't got time to explain now; I'm in a hurry—needed to pick up something."

"What?" she called after him.

"Just work stuff. You wouldn't understand if I told you."

She frowned and reached for the iron. Leaning, she picked up a pair of khakis and laid them across the board.

In their bedroom, Vic found a tote bag in the closet and quickly placed a pair of pants, a shirt, and a pair of tennis shoes in it, then hurried to the dresser.

When he came back through the living room, Peggy said, "You were with him last night—when they arrested him?"

"Yeah."

"What did—"

"I'll explain later." He walked toward the door.

"Will you be in tonight?"

He stopped with his hand on the doorknob and looked back at her. "Hell, Peggy, where else am I gonna be? Why always the questions? You like to eat, don't you? Well, in order for us to do that, I have to work to make a living, you know; it's not that I enjoy having to be out all night."

"Vic, all I want is for the two of us to . . ." The door closed and he was gone. She stared at the door, then dropped her eyes to her wedding band. After a moment, she twisted it off and laid it on the ironing board. She moved to the hall closet and lifted out a suitcase, stared at it for a second, and walked toward the bedroom.

* * *

Traffic backed up for a mile on 49 north.

"What's goin' on?" one old man asked as he stuck his head out the driver's window. The highway patrol officer stepped to the side of the car, glanced inside the front seat, then onto the floorboard of the rear seat.

"Sorry, sir, we're looking for an escapee. Would you step out of your car and let me have your keys please?"

"What for?"

"We have to look in your trunk."

The old man handed the keys out the window. "Look."

"You need to get out, sir, so you can see us when we open your trunk."

"I'm disabled."

The patrolman walked toward the trunk.

"Told you, Clyde," the old woman in the passenger seat said. "His name's Dunnigan. Local boy gone bad. More'n likely dope. You know, that started up North, was brought down here by Yankees moving South."

"Weren't no such a thing, Joyce."

"Yeah, were. And you shouldn't be lyin about bein' on disability, neither."

"Didn't say I was on it, said I was disabled."

"Same thing."

"Not any such thing."

"Is too. And a lie in any case."

Vic slowed as he passed the service station off to his left. A half mile farther he saw the rutted logging road and turned onto it. Following the edge of a wooded creekbank, he turned abruptly back to the right onto an even narrower road ending at a cattle gap into a large pasture. He stopped before the wire gate stretched across the spaced pipes of the gap.

A rabbit bolted out of a clump of bushes to the left and darted across the road in front of the car. A moment later, Brett, barefoot and with the pants of his uniform tattered, stepped from the same bushes and walked to the car.

"Thank you, Vic."

Vic stared up through his window. "What choice did you give

me, buddy? If I end up in jail, you better hope they don't put me in the same cell. I'll whip your ass daily."

He handed a Coke, two cans of Vienna sausage, and a pack of crackers out the window. "Only thing I could think of. Got you some clothes in the back."

Brett set the Coke and cans on top of the car and reached into the rear seat and lifted a shirt and pants from the tote bag. He glanced at his watch, then started hurriedly slipping on the clothes.

"Vic, she said she'd like to see inside everybody's house. That's a start."

"That's crazy, somebody keep something in their house that would show they're the killer."

"Crazy or not, I've only got two days, and I'm not going to do nothing."

"I told you, buddy, that sign doesn't mean shit. She's . . ." Vic shook his head and stared ahead through the windshield for a moment, then back out the window.

"Brett, since I talked to you, I've heard something else. They found a crowbar out in your toolshed and it had blood on it—AB blood."

Brett felt a sudden tightening in his stomach. *That still didn't mean* . . . "Still doesn't mean she's dead, Vic."

Vic nodded slowly. "Yeah, you're right. But what it also means is you're right about them not allowing you to take a polygraph now. I stopped by the bank, brought a little over twelve hundred dollars, about all the spare cash I had on hand. I can get you to Mobile and into some cheap apartment there. Give it a couple of weeks and let things cool off around here. Then I can come and get you and take you on down to Florida somewhere. Maybe by then something will happen to set all this straight. We'll at least have time to think."

Brett shook his head. "No." He finished buttoning his shirt. "I want you to go to the chancery clerk's office for me."

"To do what?"

"I've been thinking and it's the only thing I can come up with. Paige *might have* found a house she decided to check out, like if somebody in town had another place, a house out in the country, or a cabin on one of the bayous, maybe the Wolf River, someplace where something could be hidden—somebody's place."

"Which somebody?"

"It has to be a cop or an elected official."

Vic chuckled sarcastically as he looked up out the window. "Oh, that's all, huh? You really got it narrowed down, don't you? What do you have in town—twenty or so cops, and how many elected officials? Hell, you've got a couple of deputies who live there, too. Brett, you're—"

"Vic, I want you to check on every politician who lives there. But a regular cop's not going to be ruined by being caught stepping out on his wife. It'd have to be somebody prominent, the people in the area might get after them like they did Dr. Felter. The chief, elected or not, he could get in trouble."

"Seales?"

"Vic, he's the one who came back to the house and said the fingerprint was smeared. How do we know it was before he got there?"

"Come on, Brett."

"He's got a temper, too."

"Christ, buddy, not that kind of temper. He wouldn't hurt a—"

"What about the prisoner in New Orleans? Didn't he nearly beat him to death?"

"Damn, Brett. That was all media—and the thug's lawyer. Seales just kept from getting himself killed, that's all."

"He shot the psychopath, too, Vic; took a hell of a chance on hitting that little girl. How do we know Seales didn't shoot to silence him, make sure that he'd never tell that he hadn't killed Trinity?"

Vic didn't respond.

"And what about the mayor, Vic. He wouldn't want it getting out he'd been with Trinity, either. He married into the Fargo family. Old man Fargo has ranted and raved about obscenity and moral decay for the last twenty years, led groups picketing the TV stations and every place else you can think of. He's made all kinds of enemies, people who would like to tear him to pieces for what he's said about them. What if his son-in-law was stepping out, you don't think shit wouldn't hit the fan then? Vic, I know Paige noticed something, or at least somebody thought she did. That somebody lives right in town, saw her that day, and came after her."

Vic remained silent for a second, then shook his head. "Buddy, you're not talking straight. What kind of nut is going to have anything lying around his house, even a second house, that would jump up and bite him if somebody saw it?"

"The psychopath did, didn't he—the scrapbook?"

"We're talking about a crazy nut there—a maniac."

"You don't think somebody's crazy who would kill a woman to keep it quiet he'd had been out with her?"

"It's not the same, Brett."

Brett closed his eyes in exasperation. "I know that, dammit. But I can't just do nothing, just sit around and let two days pass. I've got to do something. I've got to try no matter how crazy it is. I want to know if anybody who could be the killer owns a place other than his house. Like I said, a cabin or shack someplace where he might not be worried about keeping something he didn't want anybody to know was there. Maybe . . . maybe even Paige is there now." He knew he wasn't thinking reasonably, and he didn't care.

CHAPTER 42

As Brett walked back into the bushes and disappeared down the side of the creekbank and Vic backed his car down the road, Randolph's dark eyes watched. He was ten. Peter watched, too. He was six.

When the car disappeared from view, the two skinny, dark-skinned boys stepped from the bushes and walked down the road to the spot where Brett had thrown his uniform into a patch of tall grass.

Reginald lifted the pants from the ground.

"An escaped con?" Peter asked. The county jail wasn't all that far away and Peter had a big imagination.

Reginald looked closely at the pants. They were the exact same kind of police uniform pants his uncle Armont wore.

He looked out the empty road then down the bank where the man had disappeared. If he could have heard the things nobody can, the walking of ants and the crawling of worms, he would have been able to hear the tears running down Brett's cheeks, and his heart beating too strongly at the thought of the crowbar—and two days.

"It was all right in front of our damn eyes," Applewhite growled as he threw the report onto Seales's desk. "Brett's been a cop for over five years and yet he didn't have enough sense but to go into the room at a murder scene. Not only go into the room but touch the body, knelt right down next to it and leaned over it and touched it. Hell, I read it and I just thought he was a stupid untrained redneck. But I see it now. If we found his fingerprints on the body, found a spot of blood on his uniform, found one of his hairs stuck to her body—he had the reason they were there. He was setting up the reason right then.''

"Brett's not the killer," Sergeant Green said.

Applewhite stared across the room at the big black man.

Green glared back, his jaw tight. "I know him," he said. "He didn't do it. I don't give a damn what it looks like. . . . Or what you think it looks like." There was a particular emphasis on his last words.

"Sergeant," Seales said. "You probably need to go on, I guess."

Green continued to stare at Applewhite for a few seconds, then turned and walked from the office.

Seales stared at the door and shook his head. "Hell, it's hard for me to believe it, too, even with the evidence."

Applewhite still stared at the door. "How many more cops you got like that, Chief? They see Dunnigan—are we going to know about it?"

"We'll know."

Radio and TV stations all along the coast were broadcasting constant updates on the search for Brett Dunnigan. At one television station the camera centered on a balding professor of criminology. In block letters across the screen under his face was the word EXPERT. He had just finished explaining what in Brett Dunnigan's background had shown he had a tendency to eventually commit a violent act—his unusual aggressiveness in sports while he was in high school; the accolades those sports had afforded him and then the feeling of worthlessness when that was over and he was no longer looked up to as a hero; even the fact that he sought employment as a police officer where he could carry a gun and wield authority. Add in the fact that he had sought out and married a woman with a handsome trust fund and, according to a well-placed source, was about to lose her and its money to divorce, everything was there to cause him to do what he had done.

As the camera's red light went off while a commercial aired, the attractive brunette in the chair across from the professor stared at him.

"All you did," she said, "was take background material we gave you and say it all led to the tendency."

"Something made him that way, didn't it?" the professor replied. "We're all a product of our environment, and that was his environment."

The red light came on and he immediately beamed and looked into the camera. He had told everybody he could think of that he was going to be on the program.

The camera caught a brief glimpse of the disgusted look on the anchorwoman's face. Then she put on a fixed smile and began asking questions again—and he drove his nails deeper.

Applewhite slammed the receiver back in place. "Nothing, not a damn sign of the pickup. Has the bastard gone around the roadblocks?" He stared up at the young agent standing in front of the desk. "Call Washington. I want his picture at every airport, bus depot, and cab station in the South. No, everywhere. The whole damn nation." He shook his head. "Where did he take her? He didn't have that much time between when she arrived at her house and when he called for officers to come out there. Is she alive or is she dead? He used the piece of cardboard to try and throw us off into thinking there is still a copycat out there. But he put a '2' on it. He knew the time of death could be determined. Did he take her to some place to kill her later? Where? Go on, get those pictures distributed."

The young agent handed over the report Applewhite had requested, then walked from the small office.

Applewhite opened the folder. It was as he thought. James Anderson had been hanging on to his job only by a thread. His drug habit wouldn't have allowed him to be there much longer, calling in sick almost every other day. It also looked like he was padding his expense account—some of the charges completely unfounded. Trinity Anderson hadn't been all that good a saleswoman, either. She didn't make a hell of a lot more than minimum wage according to her income tax form. They were going under—already were under. A perfect time for them to try a little blackmail. He threw the folder onto his desktop. *The trust fund*. Any way you looked at it, it came back to Paige's trust fund.

Seales appeared in the doorway. "Jerry, I've got somebody you need to meet."

As Seales came on into the room, a middle-aged, nice-looking man with wavy blond hair followed him inside. He was dressed in an expensive dark suit. A short, slightly younger, stocky brunette with short hair and in a print dress was behind him.

"H. Wayne Warren," Seales said, "this is F.B.I. Supervisory Special Agent Jerry Applewhite."

The man, obviously nervous, beads of perspiration dotting his forehead, nodded but didn't speak.

"And his sister," Seales added. "Mrs. Parret." The woman ignored the introduction, continuing to stare at her brother as the chief went on. "Or maybe I should introduce him as Hope-To-Be-Mayor Warren. Mr. Warren used to be a mayor of a small town north of here. He moved down here a year ago and has been running ever since—and the election's still two years off. It's a joke around town. And, guess what, they're the couple Trinity Anderson went by to see that night. The man she met in New Orleans."

Applewhite's eyes narrowed.

"Trinity came over to Mrs. Parret's house and confronted them," Seales said. "Mrs. Parret slapped her, told her that nobody was going to believe somebody like her brother would go out with a little whore like her. Said they'd run her out of town if she said anything about the relationship Trinity and her brother had."

Run them out of town, Applewhite thought, having a rare compassionate thought. Both Trinity and her husband were already down financially and the man might have been able to cost both of them their jobs—all they had left.

Seales continued. "Trinity told them that she had her friends, too, and they would see who ran who out of town."

Applewhite threw away his compassionate thought, and nodded slowly, knowingly. "Remember what Catherine Maddox said? The same thing. She said the Anderson woman remarked she had friends, too—but the exact words on the tape were *cops, too*. Anderson was referring to Brett. After she left this character's house, she had to have called Brett and told him what happened to her, asked him to help her. Or maybe she didn't call. Maybe she went to his house to see him. Either way she was angry, demanding he help her. He was afraid his wife would find out. Maybe there had already been a blackmail threat and maybe there hadn't. But if there was, then this just added to it. If there wasn't, it would still scare him. He became scared, panicked. Maybe she even threatened to expose him to his wife right then if he didn't help her. She had to be panicking, too, in the financial shape she and her husband were in. Brett could see divorce ahead now for sure. He had only been married a year and already screwing around. He could see himself kissing that two million plus good-bye. Greed and sex—damn near every premeditated murder committed is because of one of those two reasons—and he had both of them." He nodded at his own words and looked back at Seales.

"Chief, what happened then, is somehow his wife found out he had killed the Anderson woman. When that happened, he didn't have any choice but to kill her, too. You wait and see. When we catch the bastard, we're going to find that out." He thought again for a moment, then shook his head in disgust.

"And we're not going to find his wife alive. I was hoping maybe she was, but she's not. She's already dead and her body disposed of. He would've killed her rather than taken a chance on going back to wherever he would've put her. But with him still trying to leave the impression that a copycat's out there, he would've had to stick to the two days he put on the sign or at least make it where we couldn't tell when she died. That means he had to leave her body where it wouldn't be found until it decomposed. The swamp. Or maybe some— The river—weighted down? Where else? Chief, can you get Hastings to call the governor again? We need men to search every shack and patch of woods in a thirty-mile radius of here."

Seales nodded. "I'll tell Hastings and see what he says." As he showed Warren and his sister out of the office, the young F.B.I. agent came back through the doorway.

"What was all that about?" he asked.

Applewhite didn't answer right away. His eyebrows were knitted in thought. Finally, he raised his face.

"I haven't seen McIntyre around since Brett took off," he said.

242   CHARLES WILSON

"You'd think as good as friends as they are, he'd be here, concerned with what was happening. Have you seen him?"

The agent shook his head.

Applewhite stared at his desk a moment. "Call his office and see if he's there. If he's not call his home. If he's not there, ask his wife if she knows where he is."

The agent nodded. "What am I supposed to tell him if he is there?"

"Just make up something; I don't care. I just want to know where he is. If we can't find out, then I have a good idea where he might be—who he's with, anyway."

Randolph waited with his smaller brother outside the police station. When he saw Sergeant Green step outside, he walked toward him and his little brother followed.

"Uncle Armont."

The big man looked down at the boys and frowned. "You don't have school today?"

"Uncle Armont," Randolph said, "we was down at the creek close to the old Johnson place. I think we saw that man you all are huntin'."

Twenty minutes later, Sergeant Green stopped his patrol car a half mile from the cattle gap leading into the Johnson farm. He moved off the road to the edge of the creekbank and down it next to the shallow water, then walked slowly ahead.

Two hundred yards farther, he slowed his movements even more, and began carefully eyeing every clump of bushes he approached.

A few minutes later, he pulled his revolver from his holster. Beads of sweat glistened off his dark forehead.

Down in a clump of bushes just past an old crooked oak twisting out over the water, Reginald had said; *he's ahidin' there.* Green saw the tree and crouched, began covering the ground at a snail's pace.

He caught the movement to his right—too late. Brett smashed into him and the two rolled toward the edge of the creekbank. Brett was up first and grabbed the revolver from the ground.

Green stayed on his knees. "I know you didn't do it, Brett."

"Who came with you?"

"No one. I'm by myself."

Brett kept his eyes searching the creekbank past the sergeant. "How did you know I was here?"

"That doesn't matter," Green said. "It won't go any farther." He came to his feet. "If you come back in with me, I'm going to say you flagged me down and gave yourself up. You can get bond that way. You know Judge Jones is not going to believe you did it anyway, whatever that F.B.I. prick thinks. But Jones has to have something to hang his hat on, a reason to let you back out on bond—your giving yourself up will let him do that."

Brett shook his head. "Applewhite will have me arrested on a federal charge as soon as I'm bonded. I'll be before a federal judge. I won't get bond there."

"It's worth the try, Brett. You can't find her out here."

Brett finally quit searching the long bank behind the sergeant. "You had a lot of guts to come out here, Armont. If you'd been wrong you could have gotten yourself killed."

"No guts at all. There was never a doubt in my mind. But if somebody else sees you, you might get shot. Give my way a try. You can't get anything done out here—not about trying to find her."

"Armont, do you know any cop who has a second house, a place out on one of the bayous—*any* place?"

Green shook his head.

"What about anybody else, a public official?"

"Nobody at all. Why?"

"I think Paige stumbled on to something. She said she'd like to see in some houses."

"See what?"

"That's just Paige's mind. But maybe she was right this time."

"You going with me?"

"I can't let you go back, Armont."

"How are you going to stop me? You're not big enough to do it anyway short of that gun, and I know you're not going to use it."

"Dammit, Armont!"

"Who's been helping you already?"

"What do you mean?"

"Where did you get those clothes?"

When Brett didn't answer, Green spoke again. "I don't know anybody crazy enough on the force but me to be out here. But I guess I'm wrong." A smile crossed the big man's face. "*Vic*. That a good guess? I haven't seen hide nor hair of him since you ran. He'd have at least been by the station, wouldn't he?" He glanced over his shoulder. "I'm on my way, Brett. But if you're not going with me, I'd like for you to do one thing for me. I got a wife and four kids. I wouldn't like to be out of a job."

"Nobody will know you were out here."

"Thanks, Brett." He turned down the bank.

"Armont!"

He stopped and turned back. "Yeah."

"Where would we look other than the chancery clerk's office to find if somebody had a second place?"

"We? That's where Vic is, isn't he—looking over the records for you?"

"Do you know some other way we can find out?"

Green shook his head. "You really ought to go back in with me, Brett. You're going to end up shot."

Brett looked down at the revolver. He raised his eyes back to Green's. "You're going to look funny without this. If I give it back, are you going to jump me?"

Green smiled. "If I was going to do that, I would have already done it; the gun wouldn't make any difference. You wouldn't shoot me no matter what. If I wasn't willing to bet my life on that, I wouldn't have come out here in the first place."

Brett hesitated a moment, then reversed the revolver in his hand and walked slowly forward to Green.

He held out the revolver. Green took it.

Brett looked at the man's dark forehead. "What are you sweating for, Armont?"

Green smiled a little. "I was about 99.9 percent sure you didn't do it." He looked at the revolver and slipped it into his holster. "Now I'm a hundred percent sure." He looked at Brett's glistening forehead. "And what are *you* sweating for?"

Brett smiled. "I was about 99.9 percent sure that if I gave you the gun back you weren't going to jump me."

Green held out his arm to shake hands. "Be careful, Brett. If somebody does get close, don't try to run like you did at the jail. If you keep trying to dodge bullets, you're going to play out of luck. Then it doesn't matter what we set straight later.''

Brett stood a long time staring after the sergeant. Then he looked back at the water rushing down the creek, and at the sun rushing through the sky faster than he had ever seen it before. He slumped back and sat on the ground, collected his face gently in his hands, and prayed.

CHAPTER 43

"Dr. Little," Chief Seales said.

The slim man's face was pale. He reached across the desk as Seales came to his feet and they shook hands. "Have a seat," Seales said politely.

"No, thank you, Chief. I . . . Brett had nothing to do with my daughter's . . . with her disappearance. I'm as certain of that as I can be."

Seales didn't know what to say.

"I heard about the crowbar," the doctor went on, "but it wasn't him . . . I know him, Chief."

Seales studied the drawn face and felt deeply sorry for the doctor. He nodded. "Yes, sir. Well, when we get him back here, I'm sure that it'll all come out in the wash."

"Chief, I'm worried about something else, too. With you having all your resources concentrated on finding him, then whoever . . . whoever took my daughter might get away."

Vic stopped in front of the cattle gap leading into the Johnson place. Brett stepped from the bushes and hurried to the car. Vic held a sweet roll and Coke out the window but Brett shook his head.

Vic laid them on the seat, then looked back out of the window. "No go, buddy; nothing. I went into the courthouse record room and crossindexed every elected official I could think of. And Seales, too. None of them pay taxes on any property but their homes in town."

Brett felt a sinking sensation, but he couldn't give up. Maybe in Hancock County, or Jackson County. He looked at the light purple-and-gray clouds forming above the setting sun. There wasn't enough time. He looked back into the car. "I want you to take me back into town, to Seales's house."

Vic stared out through the window for a moment, then slowly nodded. "Okay, old buddy, I'm not going to argue with you anymore. This last thing I'm going to do for you. This last time—that's it. Then you either let me take you to Mobile or I drop you. I'm not kidding. I have a life, too. I've been thinking about it. It's not just me, it's Peggy, too. I could end up in prison with Applewhite finding out I helped you. This last thing. Period."

There were no cars parked at Chief Eddie Seales's small brick house as Vic drove slowly past it.

He looked at the last faint glow of the sun. "You sure you don't want to wait until good dark? Just be a few more minutes."

Brett reached from the floorboard to the door handle on his side of the rear seat.

"Wait a minute, dammit, Brett. Let me at least go around to the side street and stop where you can come back along the sidewalk to the back. Somebody see you dart across the front yard, they're going to know something is happening."

In a few seconds, he stopped the car a couple of hundred feet away from the house.

He leaned back over the seat. "I know all this is crazy, that you're not going to find anything. But I was thinking . . ." He looked toward Seales's house as he paused. He shook his head.

"Crazy," he said. "You're doing it to me, Brett. That's what it is."

"What?"

"You started me thinking when you said Seales is the only one who knows whether the print was smeared before he got there. He also came up late that night, remember? You told me that his wife had to go get him, that he had been fishing."

"Yeah, and he also would have been someone who Trinity and her husband would have let into their house at night without any question—the chief of police. He could have used any excuse for coming over."

Vic leaned toward the passenger door and reached into the glove compartment. "But it's still crazy—worse than crazy."

He lifted out two small radios and handed one to Brett.

"Carry this with you, buddy. I'll click mine twice if anybody drives up." He shook his head. "You know even if we're right about Seales, nobody would have anything in their house that— *Damn! Get down, Brett.*"

As Brett ducked low on the floorboard, a patrol car stopped beside them and a tanned face turned toward Vic.

It was Officer Franks, a square-faced dark-haired man of about forty.

"Are you Mr. McIntyre?" he asked out his window.

Vic smiled and nodded.

"I thought I recognized you. Any problem?"

Vic shook his head. "No, no problem."

Franks still stared.

Vic nodded ahead of them toward Seales's house. "I was going down to see if the chief was home yet," he explained. "Got a damn cramp and had to pull to the curb. Been happening ever since I tore up my hamstring in high school."

"Football?"

Vic shook his head. "Running track." He dropped the car into drive. "Well, see you."

"Chief's car isn't there, but that doesn't mean anything. He jogs to work sometimes, jogs home sometimes."

"Thank you." As they pulled away from the curb, Brett raised his head. Franks turned right at the next street and his car moved out of sight.

"Circle around by the back and I'll get out without you stopping."

"Take this," Vic said. He handed his revolver over the seat.

Brett stared at it for a moment, then stuffed it into his waistband. Three turns later, he cracked his rear door, waited for Vic to slow, and jumped from the car.

Vic watched him over his shoulder, then reached to the seat and lifted one of the sweet rolls and began peeling it of its cellophane.

A few seconds later, Brett was at the rear of the house. He found the door in through the garage unlocked.

Jogs to work sometimes, jogs home sometimes.

He pulled out the revolver and slowly opened the door. He looked into a small kitchen, a dining area to the back of it, and a living room off to the left. He walked slowly across the tile floor. There was a hall at the far side of the living room and three doorways down it.

In minutes, he had quickly gone through the different rooms, his progress illuminated only by the table lamp left on in the living room and the moonlight shining through the windows.

And there was nothing, absolutely nothing to find.

He leaned his head back against the hall wall. *What am I doing?* Crazy. Insane. Grasping at straws. God, please let her still be alive, please help me to find her.

Driving slowly by the front of the chief's house, Vic didn't see Seales, finished with his jogging, walking across the backyard of the homes next to his.

Seales, his lungs still straining, stopped at the garage door. He leaned forward, placed his hands on his knees, and shook his head. He was getting too old for this.

Straightening, he opened the door and stepped inside the house. Reaching to flick on the overhead light, he saw Brett stepping from the living room into the kitchen.

They both froze

Seales's eyes went to the revolver. Brett lowered it to his side. He spoke softly.

"Chief, she saw something; I know she did. She saw something and whoever it was came after her."

Seales remained quiet for a moment, staring. "Saw something? In my house?"

"Somebody's house—*some*place."

"You're losing it, Brett. There wouldn't be something in anybody's house—that's insane. You better give yourself up before you get killed."

"I can't. Where's your wife and son?"

"Why?"

"Where are they?"

"Went over to D'Iberville to visit her mother for a couple of days. What are you going to do?"

"I have to make sure you stay put the rest of the night."

"While you go visiting house to house? You're going to get killed, Brett." He dropped his gaze to the gun Brett held at his side. "Or kill somebody."

"You have any handcuffs here?"

Seales didn't answer.

"I can use electrical cord, Chief. But handcuffs will be more comfortable."

"They're on my dresser in the bedroom."

In a few minutes, Seales was handcuffed and lashed with belts and strips of sheet to the brass end-posts of the antique bed in his room.

"I'm going to have to gag you, Chief."

He folded and twisted a wide section of sheet and raised it toward Seales's face.

"Brett, it wasn't who she went to see that night."

Brett lowered his arms. "What do you mean?"

"She went to see Wayne Warren."

"Who?"

"You know, the one who was mayor up above us. He came in today and admitted he was the one. His sister says he was already shook up, getting ready to come in anyway, then when Paige was kill— when she disappeared, he went all to pieces, got to worrying whether he was going to be blamed for that. So there's no place for you to go looking, no killer Trinity went to meet that night for you to find."

Brett was unable to speak. Seales stared at him for a moment. "Brett, I don't know; you're putting on a hell of an act if you haven't done anything."

"Chief, you know I'm not the one who came after Paige. You know that. And I didn't kill Trinity, either. Look at me. You know I didn't. But somebody did kill Trinity and that same somebody has Paige, that has to be who it is. The smeared fingerprint at the pool house and the missing page. It *has* to be someone we all watched walk in and out of that house."

"If you didn't do it, then come on in, clear yourself. We can look for Paige, then."

"Chief, has anybody on the force got another place, another house you know about—some kind of hideaway?"

"Who do you know on the force with enough money for that? They're doing well enough if they keep up the payments on their home. Maybe a camper or something like that, but that's it. Oh, yeah, there's Franks. But his wife's an insurance executive over in Biloxi. He just married lucky."

"Franks has a second house?"

"He wasn't the one, Brett. Remember, he was over in Biloxi at the hospital with his kid—all night. A couple of the others on the force were over there with him, had been sitting with him for hours while his kid underwent surgery when they got the call about the murder. Of course, Felter has a second house. But if you're asking about law-enforcement personnel, you're—"

"Felter?" Brett's blood raced.

"Yeah, a cabin, out on the Wolf River."

"Where on the river?"

"I saw Vic a little while ago," Arnie answered from his patrol car.

The dispatcher had been the one to ask if any officer had seen Vic McIntyre today, but it was Applewhite's voice that came back over the radio now.

"When did you see him?"

At the sound of the gruff voice, Arnie glanced at the radio. "I just did."

"Officer Hatcher, this is Jerry Applewhite of the F.B.I. Where did you see Mr. McIntyre?"

"He was down the street a little from Chief Seales's house."

"Doing what?"

"I guess he had been by to see the chief."

"Excuse me, this is Officer Franks," a voice broke in over the radio. "I saw him, too. He was sitting at the curb not far from Chief Seales's place when I went by. Said he had a muscle cramp and had pulled over."

"Get off the damn radio, Franks!" Applewhite yelled. "Hatcher, you said just a little while. How long?"

"Just a little while. I mean he just drove out of sight."

"Damn, Hatcher, in what direction?"

"He was driving north toward the railroad tracks."

"Was anybody with him?"

"I just got a glance at him as I passed. I don't know if anybody was with him or not. Don't think so."

Seales strained against the looped belts and twisted strips of sheet binding him against the bedpost like a man tied to a stake. He heard the faint sound of metal twisting against metal as the rails connecting the post to the bed frame began to give. He strained harder. The post pulled loose from its connecting rods and he toppled over facefirst hard to the floor.

Still on his stomach, he angled his feet inward, grasped the post with the rubber soles of his jogging shoes and pushed hard down the length of the bright, round piece of metal. The post gradually began slipping inch by inch out of the belts and knotted sheets.

Brett shook his head as they drove north. "Seales wouldn't tell me the location of Dr. Felter's cabin. All I know is it's on Wolf River."

"I told you no more, Brett."

"This last thing . . . Please."

Vic stared through the windshield a few seconds, then looked back across the seat. "I've warned you, buddy, I told you. You need to run. I'll say it one more time. I'll take you anywhere you want to go—just name it."

"Vic, take me on out to the river. I won't ask any more. You can leave after you drop me off. Just the ride out there. Please."

Vic frowned and looked forward through the windshield. They approached a darkened service station on the right. He stared at the building, then slowed and guided his car off into the entrance and stopped next to a pay phone on a blue post. He looked across the seat.

"What's Felter's assistant's name?" he asked. "I've met him before."

"Dale Boyce."

"He'll know where the cabin is."

The restricting bedpost slid out from between his bonds and the knotted sheets now had slack in them. Seales started working at the knots, cursing under his breath at how long it was taking him.

In a moment, only the handcuffs remained. He slipped his hands under his feet to get the cuffs in front of him, then walked to the drawer where he kept the spare key. He used it to open the cuffs and discarded them, then looked back into the drawer and lifted another key.

He walked to the telephone on the bedside table and punched in the sheriff's home number.

Hastings answered on the first ring.

"Richard, this is Eddie. Brett was by here a little while ago . . . I'll explain later." He looked at the key he held. "I sent him out to Dr. Felter's cabin . . . Yeah, Felter left his key with me to watch over his place while he's out of town. I'll meet you at the intersection in the road just below his place. Make it quick. We won't have much time."

Vic stepped back inside the car and closed the door. "I got the directions to Felter's cabin." A one-sided sarcastic smile crossed his face. "And that's not all I got, either. I called Peggy. All the times I've lied to her when I was stepping out on her and she never imagined a thing. Now she thinks because I've not been at the office all day that I've been with a woman. She says she's sure of it. Swears she has her bags packed. You figure wives out."

The door opened at the top of the wide stairs and the light came on.

Paige, her hands cuffed behind her back and her arms held tightly against her sides by masking tape, another strip of tape holding her ankles together, lay against the base of a wall. She rolled to her back and looked up the stairs.

The woman, a short, attractive blonde in her thirties, came down the steps and walked past the pool table to Paige. She stared down at her for a moment, then knelt and pulled a strip of tape off a roll she had brought with her. She reached toward Paige's mouth.

Through the closed and shuttered glass of the window above them, there could be heard the faint hum of an outboard motor pushing a boat through the dark along the Wolf River behind the house.

CHAPTER 44

"This is it," Vic said.

The impressive structure before them could hardly be described as a cabin, though that's what Seales had called it. Sitting on a high, mounded rise overlooking the river, it was a sprawling redwood structure sporting a mansard roof covered with expensive, hand-hewn cedar shakes. A few hundred feet farther down the gravel road fronting the house, an old abandoned logging road circled back into the thick pines on that side of the road. They parked there and came back on foot.

The home was dark.

"Two clicks," Vic reminded. "This time I guarantee you there won't be anybody coming up on you without me warning you. I'm going to be where I can see the front *and* the back. If I click you twice, it'll be somebody at the back. If I do it once, it'll be someone coming to the front, and you go out the back. Here, take this." He held out his flashlight.

As Vic stepped toward the concealment of the bushes at the side of the road, Brett moved into the yard and around the back of the house, past the large picture windows, to a screened-in porch at the far corner of the wide structure. The sound of the swollen river rushing past the banks could be heard down the slope behind him. Downriver there was the hum of an outboard motor straining against the current.

A half mile back up the road, the car that had followed them from town pulled to a side of the road. The driver's door opened. A stocky figure stepped out into the dark and hurried down the road toward the house.

Brett went up the steps onto the wide deck at the rear of the house, walked across the planking, and opened the screen. The door was locked, but a window a few feet away wasn't. He raised it and crawled inside, emerging into a big kitchen.

The kitchen connected with a dining room which opened into a large living room spanning the entire depth of the house. The big picture windows overlooking the river took up the rear of the living room and allowed moonlight to brightly illuminate the inside of the house.

Across the room, there was a wide hall and he walked to it. Switching on his flashlight, he moved slowly down the corridor, stopping and peering into three bedrooms and two baths as he came to them.

And there was nothing.

He stopped and leaned back against the wall.

Nothing.

And there wasn't going to be anything. He knew that. He knew it when he was telling Vic to check the records in the courthouse and he knew it when he went to Seales's house. He *really* knew it when he was sloshing through the swamp in a hurry to get away and then get to a telephone. But he had to try. He had to . . .

His lip trembled and his eyes moistened. Then he was suddenly angry with himself for giving up. *Somewhere.* Somewhere. God, she was somewhere. Please let him know. He pushed off the wall and started back up the hall.

In the living room, he tried to force his mind to think that one great thought, something he hadn't thought of yet. Something.

But nothing came. He shut his eyes. *Please, God, please.*

He looked around the living room once more, turned, and started back toward the dining room—and his eyes fell on a wide double door to his left near the front of the living room area.

Chief Seales slammed hard with his shoulder, and the back door to Dr. Felter's small, ramshackle fishing cabin flew open. Sheriff

Hastings kicked open the front door and, revolver ready, quickly hurried inside. Franks came in behind him, both of them shining their flashlights quickly back and forth.

Seales rushed into the front room. Franks turned on the overhead light. Seales raised the back of his hand to wipe the perspiration off his forehead as he looked around the dingy, unkempt living area.

"Just the room back there," he said, "and a small kitchen, that's all there is besides this room. I was sure Brett would be here. He hasn't had time to get here and leave already, has he?" He looked at Hastings, and the sheriff shook his head.

"He would've had to come back past the intersection. I had a deputy there within five minutes of your calling."

Seales was puzzled. "I told him about this cabin because I knew Felter was out of town and wouldn't be here," he said. "Brett's out of his mind. Wherever he went, we've got to catch him before he ends up killing somebody."

Vic entered the rear of the big house on the river and came slowly down the hall.

Brett walked to the double doors near the front of the living-room area and slowly opened one of them. He looked down a wide flight of stairs into a basement, a place he would have never thought to look for. Almost no house along the coast had a basement—the water level was too close to the surface. But this house was built on a high mound above the river. There was a wall switch to his right and he flicked it on.

Sergeant Green glanced at the front of the courthouse in Gulfport as he drove past it. Suddenly, he threw on his brakes and stopped in the middle of the street.

Confederate Memorial Day!

Behind him, a driver locked his brakes and screeched to a halt, almost running into him.

"Armont," his wife exclaimed, looking across the seat at him and holding her chest where the harness of the seat belt had grabbed against it, "what's taken hold of you?"

He continued to stare at the darkened building. It was Confederate Memorial Day, the courthouse had been closed all day. The chancery clerk's office was located inside the building. Nobody could have gone through any land records that day.

He grabbed for his radio mike. "Dispatcher! Martha!"

"Okay, Sergeant, okay," the voice quickly came back. "What is it?"

"Get me Chief Seales's home—quick!"

"He's not there. He's in his car!"

"Chief Seales! Chief Seales! This is Sergeant Green! Will you answer the damn radio!"

"Sergeant, this is Sheriff Hastings. Just a second. Eddie's coming."

Hurry.

The driver behind Green pulled around him, holding down on the horn of his pickup as he drove past.

"Yeah, Sergeant," came the deep voice over the radio. "This is Chief Seales."

"Chief, Brett's out at a creekbank near the old Johnson dairy farm. Least he was earlier. He might be with Vic by now. Brett thinks Vic went to the courthouse to check land records for him. But he couldn't have—it's Confederate Memorial Day."

"What in the hell are you talking about, Sergeant."

Green tried to slow his words, but couldn't and just blurted it out. "Vic lied to Brett, he's not helping him, he's setting him up. Hell, Vic might be the killer!"

Brett started down the wide staircase leading to the brightly lit basement area. Below on the floor to the steps open side, a pool table took up much of the area. Then his heart stopped.

She was lying on her back close up against the wall to the far side of the pool table, her ankles taped together, her hands pulled behind her back and her arms taped securely to her body. Though a black hood was pulled down over her head with its drawstring tightened around her neck, he had no doubt it was her. He wanted to run down the rest of the stairs. Yet she lay so still, and for a moment he was frozen in place. God, let her—

She moved slightly. His pulse surged. *She was alive!*

He jammed the revolver inside his waistband, took the remainder of the stairs in two great strides, turning his ankle and nearly falling as he reached the concrete floor.

Her body turned partially toward him and she cocked her head, straining to hear.

"Paige!"

Her answer was a muffled moan.

He fell to his knees beside her, wanting to hug her to him. He undid the string and jerked the hood from her head. Her mouth was covered with strips of tape, but her eyes were uncovered, open, staring at him. She had an ugly gash at the top of her forehead, with blood caked around it. He ripped the tape from her mouth.

"It's Vic!" she screamed. She glanced past him and her eyes widened in terror.

He felt a cold chill rush over him and whirled around, springing to his feet and reaching to his waistband for his revolver in the same motion.

Vic fired and the bullet caught Brett in the shoulder, slamming him backward into the concrete wall. His revolver flipped through the air, clanged against the concrete floor, and slid under the pool table.

Paige gave a long, blood-curdling scream of anguish, trailing off into a sob.

A figure stepped in behind Vic's at the top of the stairs and followed him as he started down toward the basement floor.

Brett, stunned with shock and confusion, leaned back against the wall. The figure behind Vic was a blonde, a woman in her thirties.

Vic's voice was devoid of expression as he moved off the stairs and stopped next to the pool table.

"I hate this, ole buddy," he said. "But it got to the point where I didn't have any choice. Oh, this is Mrs. Lloyd," he added, nodding toward the woman. "Sherry Lloyd. You've spoken with her on the phone."

The woman smiled.

"He killed her husband," Paige moaned from the floor. "That wasn't the psycho, either."

Vic looked down at Paige, then raised his eyes back to Brett's.

"She's right, Brett, Mr. Lloyd was banging their maid. Mrs. Lloyd came to me for proof. She didn't want to get left out in the cold without part of his money if her husband dumped her. I convinced her she needn't settle for part when there was a way to have it all—where both of us could come out in good shape.''

"Brett!" Paige cried out. "Trinity came out to a motel room where they were and saw Mrs. Lloyd."

"I have a little place I use free from time to time," Vic said. "Took Trinity out there a couple of times and she thought she owned it. Walked right in on me and Sherry, wanting me to help her with the Warrens. Trinity didn't know Sherry from nobody. To her she was just some woman I was shacking up with. But she might have seen a picture in the paper one day—maybe something like an anniversary shot of the grieving Mrs. Lloyd. You never know what the papers are going to run. Sorry, Brett. That's just how it is."

Brett glanced at the revolver under the pool table, and Vic raised his pistol.

Paige struggled frantically against her bonds.

"DON'T MOVE, VIC!" Applewhite shouted.

Vic didn't freeze, didn't seem to even think about it as he whirled and fired, the report from his and Applewhite's weapons erupting simultaneously.

Vic was spun around and knocked to the floor. Applewhite was blown back against the wall at the top of the stairs, his pistol dropping over the rail to the concrete floor.

Vic rose to one knee and fired again as Applewhite, slumping against the wall, flipped off the lights. Brett dove headfirst toward the pool table.

Vic fired twice into the blackness. Brett felt the slugs slam into his thigh.

He grabbed the revolver from under the table and rolled to his back. Vic fired again, the flash of his gun showing where he was, and Brett emptied his pistol in that direction.

The sound of Vic's body thudding to the floor was cut off by Mrs. Lloyd's scream.

CHAPTER 45

Brett felt the warmth on his face and saw the fuzzy light. Mrs. Lloyd was framed in it, confessing, but she was laughing, too, laughing as she said she was the one who came up with the idea to carry Trinity's husband's body off and dispose of it where it would never be found. That way they would be covered, she had told Vic.

No, Brett tried to say; *don't you all remember? Vic had dumped the body when we arrived there so soon. It floated to the top of the pool. Remember, we all saw it? It couldn't have been the husband. It was Vic, he's the murderer. He was the one who came back and smeared the fingerprint. Don't let him get away. Don't!*

"DON'T!" he shouted and sat up in bed.

"Baby, what," Paige said, and laid her hand on his forearm, "what is it?"

He looked at her then back at the fuzzy light coming into focus—the window, the bright sun shining beyond it. His leg was in a full-length cast. His shoulder was bandaged; tubes ran to a liquid filled bag hanging from a rack next to the bed. He remembered being wheeled into the operating room.

He slumped back against his pillow.

"Brett?" Paige said again.

"I was dreaming," he said.

Seales stood next to the foot of the bed. He smiled. "Hey, Brett."

Brett looked toward him.

"Applewhite said to give you his best when you came out from under the anesthetic," Seales said. "He's going to be spending a few days in bed himself. But he said that before he left he was going to come by and see you, wish you well. Even going to send a letter to the F.B.I. academy telling them what a hell of a law-enforcement officer you are. That's a big difference from yesterday when he was following Vic's car to see if you were in it."

"Thank God he did," Paige said. "And thank God he did it in the way he did. If he'd pulled Vic over, Brett would be in jail now on a murder charge—of me."

"Yeah," Seales said. "If Applewhite had known Brett was in the car, he would have pulled them over. When Vic, instead of heading on toward Gulfport, turned out into the country and drove toward the river, Applewhite was sure something was up."

Paige looked at Seales. "Did Mrs. Lloyd say how Vic noticed his number in the phone directory?" she asked.

"Yeah. After he had taken off his gloves and saw they were torn, he realized he might've left a print when he looked inside the pool house. He came back, saw it, and smeared it. Then he started wondering if he might've made any other mistakes he hadn't noticed. He came back to the house after everybody else had left. He probably figured there wasn't much chance he would be seen and, if he was, he always had the excuse he was investigating the Lloyd murder and was back there seeing if any similarity might catch his eye. After he was finished looking around, he called Mrs. Lloyd, who had been waiting all this time out at the river house. He had never called her there and had to look in the directory for the number, saw his name and number written on the front page, and tore it out. He never did see Brett's number, Mrs. Lloyd said, at least didn't recognize it. Didn't know it had been there until after Applewhite told Brett the lab picked it up. I guess that when Vic's number was written, it wasn't done hard enough to leave an impression."

Paige shook her head at her next thought. "Applewhite was right about one thing—greed being the motive."

"Ten million dollars' worth," Seales said. "That's what Mr. Lloyd's estate was worth. But when Applewhite stayed around after the psychopath was dead, Vic started to get worried. That's when he decided it would look better to me if he mentioned his having gone out with Trinity rather than the F.B.I. finding out about it from somebody who had seen them together. But his main worry was that if Applewhite kept thinking long enough, who knows what he might have come up with? Of course Vic knew that you had been around Trinity and were keeping it from everybody—you told him yourself, Mrs. Lloyd said, that night at Antonio's. He saw Applewhite start wondering about you, saw how Paige's trust fund, your lie to her about not seeing Trinity—everything—started pointing toward you. The way Applewhite saw it, anyway.''

Paige nodded her agreement. "Uh-huh," she said. "And after you were arrested, broke loose, and called Vic, Mrs. Lloyd said he just wanted you to run. He knew with the evidence against you that you didn't have a chance—running just added to your guilt. And you know, he was right. You would've been convicted. You know you would have, Brett; no telling how many people have been convicted on a lot less than there was against you after he set you up. But you wouldn't leave the area, you wouldn't go on and really run. And you wouldn't leave him alone. That's when he decided to go ahead and kill you. He was going to tell everyone he helped you because he believed in you, and then he had to shoot you when you flipped all the way out and started after him.''

Paige paused and squeezed his hand. "Thank God, you called Vic as quick as you did. He hadn't killed me because he had to get back to our house, so he wouldn't be missed. If you hadn't kept him busy I'd be dead and in the river.''

Brett noticed her glance at the bend of her arm and rub the skin where it was blue.

She saw his stare. "It's where Vic used a needle to draw the blood he planted in the trunk of the car and on the crowbar,'' she said.

"Bothering you?''

"No, not sore at all, just looks terrible, doesn't it? And my head, it's terrible looking.''

He looked at the bandage and the spot where the doctors had cut her hair away before stitching the wound at the top of her forehead.

"Well,'' Seales said as he started toward the door. "I guess

I'll get on back to work. Just wanted to see you come out from under the anesthetic. I'll check in on you again tomorrow."

"Thanks, Chief."

As the door closed behind Seales, Paige looked back down at the bed. "You hurting?"

He shook his head. "No, I'm fine."

She smiled and raised her hand to touch her bandage. "We're a mess, aren't we?"

He smiled and she clasped his hand gently. "The doctor said you needed to rest as much as possible." She nodded toward the chair against the wall next to the door. "So I think I'll sit over there and read and let you go back to sleep."

"God, that sounds good—sleep, finally."

She smiled. "You've just been knocked out for hours."

"That doesn't count."

"Daddy was by," she said as she adjusted the pillow under his head. "But he got called to a patient. So what's new? And your father called from the ship. He caught me at the house when I was getting some clothes to bring over here."

"You told him I was all right?"

"He didn't even know about it. I decided I'd let you wait and tell him."

"Good. How was he?"

"Excited," she said as she turned and started for the chair. "He met a company president on the cruise and got a ton of orders from him; said it's one of the biggest orders he's ever received. He said for me to not forget to tell you that he loves you and he'll be back here by the end of the week."

Brett smiled at her words. His father, not at all the affectionate type, had never been the kind to express his love, while Brett couldn't remember his mother ever failing to say how much she loved them at every chance.

Then, when she died, his father had taken up her habit. It was his way of keeping part of her with him. Brett knew he was that way, too, keeping part of her with him by recalling things she used to tell him—usually the little moral lessons she was always stressing.

Oh what a tangled web we weave, he began in his mind, *when first we practice to deceive.*

He smiled. Sir Walter Scott, one of his mother's favorite poets. Yeah, Mom, I remember that one, too.

"Oh, by the way," Paige said as she settled into the chair next to the door and looked back toward the bed. "I had your car taken down to the garage to get the brakes fixed. I've been worried about them for a week—that's dangerous."

He smiled. Then, still partly under the lingering influence of the anesthetic, the bed soft, the sun coming in through the window warm on his face, he slowly, peacefully, drifted back to sleep.

And his next dreams were good ones.